FIRELIGHT RISING

The Lindisfarne Series
Book One

BY THE SAME AUTHOR

THE WEST COUNTRY TRILOGY
Moonshine (Prequel)
Bridles Lane (Book 1)
Hills of Silver (Book 2)
Wild Light (Book 3)

FAR FROM MY NATIVE SHORE: A
COLLECTION OF AUSTRALIAN
HISTORICAL NOVELS
One of Us Buried
Forgotten Places
Playing the Ghost

THE LINDISFARNE SERIES
In Darkened Corners (A Lindisfarne Series short story)
Moonlight Rising (Book 2)

STANDALONE TITLES
The Devil and the Deep Blue Sea

FIRELIGHT RISING

THE LINDISFARNE SERIES
BOOK ONE

JOHANNA CRAVEN

www.johannacraven.com

ISBN: 978-0-6451069-5-4

NORTHUMBERLAND
ENGLAND

AUGUST 1715

CHAPTER ONE

It's a fisherman's cottage grown wild. Rolling grassland on two sides and sea on two others, leathery and purple in the late-afternoon light. A house at the end of the world.

There are hints of its Tudor beginnings in the gabled roof and oriel windows, the forest of chimneys pegged against the sky. Walls are cobbled together in a mismatch of stone and faded brick, the red tiles of the roof washed to the colour of earth. Vines are scrawled across the house, the grass so long in places it tickles the grimy windows. Eerily beautiful in its own devastated way.

Eva waits for a prick of recognition, for some sense that this house, this island, is not as foreign as it seems. Lindisfarne had been home for the first four years of her life. But no part of it strikes a familiar chord. Whatever connection she might have had to the place has been frayed by two decades of London life.

She reaches for her niece's hand, and with their duffel bags slung over one shoulder, they slink towards the front door.

Eva rehearses her speech to her older brother in her head. An explanation. An apology for her failures.

Before she can ready herself, Nathan appears from inside one of the dilapidated out-buildings. He is clearly knee-deep in his restoration work, wearing rolled-up shirtsleeves and a tatty brown vest in place of his usual embroidered waistcoat and justacorps. His coffee-coloured hair is unpowdered and tied back messily, a few stray curls plastered to his neck. His eyes widen at the sight of his daughter and sister, here where they were never supposed to be.

Theodora calls to him excitedly. She lurches forward but stops inches from her father, as though registering his look of bewilderment.

Nathan had been adamant that London was the best place for Theodora, away from the broken beams and shadows of Highfield House. He had left his daughter under Eva's supervision, back in the neat sea-less confines of South Kensington, while he restores the shell of their family's house into something sellable.

He will not be pleased to see them. But it is not as though they have a choice. In the right moments, Eva can convince herself that none of this is her fault. But that doesn't change the fact that she and Thea have nowhere to go but out to this Holy Island of Lindisfarne to face Nathan's disappointment.

He drops the hammer he is holding and it thuds dully on the grass. "Why are you here?"

"Are you not happy to see me, Papa?" Theodora is theatrically pitiful.

"Of course I'm happy to see you, my love. I just…" He looks searchingly at Eva. "You can't be here," he says, voice low. "This is no place for a child to be running around. The house is in a state. It's dangerous."

Eva drops the bags. "She's seven years old, Nathan. She's not an infant."

Something she dimly recognises as anger flickers across his eyes. She can count on one hand the number of times she has seen her brother angry. Usually his rage is hidden behind a façade of warmth and cordiality. Today is no different— when he speaks, there's a thin control to his voice.

"Why are you here?" he asks again, slowly, as though reining in his displeasure.

Eva lets out a deep sigh. The story was devastatingly shameful when she was tossing it around in her head. Telling it to her older brother makes her wish the earth would swallow her. She had spent the long coach journey from London trying to piece the right words together.

"Mr Walton no longer wishes to marry me. He says it's for the best that Thea and I leave the townhouse." Despite how quickly she blurts them out, the words are bitter on her tongue. This is the first time she has spoken of the thing out loud, apart from the brisk, smooth-edged version she had fed her niece in the carriage as an explanation for their trek across the country.

She ought to have known better than to move to her betrothed's townhouse before they were married. Of course, Walton had not been there at the time—no, he was tucked away in his private lodgings in North London, the bachelor's hideout he used between endless business trips and pleasure jaunts across the Channel.

A year earlier, Nathan had been forced to sell the family house in Chelsea to repay the debts his merchant business had racked up, and they'd had no choice but to rent on the edge of the city. When Nathan had made his plans to head to Holy Island last month, he had welcomed Walton's offer to put a roof over the head of his wife-to-be.

All in good faith, I can assure you, Nate. I'm never at the townhouse myself. There shall be nothing improper about it.

The offer of the townhouse, Eva had discovered, after Walton had sat her down in his office of all places—as if their betrothal had not felt business-like enough—had turned out to be a fickle one.

I'm afraid this match will not be suitable for me after all...

Two days later, Eva was rattling up the coast of England with her every plan for life unravelling.

Nathan frowns. "Are you certain?"

"Of course I'm certain."

"I've heard nothing of this."

"Well," she says sharply, "perhaps your dear friend Mr Walton is not the fine upstanding fellow you imagined him to be." She gives him a wry, thin-lipped smile. "Although he was kind enough to pay for our passage up here."

Nathan scrubs a hand across his forehead. What is he thinking? Is he cursing Matthew Walton's name, Eva wonders? Or is he cursing hers?

"I'm sorry," he says finally. "I imagine this is my fault."

Eva doesn't speak. Nathan is nothing if not predictable, and she had known he would attribute the breaking of the betrothal to the recent failures of his business. Eighteen months ago, he had signed a deal with a smooth-tongued watch manufacturer whose products had not lived up to expectation. Nathan had discovered far too late that the pieces he was selling his wealthy clients were not of the quality they were used to. Word had spread and business had dried up, leading to the sale of the family home in London. No doubt he assumes Matthew Walton had changed his mind about marrying into a family in such a fragile financial state.

She ought to tell Nathan the truth, of course. Tell him the real reason Walton had ended the betrothal. She can practically see the weight of his guilt pressing down on his shoulders. But right now, all she wants is for this conversation to be over.

"I know you don't want us here," she tells her brother, "but there really is nowhere else." She meets his eyes pointedly. "We've been travelling for days. And Thea... She missed you terribly."

Nathan looks down at his daughter and his smile is suddenly genuine. "I've missed you terribly too, my love." He looks up at Eva, nodding faintly. A resignation. He looks exhausted, she realises. Older than his twenty-eight years, with dark circles beneath his eyes and grey at his temples. Flecks of blood scarring his knuckles. The restoration is clearly taking its toll on him. Perhaps having his daughter here will be good for him. Even if he doesn't know it himself yet.

"The housekeeper, Mrs Brodie, will find you somewhere to sleep," he says finally. "Tell her to put Thea in my room."

Eva manages a faint smile. "Thank you." She swings the bags onto her shoulders again.

"Leave those," says Nathan. "I shall bring them in for you."

"I can manage." And she is off before her brother can protest.

The house is a wreck. All broken beams and faded walls, like a foundered ship that has been lying on the ocean floor for decades. While the housekeeper makes up rooms for the unexpected arrivals, Eva walks the passages, breathing in the place. Two large seascapes hang in the entrance hall, their colours faded, turning their landscapes dull and wintery. Some long-buried ancestor looks down from the wall beside them, candlelight flickering on his cracked cheeks.

The vast dining room on the ground floor is swathed with dark wood panelling, bare smoke-coloured stone on the back wall. A long table fills most of the room, and a half-attended fire simmers in the grate. Next door she finds a sitting room with a worn settle and a bookshelf standing empty, the volumes piled up on the floor beside it. The room smells of dust and damp, and the faint breath of the sea. There is a vague sense of familiarity here, perhaps. But nothing solid. Nothing that tells her for certain that she belongs in this house.

Though Nathan has been at work here for close to a month, it still looks forgotten, with its bowed stairs and grime-thickened windows, and exhalations of dust from between the worn stones of the walls. Unloved and abandoned. Eva supposes that's exactly what it is. Twenty years since her family had last lived here. To the best of her knowledge, it has been empty for all that time.

For years, Nathan had shown no interest in the property. With the family in London, Highfield House had been little more than a name, a neglected and nostalgic shadow. Occasionally, he would toss in mentions of selling it, or tearing it down, or at the very least finding a tenant willing to take on such a ruin, but there was never any urgency to his plans.

And then that day a month and a half ago when he had

announced with feverish enthusiasm that he was to travel to Holy Island and bring Highfield House back from the dead. Restore her to her former glory and sell it for what he hoped would be a sizeable profit. Bring the wealth he had squandered back to the family.

The thought of selling the house feels almost blasphemous. Eva wonders what their parents would think of it. It matters little, of course. They have both been dead for years. Their father had taken his last breath right here in Highfield House when Eva was a child, their mother succumbing to consumption five years ago. She supposes Nathan is right to sell the place. The family needs money far more than they need a sentimental shadow hanging in the background of their lives.

Nathan had convinced their brother-in-law Edwin to help him with the restoration. In London, Edwin has a reputation as a fine craftsman, whittling sought-after furniture for the wealthy upper classes. The hastily patched holes in the sitting room ceiling suggest he has not worked his magic on Highfield House just yet.

Edwin had brought Eva's sister Harriet and their infant son Thomas with him. Now she is walking the dust-laden halls of the house, Eva can only imagine the displeasure with which her polished younger sister has been doing the same this past month.

The stairs creak loudly as she climbs to the second storey. The staircase opens out into a wide corridor with rooms on either side. The door to what she assumes is Nathan's bedroom is slightly ajar; several others looked unused. She can hear the sound of hammering coming from a room at the end of the hallway. She walks down the passage and peeks inside. Edwin is kneeling on the floor with his back to her, hammering new boards into place. He looks as ragged and dirt-streaked as Nathan; dust-worn and wigless, with sleeves rolled to his elbows and his dark hair in a loose queue. He doesn't notice her.

"Your room is ready, Miss Blake." Eva turns at the sound of Mrs Brodie's voice. The housekeeper is a tall woman with a thin but friendly face, and a thick Northumberland accent. Greying hair peeks out from beneath a cloth cap. As far as Eva can tell, Mrs Brodie is the only member of staff here, beside Thomas's nurse, who she knows made the journey up from London with Harriet and Edwin.

She follows Mrs Brodie down the hall to her bedroom. The room is sparse and cavernous, with a narrow, childlike bed along one wall, and a washstand and chipped chest of drawers in the corner. A tiny fire is spitting in the grate, the mantel topped by a cracked gold-rimmed mirror. It smells of dust and woodsmoke; of the past.

"I'm afraid it's a little bare," says Mrs Brodie. "And I've only just now lit the fire, so there's still a chill in the air. Summer takes its time arriving up here."

Eva offers her a smile. After a week and a half of travel, she would happily sleep on the floor of a cart shed. "It's quite all right. I know I was not expected. Thank you."

Mrs Brodie bobs her head and disappears back down the hall, leaving Eva to the faint echoes of the house. She peers out the cracked window at the sea; at the shadows of the Farne Islands dotting the horizon. An arrowhead of birds glides past the glass.

Exhausted, she sinks onto the edge of the bed. It creaks loudly; an old, hard relic, not so far removed from the floor of a cart shed. She closes her eyes, her body weighted with exhaustion and swaying slightly, as though she were still in the carriage.

When she hears delicate footsteps making their way down the passage, somehow managing to avoid the squeaking boards, she knows they can only belong to Harriet. Her sister taps on the door, then steps inside without waiting to be invited.

"I thought I was imagining things when I heard your voice outside." She reaches down and pulls Eva into an embrace that barely manages to touch her.

Even after a month in the grime of Highfield House, Harriet is still polished and golden, with blonde curls twisted high on her head, and her embroidered pink and green stomacher far too fine for a place like this. In her dark, mud-streaked travelling dress, Eva feels positively dour.

Harriet's gaze travels to the duffel bag tossed on the floor beside the bed. "Is that all you've brought with you? Where are the rest of your things?"

"I've all I need," Eva says tightly. She had abandoned most of her belongings at Walton's townhouse. Her former betrothed had offered to send her things on to the island, but she had told him such a thing was not necessary. Surely there was little point carting all her worldly goods up to the end of the earth when her family would only be here for a short time. She will simply send her brother to collect them once they are back in London.

She had shoved a few of her favourite books into the bottom of the duffel bag, along with a single change of clothes—enough to make herself vaguely presentable. She cannot find the energy for much more than that. Besides, there is something freeing about carrying only the duffel bag with her. A pleasant simplicity to this one-cloak, one-bonnet existence against the chaos the rest of her life has become.

Harriet perches on the edge of the bed beside her. "I overheard your conversation with Nathan. What happened between you and Mr Walton?"

Eva shakes her head. She does not want to speak of it to anyone. Least of all to Harriet.

To her relief, her sister doesn't pry.

"How has it been here at the house?" Eva asks. "Is Thomas well?"

Harriet huffs. "It's been dreadfully dull. The town is almost non-existent. And all I hear inside the house is the thudding of hammers all day long." She shakes her head. "It's a foolish idea, every bit of it. Nathan ought to have just sold the place and moved on. Surely it would have been far less trouble for everyone concerned." She stands and peers into the mirror. Tucks a stray strand of hair back into place. "Edwin had a coachload of timber brought in the other day and it was nearly swept away by the tide. The locals watching had a fine time of it. They're not fond of us, you know."

"I gathered." When Eva had asked a woman in the village for directions to Highfield House earlier that afternoon, she had been gifted with cold and critical eyes. A look that told her in no uncertain terms she was an outsider. "But you know Nathan," she continues. "He blames himself for the trouble our family is in. If he thinks he can make the lost money back by restoring the house, he's going to do all he can to make that happen."

Harriet hums. "It was all rather sudden though, wasn't it. He'd hardly made mention of this house in years. And now he's planning to restore the place? It's a little strange, don't you think?"

Eva gets up from the bed and tosses a log into the grate. Sparks fly up the chimney. "Well," she says, "maybe he needed something to put his mind to. Something to stop him dwelling on all he's lost. If this madness with the house is what he needs to find himself again, we ought to let him do it."

"Tell us about the journey, Thea," Nathan says, too cheerfully. "Did you see the ocean? And did you have some lovely horses?"

Theodora's cheeks are flushed, no doubt with the thrill of sitting among her entire family at this ridiculous banquet hall table. She ignores her bowl of stew and barrels into a breathless recollection of everything they saw in the coach between London and the island, oblivious to her father's displeasure at her being here.

"And four big black horses," she is saying, "just like from a story book. It was so wonderful"—neatly avoiding the rain and the mud, and the ten days of complaining she'd subjected her aunt to.

Nathan winds the handle of the pepper mill, a muscle tightening in his jaw. "I'm glad the journey was not too trying for you," he says stiffly.

Eva forces down a mouthful of stew and dares a glance at her brother. There's anger behind his eyes, but she can't tell if it's anger at himself or her. If he is to be furious at anyone, it ought to be Matthew Walton.

Edwin nods along to Theodora's story for a while, before growing bored and rattling off a list of the improvements he and Nathan have made to the house. They seem to be few and far between.

"Yes, it's coming along," Nathan puts in. "Although rather slowly, I'm afraid."

"Well," Edwin says, "you can hardly be surprised at that. Takes an age to get any of the building materials carted out here. Ordered some timber to be brought out to Lindisfarne and the fellow carried on as though I had asked for it to be taken to the moon." He snorts. "Mind you, I suppose we can't be surprised. The Jacobites have this part of the country in disarray. The troublemaking bastards." He gives a short chuckle, tucking a strand of limp charcoal hair behind his ear. "It's chaos up here, Eva. You shan't know what you've wandered into."

"Come on now," says Nathan tensely. "I think that's something of an exaggeration."

Edwin waves a dismissive hand. "It's no exaggeration at all. Can't go two minutes without hearing of another Jacobite protest. And have you not heard the rumours? Government spies on the island? Sent to hunt down those who want the Old Pretender back on the throne."

Harriet rolls her eyes. "Tell us about London, Evie." She sighs wistfully, as though it has been years since she was there, and not mere weeks. "Is it just as inspiring and wonderful as ever?"

Eva smiles wryly to herself. Her last week in London had been anything but inspiring. "I'm sure you'll find it just as you left it," she tells her sister.

Harriet directs an overt sigh in Edwin's direction. "I do hope I'll see it again soon." She gives Eva large, mournful eyes. "You must be terribly disappointed to be here."

Theodora reaches for the plate of bread and knocks over her glass of ale. Nathan swoops in with a napkin.

"Indeed." Edwin takes a mouthful of wine. "I do hope old Matthew has a good explanation for all this."

Nathan's attention snaps away from the pool of ale at his elbow. "I think we all know Matthew's reasons for doing as he did."

"Nonsense," says Edwin. "He knew what he was getting himself into. Financially, I mean. Matthew has known for months about the trouble with the business, Nate. If that was the reason for his change of heart, you'd have thought he'd have reached the decision sooner."

Eva's cheeks burn. She wills Edwin to stop talking. She had not imagined she might be able to keep the breaking of her betrothal a secret, but nor had she expected it to become dinnertime conversation.

She feels an uncomfortable prickling beneath her skin. A sense of rising panic she is barely able to contain. In the shadow of Harriet's impossible charm, Eva has always prided herself on being the sister with her head on straight, the *sensible choice* with her life under control. She had been engaged to Matthew Walton for almost a year and a half; had never seen fit to complain when his cross-Channel jaunts and business trips had continuously delayed their marriage. She had used the time to set out her plans; to determine which rooms in the townhouse would be their parlour, their dining room, their children's nursery. She planned which gown she would wear to be married in. Devised the names of their future sons and daughters. Planning gave her a sense of purpose. A feeling of faint control over this life that had been laid out for her by expectation—and her older brother. Now she is almost halfway through her twenties, and completely without prospects. Those plans—those orderly and sensible plans, of sky-blue sack gowns and sons named for their grandfathers—are trailing through her fingers like seawater, leaving nothing in their place.

She tears at her bread with far too much aggression. Harriet places long consoling fingers over her wrist.

Eva grits her teeth. A part of her had been looking forward to seeing her family. But she feels like an utter failure. And the sight of perfect Harriet, with her perfectly styled melancholia and her perfectly sympathetic eyes, is not helping matters.

Eva excuses herself, taking a candle from the mantel and carrying it up the groaning staircase. Her body is aching from days in the carriage, and from the tension she had carried in her shoulders in anticipation of her brother's disappointment. She is ready for the day to be over. Ready for morning light to make the shadows lying over the house a little lighter.

She kicks off her shoes and unlaces her stays. Wipes her body down with the lukewarm water Mrs Brodie had placed in the washstand in the corner of the room. She rolls onto the bed and closes her eyes, listening to muffled remnants of the dinner conversation floating their way up the staircase. Outside the window, the sea sighs and shifts the shoreline.

Eva pulls the blankets up towards her chin. Though she can tell from the heady smell of lye that the sheets are clean, the woollen blanket smells musty and disused. She wonders if it had been tucked away in some forgotten cupboard since her family had last slept under this roof.

And with that thought comes a sudden, searing pull of dread. She sits up in bed, gasping down a breath. Because as she lies here in the cradle of Highfield House, with gulls wheeling and the German Ocean rising to lock them onto the island, a solid memory digs itself up from somewhere deep within her. Pieces of the past come out of the dark, seeping from the walls and jostling their way to the front of her mind.

She is a child; screaming, crying; water on all sides and thick, impenetrable dark. She is wrapped in her mother's arms as she runs through the shallow sea connecting Lindisfarne to the mainland. And they flee Highfield House without looking back.

CHAPTER TWO

Nathan is awake when the first light finds its way through the window, unsure if he was ever asleep. He remembers long hours of lying awake, listening to Theodora's deep breathing as she lay in the truckle bed on the far side of the room. Remembers the creak of the floorboards when Eva had got up in the night.

His sister has ended up in the same room she had slept in as a child. So has he. It had been an almost unconscious thing. On his return to the house, he had gravitated to his childhood bedroom without a second thought. Memory had pulled him back onto a hazy but well-worn path, between his father's old study and the bedroom once belonging to his older brother Oliver.

There is something odd about sleeping down the passage from Eva again, crammed into his childhood bed. Something that is at once both comforting and unsettling, as though time has twisted in on itself. The house is just as full now as it was back then, in that time before Harriet, before Theodora.

Many of the same bedrooms are filled, the hallways again alive with footsteps. The house ought to feel warm and inhabited. But there are shadows in corners that refuse to be swept away.

Theodora murmurs in her sleep, and the sound makes Nathan start. Since her mother's death three years ago, his daughter has been prone to nightmares. But this morning, mercifully, she seems calm. Nathan is surprised by it. He had imagined the gloomy halls of Highfield House would find their way into her dreams.

He knows he has not always been like this, so rigid and fearful. He remembers a life with soft edges; a life with Sarah in it. A life in which he did not have to try so hard to keep a smile on his face. But the last three years have been almost intolerably difficult: first the death of his wife, and then his foolish choices that led to the collapse of his business. His characteristic brightness has become more forced; he knows these days his smile rarely reaches his eyes.

He watches Theodora sleep, her pale blonde hair fanned out upon the pillow. He had been protective of Thea back when Sarah was alive too, of course. But not like this. Now there is this crushing fear that something might take his daughter from him, the way it had taken his wife. With Thea in London, away from Highfield House—away from *him*—it had been easier. He had trusted that Thea would be in safe hands with Eva, and that he did not have to watch her as though she might crumble with the next gust of wind. He knew, too, that his daughter would be far happier in London with her aunt than she would be here with him poring over her every move. Infecting her with his poorly hidden panic.

He sits up, knowing there's no chance of sleeping. Best he get an early start on the seemingly endless undertaking before him. Every day, Highfield House seems to get bigger, and he becomes more overwhelmed by the task he has taken on. There are floorboards to replace, walls to paint and polish. Broken steps and windows to repair. Edwin, thankfully, has taken the reins of the restoration, giving Nathan the most mindless and mundane of tasks. This new life on Lindisfarne is far more physically demanding than his pen-and-paper-filled workdays in London. But there is something faintly comforting about ending each night with aching arms and a shirt damp with sweat. It keeps him from losing himself in an ocean of worrisome thoughts. He dresses silently and creeps out of the bedroom, shooting his daughter one final glance before he leaves.

He is surprised to find Eva sitting in front of the fire in the dining room, a teapot on the table beside her. He had not heard her get up. Dull, dish-related crashes come from the kitchen, along with the comforting smell of baking bread. Blue early-morning light filters in through the high windows, making dust motes whirl as he passes.

"Tea?" Eva asks, gesturing to the pot. "Mrs Brodie just brought it out."

Nathan nods. He sits beside her as she fills his cup.

She looks tired this morning, her blue eyes underlined in shadow. But she is tidily dressed as always, with her mousy hair pinned at her neck and her dark blue woollen skirts sponged clean.

Nathan feels a fresh pull of irritation. He had worked hard to secure her marriage to Matthew Walton. He knew it his duty to find his sisters the best matches possible, and a connection to a well-respected family like the Waltons would have done no end of good to his ailing status. Would have gone some way to restoring the Blake name to their rightful place among London's upper middle class. What had gone awry? Such a disaster he would have expected from Harriet. But not staid and reliable Eva.

He is bitterly disappointed. In her. In himself. In Matthew, who he had considered a good friend—or at least a good enough friend to come to him with his changed decision, rather than packing his former betrothed onto a coach to Holy Island. But he has trained himself not to show such things.

He reaches for the poker and jabs at the fire in an attempt to avoid eye contact. "I know you're reluctant to speak of it," he begins carefully, "but I need to know exactly what happened between you and Mr Walton." He keeps his voice steady, even. Perhaps it is not too late to fix this. But he cannot do that without knowing details. He has always been close to Eva—at least, far closer than he is to Harriet, who often seems like an entirely different species. With the right words, he is sure he can nudge the truth from her. But he senses this is a delicate subject, and the right words seem to evade him. He clears his throat. "It's important that—"

Before he can finish, gunfire splits the sky. Eva jerks, slopping tea onto the flagstones. Nathan strides outside to find two of the villagers standing close to the house with muskets in hand. Donald Macauley is standing atop the highest dune, his son Martin close behind. The two men are identically dressed in faded slops and grimy woollen caps, broad hands wrapped around their weapons. Their blue corduroy jackets are flapping in the wind.

Nathan inhales, trying to harness his anger. "I've told you before, Macauley. This is my land. I'd appreciate it if you refrained from hunting upon it."

Donald Macauley lifts the musket to his shoulder and sends another shot into the cool morning air. Birds screech and hurtle into the sky. "We've been hunting here for years, Mr Blake. Long before you showed up. Roe deer like this part of the island."

Nathan knows Donald Macauley has lived on Lindisfarne forever. Knows he is well respected among the islanders. A man with plenty of influence. He does not want to get on the wrong side of him. Nonetheless, he cannot have bullets flying all over the property, especially now Theodora is here. "I understand that," he says, trying to level his voice, "but my family is here now. So please find somewhere else to hunt. There are children in the house."

Donald Macauley chuckles to himself and trudges across the dune to stand eye to eye with Nathan. "Well," he says. "Seeing you went and asked so nicely…"

Heat prickles Nathan's neck. But he does not step away. After a moment, Macauley strides off to retrieve the fallen roe deer. He slings the small brown body over his shoulders. Blood beads on the grass. "Come on then, Martin," he says, though his son has already fallen into step beside him, "let's leave Mr Blake to all these fine acres."

Nathan watches until they have disappeared back towards the village. When he returns to the dining room, he finds Eva standing at the window, watching in the direction the men had disappeared.

"Who was that?" she asks.

"Name's Donald Macauley. One of the village elders." Nathan grabs his tea and gulps it down, trying not to let the run-in shake him. It's lukewarm now, and anything but settling.

He remembers Donald Macauley from their time on the island when he was a child. He'd been just as much of a bastard then as he is now. Nathan remembers being scolded by the man for venturing too close to his fishing boat. Remembers being afraid to sit close to him at church. When Oliver had dared him to steal an apple from the tree from outside Macauley's cottage, he had refused, even knowing the ridicule his brother would inflict on him. Even as a boy, Nathan had had a strong sense that Donald Macauley was to be kept away from.

"Don't let him worry you," he tells Eva anyway. "He's just hunting."

But he is certain the Macauleys' near-daily appearance has less to do with the deer on this part of the island, and more to do with intimidation. After all, these are unsettled times. He knows this part of the country to have more than a dash of Jacobite support. And with the placing of German King George on the British throne last year, the Jacobite movement, which has lain dormant for close to a decade, is beginning to rear its head again. With an unpopular foreign king at the helm, the Jacobites are seizing their chance to return the crown to the Stuarts.

Nathan had managed to keep his distance from the riots in London, but the movement is on its feet here in northern England, so close to Scotland and the Jacobite heartland. No doubt the people of Holy Island have little trust for outsiders from London who might be harbouring Hanoverian sympathies. Nathan has seen Donald Macauley striding around the village with the Jacobite cockade pinned to his cap. Surely a man bold enough to risk arrest by doing so would have little reluctance to scare those he distrusted. And Nathan is fairly sure he and his family fall into that category.

Eva gives him a shrewd look over the top of her teacup. "Hunting? It sounded more like they were trying to scare us."

Nathan looks at her for a long second. "Perhaps now you're beginning to understand why I did not want my daughter here."

She turns away from him and edges a little closer to the fire. "Well," she says tautly, "I'm sorry, Nathan. But we've nowhere else to go."

CHAPTER THREE

Eva is distracted as she rattles through Theodora's lessons later that morning. Her first night back in Highfield House had been restless. As she had lain in the dark, listening to the sea rattle the shore, she had tried to piece together her fragmented memories of the night they had left Holy Island.

She has no thought of why they had fled. Her mother had never spoken of that night when Eva had been growing up; the memories had sat untouched within her until she had set foot back in Highfield House.

She stares out the window as Theodora's quill scratches across the paper. Looks out at the bleak gunmetal sea, as though it might provide answers. She thinks of Donald Macauley and his son with muskets in their hands. They had done little to calm her unease. Nathan can tell her they were hunting all he likes, but she knows there is more to it. She had seen the faces of the villagers when she and Theodora had passed through the streets yesterday. Had felt the animosity coming from every look that was sent her way. She misses the blissful anonymity of London.

The Blakes are well known here. Highfield House has been in her family for generations. Her great-great-grandfather had been the one to lay the foundations; to find that slice of buildable land among the hummocks and dunes at the top of Holy Island. The story goes that it had been nothing but a fisherman's cottage back then, added to generation by generation as the family's wealth expanded. Now those riches are all but gone, thanks to decades of bad business decisions by the men in her family. But she is sure her family's reputation as wealthy landowners has done little to endear them to the villagers. The Macauleys, she feels certain, were either trying to scare them, or watch them. For what purpose, she cannot imagine.

"Auntie Eva?" She snaps out of her daze. How long has Theodora been calling her? "I've finished."

Eva clears her throat and tries to focus. She takes the book from Theodora and skims through her sums. "All right. Good. Let's do one more page."

Theodora puts down her quill. "Can't we finish now? Please? Can't we go exploring?"

Eva has vague memories of promising her niece some grand explorations once the interminable carriage ride had deposited them on Lindisfarne. "Where do you wish to go? You know your papa doesn't want you exploring the house."

Theodora sighs like a tired, widowed mother. "I *know.* He's told me *so* many times. I'm not a *child.*"

Eva smiles. "You are, actually."

Theodora huffs. "Can we go and see the village?"

"All right. Tidy your things and fetch your bonnet and cloak. It looks as though it might rain."

Theodora slams her book closed and is out of the room before Eva is even on her feet. Shawled and bonneted, with cloaks tossed over their arms, they make their way out of the house and over the grassy embankment that leads toward the village. The tide is out, revealing the planes of sand that tie Holy Island to the mainland. In the late afternoon, the sea birds are a chorus, swooping down in graceful arcs to pluck squirming creatures from the mudflats. Soon, the ocean will return, cutting Lindisfarne off from the mainland and ringing them in sea.

Wind whips up off the water and Eva slings her cloak over her shoulders. Red-coated guards peer down at them as they skirt the castle. Theodora reaches for her hand.

Lindisfarne is a grey stone shadow of a village, watched over by the ghostly ruins of the monastery that tower behind the church. There is an odd stillness to the place. It's an almost absence of sound; wind rustles the grass that lines the harbour, and ratlines knock and chime against the thin forest of masts in the anchorage. But there's an emptiness, a quiet, that feels almost otherworldly after the rattling chaos of London. This scrap of land at the top of England has seen bloodshed and miracles. Viking raids, the slaughter of monks, and inexplicable marvels at the hands of saints. In the bleak summer light, it feels as though the past is blowing in through each weather-worn stone.

Eva feels the muscles in her shoulders tighten as they step into the warren of lanes that make up the village. Two women pass, darting glances at her, then quickly look away and murmur to one another. Eva presses her shoulders back and lifts her chin, trying to conjure up confidence she doesn't feel. She refuses to let these people faze her. Her family has owned

Highfield House since Elizabeth was on the throne. This is her home, at least for now.

"Auntie Eva. Look at this place." Theodora points to a shop on the corner of Church Lane. Eva peers through the window. Shelf after shelf is overflowing with old books, with painted teacups, with tarnished tobacco boxes and dust-covered toys. Theodora's eyes light. "Can we go inside?" she begs. "Please?"

"Of course. But you're not to touch anything."

Theodora shoves open the door, a bell at the entrance announcing their arrival. They are accosted with the smell of the dusty past, mildew and grime clinging to the mad clutter of objects crammed onto the shelves.

A woman stands up from behind the counter, two old books in the crook of her arm. A pale pink kerchief is wrapped around her shoulders, clashing violently with the shock of red hair escaping out the sides of her cap.

"Good afternoon." She gives them a bright smile, one that is far more genuine and welcoming than anything Eva has seen on Holy Island so far. The woman waves a hand, gesturing to the shop. "Look as you please." Eva nods her thanks and the woman goes to one of the shelves, shoving aside a faded toy drum to make room for the books.

Theodora floats from shelf to shelf, lips parted and eyes wide as she scans the disordered display. "Look," she breathes, pointing at a doll staring down from between an old vase and what Eva guesses is some kind of navigational tool. It is draped in a silky green dress, with wide painted eyes and long, dark lashes. Theodora steps closer, until her fingertip is an inch from the porcelain face. "Can I have it?" she begs, tugging at Eva's arm with her free hand. "Please? I've been ever so good."

Eva raises her eyebrows, gives her a playful smile. "Have you just? I seem to remember an awful lot of whining during your arithmetic this morning."

"But arithmetic is just so awful. And I've not touched anything. Not a single thing." She takes a step back from the doll, as if to emphasise her point. "*Please?*"

Eva reaches into her pocket, but finds it empty. "I've not brought a penny with me. You'll have to speak nicely to your father."

Theodora's shoulders sink. "We'll be back," she tells the shopkeeper solemnly.

The woman grins. "I'll look forward to it."

They head towards the path that slices down the middle of the island. "Did you see her dress?" Theodora is saying. "All silky, like a queen."

Eva smiles. "Yes, it was beautiful." She puts a hand to Theodora's shoulder, guiding her down a narrow lane.

A wrong turn.

The moment she steps into the alley, she can feel it. That sense that they are not where they are supposed to be. That sense that they are trespassers.

At the bottom of the lane is a large outbuilding she guesses to be a barn or shed. She cannot see the house beyond, but the thick stench of animal waste suggests a nearby farm. Through the ajar door, she can see men moving about inside the shed.

Eva is about to turn on her heel when Theodora darts forward. "Look! There's a big horse inside!"

"Thea," she hisses. "Come back at once." The last thing Eva wants is to anger the villagers further by trespassing onto their land.

The door to the shed creaks open and a bristly head pokes out. Eva recognises the older man she had seen hunting outside the house that morning. Donald Macauley. Up close, his eyes are flinty and cold. Something in them makes Eva wary.

At the sight of him, Theodora scurries out of the lane and around the corner, disappearing from sight.

"I'm sorry," Eva tells Macauley. "I did not mean to trespass. I'm new in town. I lost my way, is all."

His eyes narrow. "You're one of them, then are you? The Blakes. I heard there was more of you arrived yesterday."

Eva presses her shoulders back. "Yes," she says, forcing steadiness into her voice. "Eva Blake. Pleased to meet you." She holds out a hand in greeting. This is the best way forward, surely, to try and create some amicability between her family and the villagers. Show them they mean no harm.

Macauley looks down at her outstretched hand. She can tell from the cold look in his eyes that there is to be no amicability between her family and his. She can't begin to imagine what might have caused such hatred. Had Nathan done something untoward when he had first arrived back on the island? Something he is refusing to share? Or does this animosity go back to the days when her father owned Highfield House?

She lets her hand fall. Swallows hard. She hates conflict, hates confrontation; hates the dithering mess it turns her into. "My family means you no trouble," she says, hearing her voice rattle.

"Is that so?" Macauley's eyes are cold.

Instinctively, Eva stumbles back, but he takes a step

forward, forcing her against the stone wall of the alley. She can smell earth and sweat on his skin. The faint hint of liquor on his breath. He looks deep into her eyes as though he is searching for secrets. He can sense her fear now, surely. Can sense it pouring off her in waves.

A younger man emerges from the barn, wearing a long dark coat and riding boots. He is leading the horse behind him. He nods to Macauley without speaking, then disappears down the alley without so much as a glance Eva's way.

"You are not welcome here, Miss Blake," Macauley says, voice low. "Not on this island, and especially not on my land."

Footsteps crunch towards the lane and he takes a sudden step back, allowing her to dart past him. She rushes from the alley before he can manage another word.

CHAPTER FOUR

Harriet stands in front of the easel with her paintbrush in hand. She tilts her head to examine her painting. Too much light. Or is it too much dark? The sky on her canvas is swirling, murky, and too unreadable.

The falling dusk is not helping matters. She puts down her brush and lights the lamp on the mantel.

This little room on the ground floor of the house was once servants' quarters. These days, with just Mrs Brodie and Thomas's nurse Jenny in their employ, Harriet has turned it into a workroom of sorts, with her easel in one corner and her paints cast out across the table.

Edwin enters without knocking. He stands behind her and peers over her shoulder at the canvas. She is challenging herself with this piece. A landscape—bleak and windblown, with pale sunlight pouring over a shadowed sea and forest at its edges. Inspired by the view from her workroom window, perhaps. Along with a need to paint more than the still-lifes that are expected of her as a female artist.

"That's coming together nicely," says her husband.

Harriet gives him a thin smile. He has an infant's understanding of art, but she is grateful he has allowed her to continue painting now they are married. She had been fearful he might forbid her from doing so, ever since Nathan had engineered their betrothal a year and a half ago.

He kisses the side of her neck, clearly hoping for a little attention. But the muddy sky needs far more attention than her husband does. She hopes he takes the hint and leaves.

He doesn't. He sinks into the worn armchair in the corner of the room and stretches his arms up over his head. He is still wearing the stained shirt he was working in today, and wood shavings have ended up in his dark hair. She smells ash soap on him, and a faint hint of sweat. He looks as though he's not seen a razor in days. In London, he had been careful to present himself as a professional and well-groomed tradesman, befitting of the lavish houses of his clients he spent so much time in. Doused in rosewater and fine silk shirts. Here, he and Nathan have begun to look like a pair of vagrants.

Harriet dips her brush back into the paint and returns to the troublesome sky, doing her best to ignore him.

"Well then," he says in a conspiratorial tone, "have you managed to get anything out of Eva yet? Any word on what happened between her and Matthew?"

Harriet sighs and puts down her brush. "She wouldn't say," she tells him. "Whatever it is, it's embarrassed her. She doesn't like it when things don't go to plan."

Eva's sudden appearance—and the news of her broken engagement—is the most excitement this place has seen in weeks. Harriet is determined to get the truth out of her.

Though she supposes that truth will be nothing more interesting than Mr Walton's unwillingness to marry into a family with such empty coffers. A rather dull outcome, Harriet thinks, just like Eva herself. She allows herself the faintest of smiles, but chides herself for her cruelty. She can't imagine being in Eva's position, with a life of spinsterhood laid out before her.

Nonetheless, she is glad Eva is here. Theodora too. They will add a little life to this house that seems completely devoid of it. The past four weeks have felt almost interminable. An endless cycle of inept childrearing, stolen moments with her easel and paints, and peering out of windows in search of something other than sea. Dinnertime conversation has largely consisted of Edwin listing the improvements he has made to the house each day, and Nathan saying, *Yes, it's coming along*, before the three of them run out of things to say.

When she had first arrived on the island, Harriet had told herself she would not bother making friends. There seemed to be little point. After all, this was just a temporary inconvenience. Besides, the choice of potential friends was woefully small. Most of the islanders are too rigid to accept new people into their lives—especially people from Highfield House. She is no fool; she knows the villagers would rather be rid of them. Not that she truly understands why.

She told herself she didn't care. Told herself she had no desire to be friends with these islanders anyway. What would she talk about? Horseshoes and herrings?

The loneliness didn't matter. Soon she would be back in London, among people she truly did count as friends. But it wasn't long before the boredom, and the painfully dry dinner conversations, ran her to the end of her patience. Since then, she has made a half-hearted attempt at building acquaintances, staying for conversation after church services and grinding out small talk at the market, but the villagers seem determined to keep their distance.

Edwin crosses one leg over the other and rubs his dark stubble. "This whole business is a damn shame if you ask me. I was looking forward to Matthew being part of this family."

"I'm sure you were."

Edwin, Nathan and Matthew Walton have been friends for years, the three of them serial frequenters of London's coffee houses. Harriet can't imagine how much wrangling it must have taken Nathan to betroth both his sisters to his best friends. Little wonder he's so bent out of shape now Eva has put her foot squarely in his plans.

Harriet rinses her brush. Perhaps she can sneak back down here later tonight. But best make it look as though she is finishing for the day. A wail comes from the nursery on the floor above them and she feels her shoulders tighten. She had hoped for at least a few hours' respite before having to tend to Thomas again.

Edwin pauses. "Will you go to him?"

"No," Harriet says tautly. "He cannot possibly need feeding again. Jenny can go." Her eyes drift upwards, listening for the nurse's footsteps. She is infinitely grateful that Edwin had agreed to bring Jenny along on this foolish little jaunt—and that Jenny had accepted. Harriet is sure she has only survived the first five months of Thomas's life because she has his nurse to share the load. Or shoulder it. It is not that she doesn't love her son—of course she does. She just loves him a little more when he is fast asleep in his crib.

She goes to the window and yanks the flimsy muslin

curtains closed. The sun has almost disappeared and long shadows are lying across the room.

She will hear them again tonight, she is sure; the footsteps that sound outside the window of her workroom. They come regularly, several times each week, late at night when the rest of the house is sleeping. At first she had thought it just her imagination, that rhythmic slap of feet on the path that winds around the house. Had put it down to a racing mind, or remnants of a dream, or the unmoored feeling of being out here on the edge of the ocean.

But no. The footsteps are far too regular and far too real to be imagination, or a leftover dream.

She knows, of course, she ought to pull back the curtains and catch a glimpse of whoever is out there. But she cannot find the nerve to do so. Who knows what she might come face to face with?

Edwin stands behind her at the window and squeezes her shoulders gently. "What's bothering you?"

She shakes her head. She has said nothing to her husband about the footsteps. She knows he would just scold her for her overactive imagination. Or far worse—forbid her from visiting her workroom at night. And Harriet cannot have him take her painting away. Right now, it's the only thing that makes her feel alive.

CHAPTER FIVE

Rain settles over the island the next day, drizzling in threads down the sea-stained windows of the house. After breakfast, Harriet locks herself away with her easel and paintbrushes, while Eva drags Theodora through her Latin lessons.

Hammer blows and splintering boards echo through the house. Eva has little idea what Nathan and Edwin are up to—since Theodora's arrival, her brother has ensured that the rooms they are working in are kept locked at all times. For his daughter's safety, he claims, but Eva can't help but wonder if perhaps he wishes to hide the dreadful job he's doing—and the fact that he really ought to have hired someone experienced to do the job. Not that he could have afforded it.

When the sun finally breaks through the clouds after dinner, Eva and Theodora head out for a walk. Nathan chases them down the stairs. He is dressed tidily, in bone-coloured breeches and an embroidered woollen justacorps, his dark curls tied back and powdered neatly.

Theodora bounds towards him, but stops short of taking his hand. "Will you come for a walk with us, Papa? We're going to the rock pools to look for mermaids."

He winks at her. "I'm a little too big to fit in the rock pools, don't you think?"

Theodora giggles.

"Shall I walk to the village turnoff with you? Then you and Auntie Eva can go searching for mermaids, and I can call on Mr Holland."

Theodora nods enthusiastically.

"Who is Mr Holland?" asks Eva as they step out the front door.

"From the fishing fleet," Nathan tells her. "We got speaking of the restorations at church on Sunday. He's offered me use of his frame saw."

She gives him a crooked half-smile. "I'm glad we've not managed to estrange ourselves from all the villagers."

Nathan chuckles. "Give it time."

"Do you have any idea how to use a frame saw?"

"That's what I have Edwin for." He nods towards his daughter, who is galloping ahead down the path. "Was she sleeping in London? Have her nightmares been bad?"

"Regular," says Eva. "Once a week at least. But she seems to remember little of them when she wakes."

Nathan nods. "It's a small mercy. Although I have to say, she seems more settled here than I expected."

They walk in silence for several paces, their footsteps sighing against the damp grass.

"Do you remember the house?" Eva blurts. "From when we were children?"

"Of course."

"What do you remember?"

Nathan folds his hands behind his back. "I remember plenty. Playing on the beach with Oliver. Eating at that enormous table. I remember Father taking me to look at the stars on the Heugh."

"What else?" Eva glances at Theodora. Drops her voice slightly. "What happened here? Why did we leave?"

Nathan doesn't look at her. "Nothing happened. We left after Father died because this wasn't the right place for Mother to raise us on her own. That's all."

Eva cannot tell if he is lying. "Why do the villagers hate our family so much?" Wind whips up off the water and she wishes she had brought her cloak. She tugs her shawl tighter around her shoulders. "Donald Macauley threatened me yesterday. I took a wrong turn down the alley behind his property and he behaved as if he'd caught me with my hands in his life savings."

Nathan gives her apologetic eyes. "I'm sorry you had to deal with that. But it's just that they don't trust us yet. That's all. The prospect of another Jacobite Rising has people on edge. The country could be at war again any day now." He shakes his head. "That Donald Macauley… He's a good man to stay away from."

Eva snorts. "I am doing my best."

"Father's death was awful on Mother," Nathan says after a moment. "The smallpox took him horribly quickly. You likely don't remember. And then all the worry Mother went through, terrified we would all take ill too. Can you blame her for wanting to leave the house where it happened?"

Nathan is right—Eva remembers almost nothing of her

father. She was not even four when he died. These days, he is little more than a name and a half-remembered story.

Theodora rushes back to them with a fistful of sea thrift. "Look!" She waves the pink flowers under Nathan's nose. "Isn't it pretty?"

"Beautiful, my love."

Theodora hands one stem to Nathan, and one to Eva, before darting back off down the path again. Eva twirls the stem between her fingers.

"But we left with such urgency. Didn't we?" She looks up at Nathan for confirmation. The memory of that night is fragile, but there are parts of it she is beginning to recall with clarity. It seems as though the longer she stays in the house, the more memories resurface.

She remembers her mother waking her from a deep sleep. Remembers being carried from Highfield House in her nightgown, a blanket around her shoulders. And she remembers the darkness; pools of it. Cold, ink-black air against her cheeks. Why would they have raced from the house in the middle of the night if their mother had only wished to escape her memories?

Nathan watches his feet for several paces. "Grief can make a person do strange things," he says finally. There's a thickness to his voice, a genuineness Eva rarely hears.

"You're right. I suppose I'm just…adjusting to the way of things."

Nathan meets her eyes with a look of sympathy that manages to sting. "I mean to write to Matthew Walton," he says. "Ask him to reconsider."

"No," Eva says hurriedly. "Please don't." She can't bear the embarrassment of it.

"Do you not wish for the security that will come with marrying a man like Matthew?"

She bristles. "Security for me, or for the rest of the family?"

Nathan shrugs, oblivious to her bitter tone. "Both."

Eva wraps her arms around herself, suddenly craving space. There is plenty of it here, and yet, since arriving on Holy Island, she has felt hemmed in and stifled. By Nathan's disappointment. By her own failures and the unravelling of her plans. She had spent so long preparing to be Matthew Walton's wife that without it, she feels as though she has little purpose. She needs space to breathe.

"Thea," she says suddenly, "why don't you go with Papa to visit Mr Holland? We'll explore the rockpools another time."

She waves away Nathan's queries and is marching off towards the coast before either of them can protest. Wind skims across the water, rippling the inky surfaces of the rockpools. Already, the days are pulling towards autumn; each evening arriving with a little more haste.

Eva holds up her skirts as she strides over the uneven ground. She tries to concentrate on balancing over the rocks at the edge of the water, but thoughts about the house keep tugging her back.

Is Nathan telling the truth about the night they left Holy Island? She has never known him to lie to her. But she can't shake the thought that he was not being entirely truthful. Had they really left the house so impulsively, all because their mother was consumed by grief? The mother Eva remembers was reserved and insular, not one to take risks. But was it possible their time in Highfield House had made her that way?

As she approaches Emmanuel Head, Eva sees a small wooden dinghy sitting at the edge of the water. Donald Macauley is pacing the beach, his boots crunching against the shingle.

Eva's stomach dives and she changes direction quickly.

He calls her name. Calls again, louder, when she does not answer.

Finally, she dares to turn around. Macauley is striding up the grassy embankment towards her. Heat floods her body and she fights the urge to run.

He lurches forward and grabs her arm. "You and I, we need to speak, lass." His face is close to hers, and she can smell liquor on his breath. His cap is pulled down low, thick brows poking out from beneath the grimy blue wool. He starts to walk back towards the dinghy, his fingers digging painfully into her upper arm. She tries to pull away, but his grip tightens.

"Get in the boat," he says.

"Do you think me mad?" Eva's voice shakes. Because this side of the island, wild and ocean-bound, is almost painfully empty. The curve of the dunes mean she is hidden even from the topmost windows of Highfield House. And she knows that if Donald Macauley, with his iron grip and unforgiving eyes, wants her in his boat, she has little choice but to obey.

He shoves her forward, her shins knocking hard against the bulwark. Eva stumbles and drops the sea thrift Theodora had given her, its delicate petals mashing beneath her shoe. Macauley reaches into the boat for his musket. "Get in."

Eva hears herself murmur with fear. She steps over the gunwale, legs shaking. Macauley shoves the dinghy into the water then leaps in after her. He sits opposite Eva, placing the musket under his seat. He reaches for the oars and begins to pull the boat away from the island. The oarlocks creak and groan; one looks to be held together by little more than a thread.

Eva watches the house get smaller. Watches the smoke from the chimneys melt into cloud. Her knuckles whiten around the edge of the bench seat. "Were you waiting for me?" she asks shakily. "How did you know where to find me?"

Macauley pulls hard on the oars. They are heading away from the mainland, out into the German Ocean. The boat tilts across the swell. "This is a small island, Miss Blake. Anyone can be found with a little effort."

Eva grits her teeth, trying to bury her panic. Surely this can't be merely because she trespassed onto Macauley's land. There's more to it, of course. She just cannot determine what that might be.

"I know you're not fond of my family," she says. "But trying to scare me like this is not going to achieve anything. I don't see why we cannot just get along. We mean you no trouble."

Macauley snorts. "Get along?" He keeps rowing. "I know what you are, Miss Blake. The lot of you. I know why you're here."

She frowns. "What are you talking about?"

"I know you've been sent out here by the German pig and his men. To weed out those of us who support the true king. Report back to the government on when we're about to strike."

Eva stares at him. "You think we're government spies?

Reporting on the Jacobites' plans?"

"I don't think it. I know it. I'm no fool. Your father was outspoken against the Jacobites. And your ma, well, we all know where her alliances lay."

Eva's lips part. "What do you mean?"

"That house has sat empty for two decades," Macauley says, pushing past her question. "And you all turn up now, just as our movement is finding its legs?"

Eva lets out her breath. Suddenly, the islanders' treatment of her family makes glaring sense. Ludicrous as the accusation is, she understands how they might have reached such a conclusion.

"You're mistaken," she says, with as much calmness as she can muster. "We've come to Highfield House to restore it. Sell it. Let us do that in peace and Holy Island will be free of us. Is that not what you want?"

"What I want, Miss Blake, is to see our rightful king returned the throne. And I am willing to do whatever it takes to make sure that happens."

There is no changing his mind, she realises. He has her and her family pegged as government spies, and she knows nothing she says will convince him otherwise. "Do you truly think this is what your king wants?" she asks. "For you to make such threats against young women without proof of the accusations you are throwing?"

He laughs humourlessly. "Don't pretend you're innocent. I know it's the lasses we ought to be most wary of. 'The ones they least expect,' they say. Well, I've seen enough skirts in the Jacobite cause to know you young women like to poke your noses into men's business." He shifts forward slightly on the seat, his grey eyes spearing hers. "I saw you outside my cart shed. With your eyes on the messenger."

The messenger? Eva thinks of the man in the dark greatcoat, leading his horse from Macauley's barn. Had he been passing word between the Jacobites?

She shakes her head. "You're mistaken," she says again, with as much firmness as she can muster. "My family and I are not spies. I saw nothing yesterday." She clenches her hands to stop them shaking. She cannot even begin to think about what Macauley might be planning to do with her. But she does know that, as of now, out here on the ocean, with no one else around, she has little to lose. She looks him squarely in the eye. Holds his gaze, despite the sweat prickling the back of her neck. "And you are also a fool." She hears a strange, cold clarity enter her voice, as though she has gone past fear to something else entirely. "Because if I truly were a spy, you would just have given me the very information about your rendezvous point I was seeking."

She sees Macauley's bristly jaw harden as that realisation falls over him. In his rage, he has said too much. Of course, so has she. Right now, Donald Macauley has two choices: either he believes her when she tells him she is not a spy. Or he makes sure she is silenced.

He lifts his right hand from the oar. Moves it towards the musket. And Eva is suddenly on her feet, making the boat lurch wildly on the swell. Instinctively, blindly, she reaches for the oar and wrestles it from the splintering oarlock. Macauley stands, and she stumbles backwards, the oar teetering in her fist. All she sees is the musket. He is raising it, stepping back.

Without thought, she swings. The oar misses the musket and strikes the side of Macauley's head. It's a cold, dead sound; at once both dull and sharp. His body tumbles into the sea with an almost-silent splash. The musket teeters on the gunwale for a second, before following his body into the water.

Eva drops the oar, her cry of shock dying in her throat. She lurches across the boat and reaches into the ocean, grappling after his body. The dinghy lurches violently and her hand comes up empty. And there is not a single blemish on the sea that might hint at where a man has just disappeared.

CHAPTER SIX

Sound distorts, leaving her in a sea of twisted silence. Her heart is drumming in her ears and she feels bile rising up her throat. She huddles in the bottom of the boat, clutching either side of the gunwale. The sea rocks her in its inescapable cradle. She feels the weight of the oar pressing against her thigh.

A killer.

Murderer.

No. An accident. Self-defence.

Donald Macauley had been about to shoot her. Send her to the bottom so she could not share her spy's secrets.

Hadn't he?

In truth, she does not know. It had all happened too quickly to make sense of. All she knows is that Macauley is gone. And she is alone with his death on her hands.

She tears her eyes from the patch of ocean where his body had disappeared. Thick cloud hides Holy Island from sight. She is surrounded by sea and a soupy, opaque sky. She has little idea which direction they had come from—she had been far too terrified to pay attention to where she was being taken. And even if she could row all the way back to Holy Island, how could she turn up alone in Macauley's boat? The villagers would string her up before she managed a word in defence.

And perhaps, Eva thinks, they would be right to do so.

Wind whips across the water and she shivers hard. Her bare forearms prickle with goosebumps and she picks up her shawl from the bottom of the boat, where it had fallen during the altercation. She pulls it tight around her body, feeling patches of dampness on the wool.

The boat is drifting. In which direction? Is she being dragged back to Holy Island, or away from it?

Perhaps she ought to try for the mainland, and the anonymity that will come with it. And do what? She has not a thing with her but the clothes on her back.

All her mind can make sense of is that she cannot stay in this horrifying limbo. Tentatively, she picks up the oar with which she had struck Macauley. She cannot look at it too closely. Cannot inspect it for blood, or hair, or any other hint of what she has done. She settles it into the broken oarlock, careful not to lose it over the side. Without releasing her grip on the handle, she shuffles around on the bench and begins to row.

The oar slides and groans in its broken casing, but the boat begins to move. She has no idea which direction she is going, but the movement steadies her a little. Perhaps she may still die, but she will not sit here waiting to do so.

She rows until her arms are screaming. The pain is a welcome distraction. The haze is thick and close, but when she turns to look over her shoulder, nuggets of land are peeking through the cloud bank. She hears herself murmur in relief.

These jagged jewels of rock, they must be the Farne Islands. She must have drifted south from Lindisfarne. South from that unplaceable circle of ocean where Donald Macauley's body had been swallowed.

She tugs harder on the oars, guiding herself towards the closest island. Mist is threaded over the rocky outcrops, but as she draws closer, a dark shape emerges from within the cloud. A cottage—as impossible as that seems out here. A small stone tower stands beside it, an unlit iron brazier hanging from it. A shipping beacon, perhaps? It is the only sign of human life she can see on any of these islets.

She pulls towards the cottage. The boat moves in a jagged path and she trains herself to guide it this way, that way, slowly growing familiar with the workings of the oars. The sea knocks the dinghy into protruding rocks; she hears it grind against undersea stone. Sucking in a breath, Eva leaps from the boat and scrabbles up the edge of the island. Pain shoots through her shin as it slams against rock. She pitches forward, making flecks of blood appear on her palm. She drags the boat higher up onto the island, its flat bottom scraping noisily.

The land around her is nothing but rock, glittering with pools and flecked with green and yellow moss. A purple curtain of dusk is beginning to fall across the island, and she hears the wild squall of sea birds from somewhere within the cloud.

Eva stumbles towards the cottage, wet skirts tangling around her shins. The house is made from the same dark stone as the island, and almost looks part of the landscape.

Both the cottage and the crooked outbuilding beside it are built on high stone foundations. Half-towers, with two large rainwater barrels beside them. The firebasket swings slightly in the wind, the chain groaning, a thin stream of ash skittering out between the gaps in the brazier.

In the fading light, she cannot see any sign of the lightkeepers, though a larger boat is roped to a mooring post not far from the cottage. For a moment, she thinks to call out, to announce her arrival. But something stops her. She does not want to break the strange stillness that hangs over this place. It feels the right kind of stillness, given she has just sent a man to his death.

She climbs the stone stairs at the front of the house and peeks through the salt-speckled window. Through the grime she can just make out a narrow bed with blankets thrown over it haphazardly. A single plate and tin cup sit on the table. The remains of a fire glow in the grate.

The place is clearly inhabited. It is also clearly a house for one. Even with her limited knowledge, Eva knows keeping the light is not a job for just one man. At least, it shouldn't be. What kind of person would agree to such a life? To such isolation, such responsibility? She doesn't know. But in her rattled, fearful state, she knows she does not wish to meet him. Surely it's no sane person that lives out here alone like this.

She hurries down the stairs and slips into the shed beside the house. Inside the thick stone walls, the shrieking wind is muted, and there is a close earthy smell to the air that Eva feels in her throat. In the long shadows, she can make out mountains of chopped wood, and great heaps of what she assumes to be coal and peat. She finds a lightless corner at the back of the shed and sinks to the ground between two enormous woodpiles. Sudden tears escape down her cheeks. She cannot tell if they are tears of grief over all that has happened, or vicious relief that she is still alive. Perhaps a little of both.

As the darkness thickens, footsteps emerge from within the constant sigh of the sea. Closer they come, rhythmic and sharp over the rocky ground. The door of the shed creaks open, letting in a shaft of dusk. Eva holds her breath. Half-hidden behind the woodpile, the lightkeeper is no more than a dark shape. A tall man, broad shouldered. She sees the outline of a short and rugged beard. A long greatcoat and woollen cap. He digs a shovel into the mound of coal and disappears from the shed.

Eva lets herself breathe.

His footsteps fade slightly and she hears the groaning of the firebasket chain. She smells the chalky odour of the flames, sees orange firelight squeezing through the gap beneath the shed door.

The footsteps return. Eva sits up straight, grips her knees with frozen fingers. The door groans open and the lightkeeper steps into the shed, tossing the shovel back against the wall. Then he freezes. Listens. Eva presses a hand over her mouth to silence her noisy breathing.

"That you, Macauley, you bastard?" The man's voice is rough and northern. He snatches his shovel again and comes striding towards the woodpile. He raises his makeshift weapon.

Eva scrambles to her feet. Holds up her hands to shield her face. "Please, no."

The man drops the shovel. "Jesus Christ. Who in hell are

you?"

"No one. I'm no one." She tries to shuffle past him, but he grabs her arm roughly.

"What are you doing in my shed?"

"I'm sorry. I'll leave at once. I—"

"How d'you get here?"

"The boat..." she manages. She hears her breathing get faster, louder. She gulps down breath, swamped in fear.

"You came in a boat? Alone?"

"No. I mean, yes. Yes. Alone." Her voice rattles.

He frowns, eyes shadowed in the half light. "Is there someone else out there?"

Eva opens her mouth to speak, but freezes. It feels as though his eyes are boring into her. Piercing her.

He shakes her arm, as though trying to yank her from her mania. "I said, is there someone else out there? Has your vessel gone down? Are there people that need help?"

"No," she coughs. "No. There's no one else. I..." She hunches over, gasping for breath. Fresh tears spill down her cheeks.

"You what?" he pushes.

"There's no one else," she sobs. "He's dead. He's dead because of me."

CHAPTER SEVEN

The man lets his hand fall from her arm. "Right, then. I see."

Eva turns her back, hunching, hiding her tear-streaked face. What in hell had she been thinking, confessing to such a thing?

"It was an accident," she blurts. "I swear it. I thought he was going to hurt me. I swung the oar to defend myself. I didn't mean to knock him over."

Dread pulls at her stomach. What will he do with her now, this killer who has arrived on his island? Strike her with his shovel? Shoot her? Turn her in to face the hangman?

He scratches his beard, shadowed in the dancing light of the shipping beacon. "Is anyone after you?"

"No." Eva shivers. "No one knows what I did. Except you." She tries to edge past him but he blocks her way.

"Where's your boat?"

"What?"

"Your boat," he says impatiently. "Where d'you land?"

"I…" Eva's thoughts knock together. "I don't know. I just… I saw the cottage…"

"Where d'you come from?"

She hesitates. Surely it can do her no good for him to know where she is from.

He looks at her expectantly. "Do you not know that either?"

"Holy Island," she murmurs.

He strides out of the shed. Eva races after him. He grabs a lamp from the table inside the cottage and hurries back down the stairs.

"What do you want with the boat?" she asks desperately. That flimsy little dinghy is her way off the island. Her way out of this man's life.

He lifts the lamp, panning it in a wide arc. Light falls on the sorry shape of the dinghy beached against the rocks. He marches towards it and shoves it out into the sea.

Eva panics. "What are you doing?"

"Can't have a dead man's dinghy on my island, aye? What will people think?"

Eva stares transfixed as the boat is tugged into darkness. She closes her eyes, forcing herself to breathe.

"I can't take you back to Holy Island tonight," he says. "Not in the dark. We'll strike the reef."

Eva nods faintly. She cannot bear to think how worried her family will be.

Now he has sent her boat away, he has her as trapped as a rabbit in a snare. And what will happen when people find out Donald Macauley is missing? Will there be a reward on her head? Is the lightkeeper thinking of making his fortune by turning her over to the hangman?

He glances at her bare arms, and the wet skirts clinging to her ankles. "I've a fire going in the cottage," he says. "You'd best come inside."

She does not want to be in this man's company. She has told him far too much, and she has no idea how to navigate his brusque, unpolished words. But she knows she has no choice. The night is growing cold, and her way off this island has just floated out towards Donald Macauley's grave.

She follows the lightkeeper into his cottage, finding thick, smoke-scented warmth, and flames dancing in the grate. The place is at once both sparse and messy, with blankets bunched at the bottom of the bed and breadcrumbs littering the table. The mantel is cluttered with candle stumps and rolls of twine, and old brassy shapes she assumes are navigation tools. A worn sideboard leans against one wall, partially blocking what she assumes is the back door of the cottage. Light from the firebasket blazes through the window, making shadows dance across the walls. Heavy wooden shutters are folded open against the windows.

"You keep the light alone?" Eva asks shakily.

"Aye."

She hovers by the door, waiting for further explanation. Nothing comes.

The lightkeeper throws another log on the fire. Jabs it with the poker. "Warm yourself. You're shivering." It sounds like an order.

Eva edges closer to the hearth, eyes drifting to the firebasket and the reams of black sea beyond. How can a man commit to a life of such solitude, such responsibility?

"Why?" she blurts. She wants some rational explanation, like a colleague's illness, or a fellow lightkeeper flitted off to the mainland for supplies.

He looks back at her. "What?" He slides off his coat and tosses it over a chair.

"Why do you keep the light alone?"

He gives a single, humourless chuckle. "D'you really think yourself in a position to be asking questions? After all you just told me?" There is no darkness to his words, but she senses the veiled threat beneath. And she sees her own foolishness. Of course, she is no place to do anything other than keep her mouth shut and make herself as small and unimposing as possible.

Especially now she is relying on this man to get her off this island.

She swallows. "I'm sorry. I didn't mean to pry."

For a fleeting second, she meets his eyes. There is something magnetic about his gaze that makes her oddly reluctant to look away. His walnut-coloured hair is tied back in an attempt at a tail, but most of it hangs loose, tangled on his shoulders. His thick beard is unevenly trimmed to his chin, his skin tanned and weatherworn. But there's a youthfulness to his brown eyes, to the ropey muscles in his forearms that show beneath his rolled-up shirtsleeves. He is older than her, yes. But not by as much as she had first imagined when she had seen him stalking towards her in the coal shed. Perhaps close to Nathan's age.

He clears his throat, pulling his eyes away. "You can use the bed. I'll not need it."

"No," Eva says quickly. "No, I couldn't." Spending the night in this stranger's house is bad enough. Climbing into his bed is unthinkable.

He shrugs. "Suit yourself. There's bread on the table if

you're hungry."

Her stomach is churning far too violently to eat. All she wants is to curl up in a corner and disappear. Hopes that when the light comes it might shine on something other than this bleak corner of reality.

Harriet paces the nursery with Thomas on her shoulder. She knows there is no chance of sleeping tonight, not with Eva missing.

When she had not returned by dusk, they had told themselves not to worry. She needed the space, they'd said, turned upside down as she has been by Mr Walton's rejection of her. At nightfall, Nathan and Edwin had gone into the village asking after her. And now, with midnight long past, Harriet is finding it hard not to imagine the worst.

Thomas is restless, as though sensing his mother's unease. Somehow, the house seems to sense it too, creaking and groaning like a ship upon the rocks. Harriet rubs the baby's back, the way his nurse had shown her. He's faintly sticky, the sleeve of his nightshirt inexplicably wet. He wriggles in her arms like a fish plucked from the water. Harriet's shoulders tighten as he paws at her neck and whines.

"I know," she says, "I hate this place too."

Unlike Nathan and Eva, she was not born in this house; their mother had left the island not long after her husband's death, with her youngest child growing inside her. There is not a single thing about Highfield House that makes it feel like home. Nor does she have any desire to make it so.

She decides to ignore the stickiness and the wet sleeve.

This child seems to be eternally damp and filthy, so there seems to be little point in rectifying the situation. She paces across the nursery, trying to coax Thomas towards sleep. Finally, she settles him into the crib in the corner of the room, rocking it mindlessly until his eyes droop closed. For a moment, she considers going downstairs to paint, but her mind is too cluttered, churning through all the terrible possibilities of what might have happened to her sister. She finds herself standing at the window, a corner of the curtain pulled back in wait. Tonight, with Eva missing, Harriet feels unsettled and reckless. Too bold for her own good. Tonight, when the footsteps come, she will catch the prowler in the act.

She had waited for him last night in her workroom. After Edwin had fallen asleep, she had slipped out of bed and locked herself away with her easel, painting until long after midnight, with her ears open for the footsteps. But there had been only silence, and Thomas's early-morning shrieking. Tonight though—she hears it. Footsteps on earth as the prowler emerges from the dunes onto the path surrounding Highfield House.

Harriet blows out the candle flickering on the mantel. She returns to the window and pulls the curtain back an inch.

She sees a man, lit only by the faint glow of the moon. He is dressed in long boots and breeches, a large greatcoat pulled over his shoulders. Harriet's heart jolts, scared of her own bravery.

She squints, trying to catch hold of any distinguishing features. But the figure's face is hidden beneath a cocked hat. Shielded by the darkness.

She knows she ought to fetch her husband, or her brother.

Have them confront the intruder and demand an explanation. But she cannot do that. Nathan will fret, and Edwin will fold his arms and announce she is to stay locked up safely in their bedchamber at night.

It's selfish, of course, to gamble with her family's safety for her own gain. Once, Harriet had assumed motherhood would whittle that selfishness out of her. But it seems to only have made it worse. Well, she thinks, she can blame her husband for that.

She presses her forehead to the glass, watching as the figure moves past her window. And then he turns the corner of the house and is swallowed by the night.

CHAPTER EIGHT

Eva wakes in a corner of the lightkeeper's cottage, curled up on her side in front of the hearth. Morning light is filtering through the dirty window. Outside, a thin line of smoke rises from the extinguished fire basket.

The lightkeeper is snoring lightly in his bed. He lies on top of the blankets, still fully dressed in his ash-streaked shirt and breeches, sleeves rolled to his elbows and one hand tucked beneath his head. His boots lie tipped over beside the bed.

Throughout the night, they had barely spoken. In spite of all Eva had confessed, the lightkeeper had had no questions. Was he simply not fazed by the foolish admission she had dropped at his feet? Or was he staying as far away from it as possible?

He had moved around the cottage like a ghost, tending the fire, darning a shirt, scrawling in a notebook, and heading out to restoke the firebasket each time the flames began to dwindle. Eva had curled up in a corner of the cottage in an attempt to disengage herself from the lightkeeper's strange world. She had done her best to stay awake, stay watchful, but her physical and mental exhaustion had finally pulled her down. She has vague memories of the lightkeeper climbing into bed with the dawn, as the beacon burned itself out.

She sits, rolling the stiffness out of her neck and shoulders. Her skin feels sticky, her woollen skirts streaked with salt.

Now her thoughts have settled slightly, she sees she must get back to Holy Island as soon as possible. She knows her family will have gone into the village asking after her. And she does not dare think on the conclusions the islanders will reach when they learn her disappearance aligns with Donald Macauley's.

Eva finds herself staring at the lightkeeper as his chest rises and falls with breath. She is completely at his mercy. Will he take her back to Lindisfarne this morning? Or does he plan to turn her in? Either way, there is nowhere to run.

He opens his eyes, catching her watching him. She turns away suddenly, her cheeks flushing. She busies herself folding the worn blanket he had given her and setting it on the table. He sits up and rubs his eyes. Swings himself out of bed and pulls on his boots. "Come on, then. Let's get you out of here."

Her shoulders sink in relief.

He grabs his greatcoat from the back of the chair and tugs it on over his broad shoulders. His slides his hair back from his face in one swift movement, tying it at his neck with a leather band pulled from his pocket. He cocks his head, gesturing to her to follow him. Eva pulls on her damp shoes and grabs her bonnet from the floor.

She steps outside. Gasps. Much of the island has vanished beneath the sea, leaving only a small circle of rock around the cottage and firebasket.

"The water," she breathes, "it's so close to your house." At once, the raised foundations of the cottage and shed make perfect sense. With the high tide, the sea is impossibly close.

The lightkeeper turns up the collar of his coat, nonchalant. "Tide won't get much higher than this."

In the early morning, the sea birds are a chorus, great gusts of them flocking around the nuggets of land not swallowed by the sea. The other Farne Islands dot the ocean ahead, sitting similarly low in the water. There's a bleak beauty to the place, a sense of otherworldliness and intense isolation. "Does it not frighten you? Being so remote? So vulnerable to the sea?"

He gives a short chuckle. "I've not been swept away yet." He steps onto the jetty. His boat is a much more solid thing than the battered dinghy Eva had arrived in, with a single mast and neatly furled sail. It knocks against the moorings with each inhalation of the sea.

The lightkeeper climbs aboard with a large stride, and takes up the oars from beneath the bench seats.

He can have had no more than a couple of hours' sleep, but his movements are brisk and energetic, while Eva's legs ache with exhaustion. Perhaps his body is accustomed to the lack of sleep. She wonders how long he has been living out here.

"Which island is this?" she finds herself asking.

"It's Longstone."

"I thought Longstone was uninhabited," she says.

"It's not." He nods towards the boat. "Get in."

Eva waits for him to offer his hand to help her climb inside. When it is not forthcoming, she bundles up her skirts and clambers ungracefully into the boat. He waits as she staggers onto the bench seat opposite him, then unties the mooring rope and uses the oars to push away from the jetty.

"Last night in the shed," says Eva, "you thought I was one of the Macauleys. Do they come here?"

"No one comes here." He looks at her with sharp brown eyes. "Where am I taking you then? Back to Lindisfarne? Or are you a woman on the run?"

Eva hesitates. She does not know which is more foolish—to step onto Holy Island with Donald Macauley's blood on her hands, or to abandon the only place in the world she can right now call home. Either way, she needs to tell her family she is safe. Or alive, at least.

"Take me back to Holy Island," she says. "Please."

He reaches up to release the sail, then tugs hard on a line, opening it to the wind. Neither of them speak as they begin to fly across the water. Sea spray flies across the bow and Eva wraps her arms around herself, shivering.

The shapes of Lindisfarne emerge from the cloud within minutes.

"Will you land on the north side of the island?" she asks. "At Emmanuel Head?"

She does not dare to show her face in town. Who knows what questions are being asked, what stories are being told? But she imagines that appearing in a boat with this strange man from Longstone will only raise more questions. Make her look more guilty.

His lips part. "Emmanuel Head. Near Highfield House."

Eva swallows, surprised at his knowledge of the manor. She nods faintly, but doesn't reply.

The lightkeeper skirts the island on its ocean side and eases the boat around the rugged north coast. There is Highfield House, dark and dominant, smoke rising steadily out of two chimneys. Eva is relieved to see it. But when she glances at the man in the boat beside her, she sees a hint of unease in his face.

In the high tide, the sea is knocking up against the embankment. The lightkeeper jumps into the shallows and shoves the skiff over the thin line of pebbles at the water's edge. Eva lurches over the bow, not waiting for his hand this time. Seawater sloshes into her shoes.

The lightkeeper steps out of the water and looks up at the smoke puffing from the chimneys. A frown creases his forehead. "Someone living there now, then? Is it you?"

"I…" Eva's words fade at the sight of a figure on the dunes. She can make out his face as the sun washes him with golden light. Donald Macauley's son, a hunting musket in his hand.

Her stomach dives. Is it just coincidence that he has appeared here now, at the very moment she is stepping back onto Holy Island?

It does not feel coincidental. It feels as though he has been watching, waiting for her. It feels as though he *knows*.

How could he know?

Hunting, she tells herself. He is just out here hunting.

He sees her—she has no doubt. Because his gaze is suddenly trained on her, and he lifts his musket to his shoulder.

The lightkeeper shoves her forward, out of Macauley's eyeline. "Run," he hisses. "Get away from him."

Eva lurches over the embankment. She hears the crack of the musket and a cry of shock escapes her. She tears across the rocks and uneven grass without looking back, waiting for the pain to hit, for her legs to give way beneath her.

She fumbles with her key, then flies through the front door of Highfield House, slamming it behind her. There is no pain, she realises. Somehow, she has made it inside without being hit.

Footsteps patter down the staircase and Harriet rushes at her. "Evie. We were so worried."

Eva lets out her breath and sinks to the ground, her dirty skirts pooling around her. Harriet kneels beside her, gripping her hand.

"What happened? Where have you been?"

"I…" Her words tangle. Heart racing, she reaches for her sister, pulls her into an embrace.

"You're safe now," says Harriet. "You're home."

Right now, Highfield House feels neither safe, nor like home, but she doesn't say it. She leaps to her feet and rushes into the dining room. Looks out the windows to the sea. Donald Macauley's son is no longer visible, but there is that handkerchief of a sail, growing smaller as the man from Longstone disappears back towards his island.

Nathan's footsteps thunder down the staircase, Edwin and Theodora close behind. Theodora flies at her, throwing skinny arms around Eva's waist. Nathan lets out a breath of relief.

"Eva. Thank God. Are you all right?"

She nods faintly.

Nathan looks at his daughter. "Upstairs, Thea. Finish your letters." Clearly rattled by the gravity of the situation, Theodora disappears upstairs without a word of complaint. Nathan turns back to Eva. "I heard a gunshot."

She glances towards the window. "He didn't hit me."

"He," Nathan repeats. "One of the Macauleys."

She nods. "Donald's son."

"Harriet, have Mrs Brodie bring us a pot of tea." Nathan looks at Eva. "Come and sit down. Tell us what happened."

With a teacup in trembling hands and her shoes drying by the fire, Eva sinks into the settle in the parlour and tells them everything—from Donald Macauley's accusations and his swift and sickening death, to her night on Longstone and the lightkeeper who had brought her home. Nathan paces in front of the hearth as she speaks, rubbing his shorn cheek.

Eva grips her teacup. She can smell the night on her skin; woodsmoke and sweat and sea. "I know what everyone will think. They'll believe I knocked him overboard on purpose."

"That's not true."

"He accused us of being spies, Nathan. They think we're reporting on Jacobite plans. Who knows how many of the other villagers think the same?"

"Spies," Edwin snorts. He is leaning against the wall in the corner of the room. "The damn fools. She's right though, Nate. We asked after Eva all around the village last night. Once people realise Donald Macauley went missing that same night…" He trails off.

Nathan paces, paces, scrubbing a hand across his forehead. Eva has never felt like more of a burden. And she has never felt more guilty.

"If the villagers ask, we'll tell them you crossed off the island in the low tide yesterday afternoon," Nathan says at last, "and got caught out by the rising water. You were forced to spend the night lodging at the tavern in Beal."

Eva rubs her eyes. "Mr Macauley's son saw me return with the lightkeeper."

"So we'll simply say you met him in Beal and he offered to bring you home."

Eva says nothing. The story is far too easy to poke holes in, of course. Anyone who saw the Longstone beacon brightening the horizon last night would know the lightkeeper had not spent the night in Beal. But she knows she has little choice. A story with holes in it is still preferable to the truth.

She picks listlessly at the dirt beneath her fingernails. "I fear Donald Macauley's son already knows what I did. When the lightkeeper brought me back to Lindisfarne, he was there waiting. He was quick to raise his musket."

"How could he possibly know?" says Nathan. "You were out at sea when it happened. Surely Martin was just hunting. You were frightened. It must have felt like he was shooting at you."

Edwin raises his dark eyebrows. "Or he was shooting at you because they believe you a spy."

Eva nods faintly. She knows Edwin's is the most likely explanation. She had seen the way Martin Macauley had aimed his musket so carefully in her direction.

Nathan goes to the window. Does he see Macauley's son prowling? Does he see that sail disappearing towards Longstone?

"We say nothing," he says, turning back to face his family. "But if anyone asks, we tell them Eva was simply caught out by the tide. Agreed?"

Edwin folds his arms across his chest. "Agreed."

Harriet nods, echoing her husband.

"Eva?"

She sighs inwardly. "All right," she murmurs finally. She stares into her cup. Doesn't drink.

"Perhaps it's best if you leave the island, Evie," Harriet speaks up suddenly. "Thomas and I can come with you. We can—"

"I can't run," says Eva. "It will make me look even more guilty." Her words are followed by silence. No one argues. Harriet's shoulders sink.

When the men head back upstairs to work, she gets up from the armchair and comes to sit beside Eva on the settle. She flicks her long blonde plait over her shoulder. "So. You met that strange fellow that lives on Longstone." She refills the teacups with a new light in her eyes. "I've heard talk of him. At church. They all say he's rather mad. Out there keeping the light all on his lonesome."

"That does not sound like a particularly Christian thing to say." Eva shuffles forward in her seat, reaching towards the fire. A violent shiver goes through her. It feels as though not an ounce of summer warmth has made it through the thick stone walls of Highfield House.

Harriet ignores her comment. "His name is Finn Murray. They say he's not set foot on the mainland in his whole life."

"I'm sure that's not true."

"Why do you say that?"

"That island is nothing but a rock, Harriet. No one could

survive out there without going to the mainland for food. Coal and peat for the firebasket…"

Harriet's lips break into a crooked smile. "I did not expect you to take his side. I thought a night out there with him would have terrified you."

"It did," she says. "But it was the situation that terrified me. Not the lightkeeper. Not really."

Harriet hums to herself. "How interesting."

"What is that supposed to mean?"

She shrugs airily. "Nothing."

Finn Murray. They all say he's rather mad. Eva feels oddly indignant on his behalf. And oddly irritated at her sister. She finishes the rest of her tea in silence..

CHAPTER NINE

The bells of Saint Mary's echo across the island, calling the village to Evensong. Nathan's instinct had told him to keep his family locked within the walls of Highfield House and refuse to show their faces at church. But he knows all too well how that will look.

It has been two days since Eva's return. Three since Donald Macauley's death. No doubt his son will be concerned. People will be asking questions. They need to show their faces and pretend nothing is wrong. Provide an explanation for Eva's night away from Holy Island.

He had known from the beginning it would be a risk coming to Lindisfarne. Had suspected the locals would not trust the arrival of Londoners during a time of such political and social unrest. But he had not imagined things would take such a turn as this.

Nathan can count on one hand the number of times he had heard his mother speak of Highfield House after they'd left. Once they had arrived in London, it was as though the place had ceased to exist. For Nathan, eight years old when they'd left the island, their former life had begun to feel like a dream. But there has always been a bitter taste in his mouth at the thought of this place. That bitterness is not helped by the half-truths he had told Eva when she had asked why they had left the house.

He had hoped she had no recollection of the night they had fled. She'd been barely four, clinging to their mother's neck and wailing as they had traipsed across the sand back to the mainland, the rising sea licking at their ankles. Still, the story he had fed her—that their mother had left the house out of grief—is not a lie. And how on earth would Eva benefit from knowing the whole truth of the matter? Especially now, after the horror of Donald Macauley?

When he'd first returned to Highfield House, he had found it drenched in evidence of their hurried escape. Tables and chairs and sideboards and desks just as his mother had left them. The same worn cushions tossed across the settle, the same blankets now faded over the beds. Long-cold ash in the grates and unopened jam jars in the kitchen. Dusty cloths and plates in the pantry had hinted at food that had long disintegrated. Everything had been covered in grime and earth and crumbling mortar, and an unplaceable heaviness had thickened the air.

They walk to church in near silence, beneath a weighted sky that looks closer to winter than the midsummer not long passed. Edwin is leading them down the path, a hand pressed to Harriet's back as she walks with the baby in the crook of her arm. Nathan is at the back of the group, Theodora by his side. Unspoken, they have surrounded Eva like pack animals, and she walks with her eyes down and her cloak pulled tight.

Walking as though she is guilty.

None of them had suggested that they not attend Evensong. A wordless agreement that pretending nothing is wrong is the best way forward. Since their hushed conversation the morning Eva had returned, none of them have spoken Donald Macauley's name, even within the impenetrable walls of the house.

Nathan knows he needs to be aware at all times. If Donald Macauley was willing to kill Eva on account of his belief she is a spy, there is nothing to say his son will not have the same idea about the rest of them. Nathan does not even want to consider what might happen if Martin Macauley discovers what happened to his father. Having Theodora here among such uncertainty fills him with dread.

People are filing steadily into the church, a dour parade of sea-stained greatcoats and patched cloaks. Nathan's shoulders tighten at the sight of Martin approaching the gate. He feels a sizeable amount of guilt over the secrets and lies he has goaded his family into. But he also feels anger. Because although he had tried to convince Eva that she had just dodged a wayward hunting shot, he can't quite make himself believe it. Had it been a warning shot? Or had she evaded a bullet intended to kill her?

As much as he wants to avoid Martin Macauley for fear of his questions, he knows he cannot do so. Only a man with something to hide would let another fellow fire his weapon across his doorstep without consequence. Nathan is all too aware that this is a game. One that must be played with care.

Edwin hangs back from Harriet to fall into step beside him. "You need to confront Martin about the shooting. Before he comes to you."

Nathan nods faintly. "I know." Edwin is right, of course, but he has never been one for confrontation.

Edwin catches his eye. "Perhaps I ought to speak to him."

Nathan bristles. "I'm more than capable of defending my family."

Edwin lowers his voice when Theodora looks up at them curiously. "Of course you are. I just mean… You need to be firm with him, Nate. And I know firmness is not your strong suit. The man's a bastard. Whatever else has happened, he—"

"I said I shall speak to him," Nathan says irritably. "I do not need you to fight my battles."

But perhaps he has lost this game already. Because Martin Macauley is approaching. Weaving through the crowd to seek him out.

Nathan nudges his daughter in Eva and Harriet's direction.

"My father been hunting out your way lately, Blake?" Martin asks without greeting.

Nathan looks at him squarely. "No. Not for days." He feels a line of sweat run down his back. Feels Edwin's eyes on him. "And I'd appreciate it if you stayed off our property too." There's a sourness in his voice, but Nathan knows he sounds far from intimidating.

Edwin steps suddenly in front of him, menacingly close to Martin. "Come near our house again and we'll have the authorities after you," he hisses. Several churchgoers stop to watch the confrontation. "My sister-in-law could have been killed the other morning."

Something passes over Martin's eyes. What is he thinking, Nathan wonders sickly? Have they just put Eva in his line of fire again?

Martin looks between Nathan and Edwin, hesitating. Finally, he says, "Your sister ought to learn to keep better company. Wouldn't trust that lightkeeper further than I can spit." He turns and walks into the church, without looking at them again.

Thomas is grizzling determinedly as the priest rattles through his sermon. It's as though he's aware of it, this grand deception his family has taken on. Harriet rubs his back, coos to him, but he just cries harder. She feels like a fool, with her mindless jabbering and pointless lullabies. Poisonous looks fly her way.

Edwin leans over to whisper in her ear: "Take him outside."

Harriet grits her teeth. She hates when her husband gives her advice on mothering. She shuffles out of the pew and slips from the candlelit church, feeling heads turn as she passes.

A part of her is glad to be out of there; that damp, righteous building with a smell of earth that reminds her of the grave. Divine eyes staring down at her, reminding her of the lies and secrets her family has agreed to.

Outside is just as gloomy, the late-afternoon sun drowned in banks of cloud. Lamps in the churchyard cast long shadows into the ruins of the monastery. She paces the churchyard with Thomas wailing on her shoulder; past worn and crooked headstones, between the pillars and towers of the crumbling priory.

Footsteps sigh through the grass and Harriet turns to see a young woman in striped blue and white skirts. Red curls are escaping out the sides of her bonnet. She offers Harriet a sympathetic smile.

"When my son was a little one, he used to stop if I hummed to him. I think he liked feeling the vibrations in my chest. Perhaps you've not tried that?"

Harriet is grateful for the assistance. When it comes to Thomas, she welcomes advice from everyone other than her husband. Unable to grasp at a melody, she hums a broken collection of notes, holding the baby close to her chest. To her unfathomable relief, Thomas's howling begins to ease. She lets out a breath. "Thank you." She shakes her head. "Sometimes I've no thought of what to do with this child."

The woman grins. "I gave up trying to get my son through church years ago." She nods towards the back of the churchyard where a dark-haired boy is balancing on the low stone wall. "Although I figure at least one of us ought to make an appearance."

Harriet shifts Thomas to her other hip. "I'm sorry to disturb the service."

The woman shrugs. "No bother to me. Just thought you could use some help."

"You came out just to stop my baby crying?"

"Well. That and the fact that I downed three cups of tea before the service and I'm absolutely bursting." She hoicks up her skirts and squats beside one of the gravestones, not a hint of embarrassment on her face. Harriet can't hold back a smile.

The woman stands and smooths her skirts. "Your family means to sell the house, I hear?"

Harriet raises her eyebrows, caught off guard by the abrupt change of subject.

The woman flaps a hand as though waving away her own discourtesy. "I'm sorry. Didn't mean to poke my nose in where it's not wanted. I'm Julia Mitchell. I run the curiosity shop on Church Lane."

Harriet accepts her outstretched hand; introduces herself.

"I think I met your sister earlier in the week," says Julia. "And her daughter."

"My brother's daughter," Harriet tells her. "Theodora has been talking endlessly about your shop."

Julia smiles. "Aye, she liked the doll in the silk dress."

"She's been begging her father for it for days." Harriet bats Thomas's hand away from the strings of her bonnet. "You're right," she says. "My brother means to sell the house. He and my husband are restoring it, but I can't see much of an improvement yet. I feel as though we'll be here for an eternity."

"There are worse places to be," says Julia.

"I suppose." Harriet shrugs. "It's just that we've not been made to feel particularly welcome."

A look of regret passes over Julia's face. "The people here are suspicious of outsiders. That's all. And poor old Donald Macauley's vanishing has people in a twist."

"What do you think happened to him?" Harriet asks, trying to keep her voice level.

Julia shrugs. "An old drunk like him? Probably took himself out to sea and couldn't find his way back."

Harriet hopes the rest of the village has come to the same conclusion.

Julia heads towards her son at the back of the churchyard,

making it clear she has no intention of returning to the service. "You're welcome to come and see me at the shop anytime you need a little company," she tells Harriet. "And I'll put that doll aside for your niece. In case her da decides to spoil her."

Eva flies out of the church the moment the service is finished. Harriet is waiting by the gate, Thomas now angelic in the crook of her arm. Eva takes her sister's free elbow and hurtles away from the village.

"That was unbearable," she hisses. "It felt as though everyone knows what I've done. Felt as though God were staring down at me, cursing me for my lies. And for…well…" *Killing a man.* Speaking it makes it far too real.

"What choice did you have but to lie?" asks Harriet, sidestepping a mound of sheep dung. "What else were you to have done? Stand up in front of the congregation and confess to Donald Macauley's murder?"

Eva wraps her arms around herself. "It wasn't murder."

"Of course it wasn't. But you know that's how the villagers will see it."

Eva says nothing. Harriet is right, of course, and the weight of that knowledge presses down on her, making it hard to breathe. Over and over, she hears the dull thud of the oar striking Donald Macauley's head. Hears the faint sigh of water as his body disappeared below the surface. Guilt pulls at her chest.

She takes the baby from Harriet and squeezes him to her, needing the comfort of his warm body pressed close to her heart.

For a while they walk in a heavy silence, broken only by the slosh of their footsteps and Thomas's sporadic babbling. When they reach the path that cuts through the dunes towards the house, Eva keeps walking. She is not ready to venture back into the darkwood world of Highfield House. The manor is stifling in the weight of the secrets they are keeping. Stifling with the weight of a past she can't quite make out.

She steps out onto the beach and closes her eyes. Lifts her face to the wind. Harriet slips an arm around her shoulder and squeezes. Though Harriet's presence is rarely a calming one, Eva is glad she is here now. In spite of everything, she had missed her sister in the month they were apart. And there had been more than one moment while she was stranded on Longstone when she imagined they might never see each other again.

She opens her eyes. Trudges back to the top of the beach, her shoes sliding over the pebbles. And she sees it then: that rusty splatter across the white shingle at the top of the embankment. Blood. There can be no mistaking it.

Her mouth goes dry.

"Eva?" she hears Harriet say. "What is it? What have you found?"

It's the blood of a sea bird, she tells herself. A fish, or a seal. Or some poor roe deer Martin Macauley has blasted from the dunes. These, she knows, are all likely explanations. But she can't shake that possibility that is making her heart pound and the sounds in her ears feel distant.

That when Martin Macauley raised his musket on her, his bullet struck Finn Murray.

Impossible, she tells herself. She would have heard him cry out. Perhaps seen him fall. But when she thinks back to those terrifying moments, she remembers screaming, remembers running, remembers not looking back at Finn until his boat was moving towards the horizon. It is possible, she knows, that Martin Macauley's bullet found him without her being aware of it. It is more than possible. She presses the baby back into Harriet's arms, unable to tear her eyes from those darkened petals of blood.

And she knows she must return to Longstone.

CHAPTER TEN

Eva rushes back to the house. She shoves spare skirts and stockings and petticoats into her duffel bag, along with her shawl and gloves and a small pouch of coins.

Harriet ploughs into her bedroom with Thomas under her arm, a barrage of questions. What is she doing? Where is she going?

"I have to go back to Longstone. Finn Murray... He may be hurt." She is off down the stairs before Harriet can gather a response. She blusters towards the kitchen, passing Mrs Brodie in the hallway as she returns from Evensong.

"All right, Miss Blake?" asks the housekeeper, following her into the kitchen.

Eva flings open the pantry. "I need to go to Longstone. I'm afraid Mr Murray has been hurt."

"Mr Murray? The lightkeeper?" Mrs Brodie frowns. "What do you need?"

Eva rifles past jam jars and potted meat and baskets of potatoes. "Food. Tea. I don't know, I..." She has no idea what she will find when she steps back onto Longstone, and no idea what she will do if the lightkeeper truly is hurt—all she knows is she must go. What if Finn Murray has bled to death in that lonely cottage? Or what if he never made it back to the island at all? What if he is lying dead in that little boat, his body at the mercy of the waves? Dread squeezes her chest. She cannot live with another death on her conscience.

She scrubs a hand across her eyes, trying to tamp down her panic. She has no idea how she will even get back to the island.

Mrs Brodie goads her out of the cupboard and produces a block of cheese and a loaf of bread from the shelf, along with a jar of potted meat and a tin of tea. She wraps the bread in a cloth and hands the food to Eva. "These should last you a few days. How long will you be gone?"

She shakes her head. "I've no idea."

The door cracks open and Harriet appears in the kitchen. "Evie. This is madness. You cannot seriously be going back there."

"I have to."

Mrs Brodie emerges from the pantry with another small jar. She hands it to Eva. "Here. It's figwort ointment. If the fellow is hurt, this will help it heal. It will keep the wound from festering."

Eva shoves it in her bag and nods her thanks. She flies past Harriet before she can stop her.

Out the front door she runs. There are Nathan and Edwin, deep in conversation as they walk the inland path back from the village. Theodora is just ahead of them, skipping backwards and chatting animatedly.

Eva darts towards the coast path, hoping she will not be

seen. Harriet will tell Nathan everything, no doubt. Right now, Eva has neither the time nor the inclination to explain things to her brother.

She hurries onto the wharf, praying she will not see Martin Macauley. A young fisherman, barely older than a boy, is kneeling on the jetty, wrestling with a tangled fishing net.

Eva holds out a handful of coins. "I need to get to Longstone. Will you take me?"

Confusion crosses his freckled face. "There's nothing on Longstone. Nothing except the firebasket."

She holds his gaze. "Will you take me?"

The young man stands. He looks out to sea, then down to the money in her outstretched palm. "You're one of them, aren't you. The Blakes."

Eva grits her teeth. "That has nothing to do with anything. Will you take me or not?"

The fisherman grabs the coins and shoves them into his pocket. He nods towards his boat. "Get in."

Eva sits at the bow, eyes fixed to the dark shape of Longstone. The fisherman's boat pitches over the swell, sea spray stinging her eyes. She can make out the shape of the cottage on its distended foundations, the coal shed behind it. Can make out the stone tower of the firebasket, unlit in the pink twilight. She grips the gunwale. "Can you not go faster?"

"I'm sorry, Miss," says the fisherman. "Big swell today. Got to be careful around the reef."

She clenches her hands until her nails dig into her palms. The need to get to the cottage is overwhelming.

After what feels an eternity, the fisherman draws close to the jetty. The sight of Finn's boat knocking against its mooring eases a little of Eva's panic. At the very least, he has made it back to the island.

The moment the fisherman's boat touches the jetty, she leaps out, clutching her duffel bag to her chest.

"I can't wait for you," the fisherman calls. "I've to get back…"

Eva nods. She casts a single glance back over her shoulder and sees the boat moving away from the jetty. She rushes towards the cottage, stumbling through a shallow pool beside the staircase.

She is breathless when she pounds on the door. Throws it open without waiting for a response. And there is the lightkeeper, yanked from sleep as she clatters into the cottage.

An unreadable expression passes across his face as he sits up in bed. Anger or amusement? Maybe somewhere between the two. "You. What in hell are you doing here?"

Eva swallows. Water drips from her wet skirts and pools at her feet. "Martin Macauley," she garbles, "I thought he hit you. I passed the beach on the way back to the house today. And I saw blood on the rocks, and I thought…"

He raises his eyebrows as he shoves back the bedclothes. Tangled brown hair hangs loose on his shoulders, dishevelled and flattened on one side. "You thought you'd come fleeing back here to see if I was dead?"

"Yes." Why does it sound so foolish when he says it? Eva swallows, her fingers tightening around the strap of her bag. "I may have overreacted."

A faint smile quirks his lips. "You think?"

Eva hesitates. "The firebasket is not lit."

"No." He looks down, away from her eyes. "It's not."

And she sees it then—that pile of bloodied cloths in the

81

chamber pot beside the bed. Sees the discoloured strapping around his calf, peeking out from beneath his woollen slops.

"He did hit you." She rushes towards him.

He jerks away, holding out a hand to keep her at a distance. "What do you think you're doing?"

Eva straightens indignantly. "I'm checking to make sure you're not bleeding to death."

He snorts. "I'm not bleeding to death. It's just a scratch."

Up close, she sees his cheeks are flushed beneath his beard. Sees the sweat glistening on his forehead. She thinks of him sailing back to Longstone with Martin Macauley's bullet in his calf. Thinks of him tending to his own wounds, alone on this island with the sea closing in. It makes her chest ache. But she takes a step back, suddenly aware of how close she is standing to him.

"You don't need to be here," he says. "I'm fine."

Eva looks at him squarely. "You are clearly not. I am not leaving you on your own like this."

His lips part at her directness. No doubt he thought her capable of nothing more than panic-stricken tears and snivelling. "I don't need a house guest," he snaps. "I don't know what you were thinking, charging in here uninvited." As if to prove his point, his hand tightens around the bed head and he attempts to stand, swallowing a grunt of pain. Eva puts a firm hand to his shoulder, forcing him back onto the mattress.

"Don't be so damn foolish. You need to rest." The conflict is making her whole body hot, but she refuses to back down. "You can be as angry at me as you wish, Mr Murray. But I am not going anywhere until you are healed. So you may as well accept it."

His eyebrows rise; she knows his name—she has clearly been discussing him. But her outburst seems to have shocked him into silence.

Flustered, Eva looks around. Now she has made her grand proclamation, she has no idea what to do. "I need to see the wound," she says, trying to conjure up confidence she doesn't feel.

He gives a short, humourless laugh. "Nah you don't."

She rifles through her bag for the jar of figwort. "Please. This will help fight off the fever."

"No need for that," he says dryly. He picks up a bottle of whisky from beside the bed and lets it dangle in his fist. "Already cleaned it out with a little moonshine."

Eva hesitates, debating whether to argue. She senses pressing the issue will only cause him to push back even harder. She puts the jar of figwort on the mantel beside a burnt-out candle stump and sets her bonnet on the table. The cottage is in disarray. Finn's greatcoat has been flung over a chair, bloodstained breeches on the floor beside the bed. A half-eaten loaf of bread sits in the middle of the table, a knife poking out of a jam jar beside it. The place smells of whisky, of sweat, of sea. Eva shivers hard. The cottage is freezing.

She spots the kettle sitting beside the unlit fire. Tea, she decides. She will make tea. At the very least, it will calm her, order her mind a little. And perhaps settle a little of Finn's anger.

She can feel his eyes boring into the back of her as she crouches by the blackened bricks of the hearth and carefully arranges the kindling from the basket beside the grate.

"D'you know how to do that?" he asks with a hint of mockery.

Her cheeks flush, but she does not give him the satisfaction of seeing it. "You think I cannot lay a fire?" she asks, keeping her back to him.

"I think a lass who dresses like you and speaks like you has always had these things done for her."

Eva hates how true his words are. Hates that she only knows how to lay a fire from having watched her housekeepers do it. And she hates how terrified she is that this fire won't take. Asking for help, after she has appeared here so impulsively—and after she has made such a scene about caring for him—would be close to the worst thing she can imagine. She strikes the tinderbox once, twice, before it sparks. After several minutes, the tiny flames licking the kindling have grown into something warming and bright. She fights the urge to give Finn a self-satisfied look.

Finding the kettle still half full of water, she hangs it on the hook and rummages in her bag for the tea Mrs Brodie had given her. In the back of the sideboard, she finds a cracked floral teapot. A single tin cup and plate sit abandoned on the table. She wipes the thick layer of dust from the pot and cracks open the lid, startling a spider out from its depths. She uses a little of the water from the kettle to rinse it. Her wet shoes leave footprints across the floor as she paces between the hearth and the table.

When steam is curling from the nose of the kettle, she fills the pot and pours the tea carefully into the cup. She cuts a little of the bread and cheese and sets them on the plate. Holds the food out to Finn.

He eyes it, before looking up at her. "I'm not hungry," he says dryly. "And I don't like tea. But well done. On managing the fire and all."

Eva presses her lips into a thin line. She dumps the cup and plate on the table, cursing under her breath as hot liquid splashes onto her finger.

Finn tilts his head, taking her in. "What would you have done if I were dead? Stood waving on the shore until a ship passed?"

Her cheeks flush. "I don't know," she admits. "It was foolish. I just… I saw the blood on the rocks and I panicked. I knew I had to come and see if you needed help."

She waits for his taunt, but it doesn't come. He lowers his eyes.

"Is there anything else you need?" Eva asks.

Finn opens his mouth, but says nothing.

"What?" she presses.

When he speaks again, a little of the mockery is gone from his voice. "The firebasket. I've not managed to light it."

"The firebasket," Eva repeats. "Of course." She looks out the window at the brazier swaying gently on the end of the chain. The dusk is thick now and the jagged shards of the Farnes are being swallowed by the night.

Building the fire was one thing, but lighting the beacon with the wind whipping up off the ocean feels like something else entirely. Finn makes to stand, but she holds out a hand to stop him. "No. I can manage. Just tell me what I need to do."

She waits for that ridicule; that comment that a well-to-do lady like her will never spark that basket to life. But Finn says:

"Unhook the chain and use the pulley to lower the brazier. The fuel is in the shed. Use the kindling to get it started, then bank it up with coal. The same way you lit the fire in the hearth."

Eva nods. She takes the tinderbox from the mantel and shoves it in her pocket, then goes out to the shed. Her wet shoes squelch loudly as she carries armfuls of wood towards the firebasket. Wind is swirling off the ocean, and she sees dark planes of sea rising and falling against the edge of the island. Slowly, carefully, she unhooks the chain from its moorings and lowers the brazier down to the earth, the rusty metal leaving orange streaks on her palms. Carefully, she arranges the wood in the firebasket and strikes the tinderbox, sending a spark into the kindling. Wind whips off the water and snatches the tiny flame.

Eva grits her teeth. She rearranges the kindling and snaps the tinderbox again. This time, the fire sparks, and with a little coaxing, it spreads. Orange light blossoms, illuminating the night. For a moment, she stares into it, feeling the warmth against her cheeks. Her arms strain as she heaves on the chain, sending the brazier into the sky. Using all her strength, she secures the chain to its hook. Light arcs out across the sea.

Inexplicably, Eva feels tears prick her eyes. After Walton's rejection, after Nathan's disappointment, and worst of all, after Donald Macauley, being capable of this felt like the air she needed to survive. She blinks her tears away quickly. She cannot let Finn Murray see them.

When she comes back inside, the cottage is bathed in orange light from both inside and out. The fire in the grate is starting to warm the frozen corners. She feels a soft sense of accomplishment.

She goes to a corner of the room and pulls off her wet shoes and stockings, replacing them with a dry pair from her bag. Her damp skirts and petticoats soak through the dry wool quickly, but she will have to wait until Finn is asleep before she can change her clothes. She shoves her wet stockings back into her duffel bag, then goes to the table and begins to eat the bread and cheese she had cut for Finn. She is famished, she realises. She has barely eaten a thing since Donald Macauley's death, and now, in the relief of finding Finn alive, her hunger has returned with force. She can't help but glance at him as she eats. He is watching her with a look of open curiosity.

"Who are you?" he asks. "What's your name?"

He knows not a thing about her either, Eva realises. Beyond the fact that she killed a man, and took Finn back to Holy Island to face Martin Macauley's musket. Little wonder he had looked so unimpressed when she had barrelled back through his door. "Eva," she says finally. "Eva Blake."

Something passes across his eyes. "Blake. Your family owns Highfield House."

She nods faintly. And she feels a strange heaviness in her chest that, even out here in such vast isolation, the shadow of the house might still manage to reach her.

CHAPTER ELEVEN

Finn's chest is heaving.

Eva Blake, of Highfield House.

She cannot stay here. Of all the people in the world, *she* cannot stay here.

But what are the choices? He is in far too much pain to take the skiff back to Holy Island tonight. And no one else is coming for her.

Besides, as much as he can't bear the thought of having one of the Blakes under his roof—and as much as he doesn't want to admit it—he needs her help.

The wound to his lower leg could have been far worse— Macauley's ball had made both a clean entry and exit, neatly finding the stripe of flesh between his breeches and his boots. But even a few steps is enough to have sweat beading on his forehead. He can feel a fever closing in.

This life is a physically challenging one, even without such an injury. Last night, he had made it as far as the coal shed, but carrying shovelfuls to the firebasket had been a step too far. He had lain in bed in thick, unsettling blackness, kept from sleep by pulsing pain.

He looks through the salt-speckled window at the bloom of orange light in the sky. He's surprised to see the fire roaring in the basket. Was sure he'd be hobbling out there himself to tell her where to find the coal. He has to admit, he's a little impressed.

Eva sits at his table, chewing through bread and cheese like she hasn't eaten for a week. She is oddly fascinating, with her stockinged feet and the thick blue cloak still wrapped around her shoulders. Is she cold? Or too enthralled by her supper to realise she is still wearing it? Strands of brown hair have come loose from the knot at the back of her neck, spidery against the white skin above her collar. Something about her is impossible to look away from. Maybe it's just the novelty of having another person in the cottage with him. He was a child the last time that happened.

When she has finished her food, she looks around, he supposes for a trough or washcloth. She'll find neither—the bucket he uses for washing his dishes is lying on its side behind the coal shed. He barely uses it at the best of times.

She leaves the plate on the table and looks over at him, wrapping her arms around her body.

"You ought to try and sleep," she says. "I can watch the light."

He shakes his head. "I'll not sleep til dawn." He nods towards the door half-blocked by the sideboard. "You can sleep in there."

Eva goes to the sideboard with a curious frown on her face. She throws her weight against it and it groans along the floor. She opens the door and peeks inside curiously.

The room is dark, the shutters fastened over the windows to keep the sea from finding its way through the glass. Finn can't remember the last time the room saw sunlight. An orange glow from the lamp on the table reaches inside, and he can see the shape of the narrow wooden bed in the centre of the room. No blankets or pillows, but a cotton-stuffed mattress, which he hopes is still intact. He can tell the room is shadowed and cold, the chill of unused decades trapped in its rugged stone walls. He has vivid memories of lying awake on that narrow bed, listening to his parents chatter, tracking his father's footsteps across the cottage and out towards the beacon. How many nights had he lain awake in that room, making up stories about the shadows the firebasket cast on the wall?

He is sure the room is filthy, filled with the sour breath of forgotten years and sea. A part of him is embarrassed to offer it to a lady like Eva Blake.

She turns to him with raised eyebrows. "You have another room? Why did you not tell me that last time I was here?"

"I offered you the bed," Finn says tautly.

"Who did it belong to?" she asks. "It looks like it's not been used for years."

He swallows. "D'you want it or not?" He desperately hopes she will take the room. Disappear into it for a few hours. He needs the space—especially now he knows who she is.

He's become too used to being kept company by only the light and the tides. These days, he needs to prepare himself for any disruption to his solitary existence. And he most certainly was not prepared for Eva Blake to appear at his door with panic in her eyes and figwort in her hands.

"Yes," she says. "Of course I want it. Thank you." She dumps her duffel bag inside the door, then looks at him with intent blue eyes. "But not tonight. Tonight you need to rest. And I will watch the light." Her words are thin and he can tell her confidence is forced.

Finn reaches down for the bottle of whisky beside the bed. Takes a long gulp. The liquor is awful, but he swallows it smoothly. His body has grown far too used to it over the last few days. The alcohol dulls the pain in his calf, but does nothing for the fierce thumping behind his eyes.

He opens his mouth to argue, but can't quite form the words. He is exhausted, from two sleepless, pain-filled nights—and from five years of keeping the light alone. He has trained himself to sleep in short spurts; a few hours at dawn, a few before dusk. But he is not immune to the rhythms of nature, and his body's inherent need to sleep in the darkness. There have been far too many times that he's woken at the table to find himself in blackness, with the firebasket spitting ash. Still, he supposes a sporadic light on the shore is better than no light at all.

Tonight, though, with a second person to keep the flames alive, he finds himself closing his eyes.

It's a broken, fevered sleep, though it's far more than he's managed in the past two nights. Eva is constantly there on the edge of his awareness, pouring water down his throat, pressing a damp cloth to his forehead, trudging out into the night to restoke the basket.

Sometime before dawn, he opens his eyes and watches her in the firelight. She puts the jam jar in the sideboard and wipes crumbs from the table with a cloth she has magicked from somewhere unknown. She lets out an enormous yawn;

doesn't bother to cover it. There is something oddly thrilling about watching her without her being aware of it. Like observing a swan through a bird hide. Her black leather shoes are drying by the hearth, lined up neatly with their buckles side by side. Her feet are soundless on the floorboards as she moves back and forth across the cottage.

In spite of everything Eva's presence has stirred up in him, he can't deny there's something faintly comforting about having another soul on the island tonight. Even if that person does come from Highfield House. In spite of everything, as he had stitched and bound his wound, dousing it in whisky to fight off the fever, he had been unable to shake the fear that he might die alone on this island.

What would happen to his body? Would he disappear back into the earth or the sea, with no living soul any the wiser? There is a certain beauty to that, he supposes. But it is more than a little unnerving. The thought of it, just like Eva's presence, reminds him of things he would rather forget.

It's been years since anyone else has set foot on Longstone. Even the churchmen who own this land never venture out here. His willingness to keep the firebasket lit, even without a real commission, keeps them from venturing his way; keeps them from demanding payment for the land. An arrangement that has been in place since his father was alive.

Eva Blake, a child of Highfield House. Eva Blake, who had knocked a man into the sea and watched him drown. There is something faintly settling about the terrible deed she had confessed to. She is carrying her own crime, so she is unlikely to dig too deeply into his.

An accident, she had told him. Who was the sorry soul?

And why was she out at sea with him so close to dark? The question has been swirling through his mind unbidden since he had plucked her from his coal shed three nights ago. But he can't ask. Won't ask. He cannot set a precedent of them being open with each other. Nonetheless, he's achingly curious about her. What brought her back to Holy Island? Because that polished London accent tells him it's been years since she last set foot in Northumberland.

She turns her head, catches him watching her. "I'm sorry," she says, "I did not mean to wake you." She takes the waterskin from the table and strides purposefully towards him. "Here. You ought to drink a little while you're awake."

The rainwater tastes of the sky, and faintly, somehow of the sea. Everything out here comes to taste like the sea. A stray drop slides through his beard, cooling his heated skin. He nods his thanks, then turns away quickly, to prevent conversation.

He shakes his curiosity about her away. It doesn't matter why she's here. All that matters is that she does not stay under his roof for a minute longer than necessary.

CHAPTER TWELVE

In the lamplight of her workroom, ripples of painted sunshine are coming alive. Harriet's brush moves across the canvas, and she is dimly aware of a smile on her face. Around her, the rest of the house is silent. Has been for hours.

She has been painting for what feels like her entire life. Does not dare to imagine what she would be without it. She remembers the friend of her mother who had taught her her craft: Madame Octavia—self-styled, of course—with her loose-flowing grey hair and silk robes that billowed out behind her like windblown clouds. Madame Octavia used to brag she had studied with Sirani; would toss Italian phrases into Harriet's lessons, all for the purpose of the exotic.

They would not be constrained, Madame Octavia would say, by the limitations the art world placed upon their sex. They would not be content to paint meagre still-lifes and visions of the home—*we are far better than that, are we not, Harriet, dear?*

How she craved those lessons, when the madame would

flounce around the sitting room of her townhouse on the Strand, her bare, paint-speckled feet pattering against the floorboards. They would paint with their easels side by side, and with the madame's careful tutelage, Harriet brought to life grand seascapes and portraits and imagined visions of worlds she had never seen. Those lessons had been full of inspiration, of freedom. They had been some of the happiest days of Harriet's life. They feel impossibly distant.

Before she had died, Octavia had introduced Harriet to her fellow artists across the city. Men and women with whom she could lose herself in conversation, spending hours in discussion over this painter's use of shadow, the drama captured in this artist's work. People who understood her. Passionate, single-minded people she felt she could relate to. She misses them with an ache that seems to reach her bones.

"Harriet. What are you doing?"

She doesn't turn. "I am sure you can work that out for yourself, Edwin."

Her husband sighs loudly from the doorway. "It's far too late for this."

She does not tell him she has been creeping down here at midnight almost every night since they arrived in this place. Does not tell him how irritated she is that he has finally woken up and caught her. Instead, she says, "I like this time of night. It inspires me."

These nights in front of her easel have begun to feel like her saviour. The only time she can live something close to the life she wants to live. Never mind the figure creeping around outside the window, perhaps seeking to punish her family for their spying ways.

Two days ago, Harriet had ventured to Julia Mitchell's

curiosity shop for tea and conversation, and had left with the sense that she might actually have something close to a friend in this place.

As she and Julia had chatted easily over their teacups, Harriet considered telling her about the figure she had seen around the house at night. But something had held her back. Perhaps a fear of being ridiculed. Or perhaps a reluctance to share the goings on of Highfield House with a village that seems fixated on her family.

Edwin steps through the doorway, glancing around the shadowed, lamplit room. "It's dreadfully dreary down here. How can a place like this inspire you?"

Harriet looks back at the canvas. In a way, he is right. The light is far too poor to allow for any great accuracy. But this gloomy hovel has become her saving grace. "You're a craftsman," she says. "I thought you considered yourself an artist. I would have thought you understood the way inspiration works."

Edwin takes her wrist, lifting the paintbrush from the canvas. "Come to bed." There is a firmness to his tone now, and Harriet can tell his words are not merely a suggestion. She hesitates. She knows she cannot push back too hard, or she risks her husband taking her painting away from her. But this impossible streak of sunlight cannot wait. She steps closer to the canvas, examining the arc of her brushstrokes.

"I will be there shortly," she says.

"No." His fingers tighten around her wrist. "You will come upstairs now. We've barely spent time together all week."

"Because you're too exhausted to keep your eyes open at the end of every day."

"Yes," he says pointedly. "Securing our future. Our son's future."

Nathan has offered Edwin a handsome cut of the profits once the house is sold, in addition, of course to a return of all the funds her husband has invested in the project. Harriet does not even dare imagine when that might happen. Lindisfarne feels like a purgatory she will never escape.

She does not miss the undertone in Edwin's comment, the words that go unsaid. The warning that in order to be permitted to keep a brush in her hand, she must remember she is first and foremost a wife. A mother.

She must remember that her husband is not to be neglected.

She sighs heavily, defeated. She places her palette into the water tray she has set up on the table beside her. And she trails Edwin back down the hallway to their bedroom, deliberate in not cleaning the paint from her hands. The streaks of light and dark staining her wrists and fingers serve to keep her mind focused on her work, rather than the task that lies ahead. Specks of sunlight on her palms to take her attention away from reality.

Edwin is brisk, efficient as he sifts through layers of clothing and eases her back on the wide curtained bed. Harriet looks up at the canopy; forces her mind to other places.

It is not that she is repulsed by her husband. Edwin is fine-looking enough, with thick dark hair that has not yet begun to thin, and a narrow, unblemished face that could almost be described as handsome. And yet it does nothing to warm her, or to persuade her closer. In the first days and weeks of their marriage, he had been attentive to her needs—or had at least attempted to be. These days, he seems to have given up the pretence entirely. Harriet is glad of it.

Nonetheless, it is not the act itself that she dreads so desperately, but the fear of finding herself with child again. Such a thing would be worse than having her painting taken from her. Being Thomas's mother is already far too big a weight to carry. Having another child in tow is a horror she cannot even begin to contemplate.

Before she sleeps tonight, she will pray for a reprieve. Reacquaint herself with a god she only speaks to while lying on her back beneath the bed curtains, with her husband's scent on her skin.

CHAPTER THIRTEEN

By dawn, Eva's eyes are heavy. She sits wearily at the table, staring out the window as the last threads of firelight are sucked away by the morning. There's an allure to this beautiful solitude, she realises. Out here on Longstone, with the rest of the world feeling far away, that weighted regret over Donald Macauley's death is sitting a little lighter on her shoulders.

Thanks to her efforts during the night, the cottage is in slightly better order, with the table cleaned of food scraps and jars tucked away in cupboards. Today, she will scrub down the plates and cups that don't seem to have seen a wash cloth in decades. Soak Finn's bloodstained clothes and air out the bedroom.

She yawns. Hopefully she will manage a few hours of sleep this morning too.

She looks over at Finn. His chest is rising and falling with sleep, his breath slower and steadier than it had been throughout the night. She hopes it means his fever is beginning to pass.

"If I die," he'd mumbled at her during the night, "take the skiff back to Lindisfarne."

And avoiding the prospect of being back on that ocean alone, Eva thinks, is as good a reason as any to keep this man alive.

She knows that, as impulsive as this journey to Longstone was, it was the right thing to do. Whether Finn Murray plans to admit it or not, she knows she is needed here, and after the devastation of the past few weeks, it feels good to be of service.

She is fairly certain he is not going to admit it.

Eva takes the knife from the table and begins to slice through the bread Mrs Brodie had given her. Decides to leave the brick-like remains of Finn's loaf to the birds.

The bed creaks and she turns to see him open his eyes. His gaze drifts to the hearth, where her wet stockings hang drying over the fireguard. Eva leaps to her feet and snatches them hurriedly, cheeks flushing with embarrassment.

"Good morning," she says guardedly, stockings in one hand and knife in the other. "How are you feeling?"

"Grand," he says wryly. "Just grand." He looks bleary-eyed and disoriented at having slept through the darkness. But in spite of his saltiness, he seems a little better this morning, his eyes somewhat brighter and the shadows in his cheeks less pronounced.

Eva shoves the stockings into her pocket, hovering in front of the bed. This is a far more awkward thing now Finn is not half vacant with whisky and sleep. She is all too aware of the impropriety of their situation.

She fills two plates with slices of bread and cheese. "Here.

You ought to eat something." She attempts a smile. "The cheese is good. I think you will like it." Finn takes the plate. Says nothing. His complete lack of gratitude—and manners—stings. "Or do you dislike cheese as well as tea?" She is unable to keep the sharpness out of her voice.

Finn studies her for a moment before taking a bite. "It's good," he says. His words sound somewhat begrudging.

Eva sits at the table, the chair creaking loudly beneath her. For long moments, they eat in silence. Wind pushes against the glass, making the window frames creak.

This stiltedness, Eva realises, it's new. When she had first blown onto Longstone and disrupted Finn Murray's solitude, he had been brusque and rough spoken. But he had not been reluctant to talk to her. Now, getting a word out of him is like trying to squeeze blood from a stone.

It's the pain, she tells herself. No doubt he's in little mood for conversation.

Or perhaps there is more to it.

Because this coldness, she realises, it started the moment Finn learned her name.

"You know my family's house," she says.

He keeps his eyes on his plate. "Everyone knows your family's house."

"Well," she says, "it won't be ours for much longer."

He looks up in interest.

"My brother is restoring it. He means to sell it."

Finn takes another bite of bread. Chews slowly. "You live there with your husband?"

She smiles wryly. Does he really imagine a husband might allow her to come out here alone like this? "My brother. And sister. And their families." She tears the crust off her bread and breaks it into pieces. "We are not government spies. If that's what you think." Because that's what this new coldness is about, isn't it? Is that not why Finn Murray closed down the moment he heard her name? Because he knows Highfield House, and he knows the rumours surrounding the Blakes, and perhaps he has his own involvement in the Jacobite cause he wishes to hide from her and her fictitious contacts within King George's government.

"What I think?" he repeats. "What does it matter what I think? What your family does is of no concern to me."

Eva grits her teeth. She had tried to nudge the conversation towards some semblance of openness; lay their cards on the table so they might get through this ordeal without blood being spilt—at least no more than it has already. But she can tell there is to be no such thing.

"Well," she says tautly, "it concerns you to the degree of Martin Macauley putting a bullet in your calf."

Finn looks at her squarely then, and it catches her off guard. His brown eyes seem to bore into hers, making her feel suddenly exposed. He opens his mouth to speak, then seems to change his mind. He turns back to his plate and shifts on the bed, tries to hide a grimace.

Eva forgets the need to exonerate her family. "Please," she says tentatively. "Will you let me see the wound? I'm sure the figwort ointment will do it good. Our housekeeper says it will help it heal." She takes the jar from the mantel and holds it out to him. "Please?"

Resignedly, Finn pushes back the blanket and tugs his woollen slops above his knee. He unwraps the strapping he has tied around his calf. The wound has been jaggedly stitched closed, tracking the path Martin Macauley's bullet had carved through his flesh. Though the skin around the wound is pink and swollen, and still flecked with blood, Eva is relieved to find it looks somewhat clean. Not that she really has any damn idea what she is looking for.

She swallows heavily and takes a step closer to the bed. She can smell the salt and woodsmoke on Finn's skin. Can feel the heat rising from his body. Her heart begins to quicken.

When she had thrown herself into the fisherman's boat, desperate to return to Longstone, she had not stopped to consider the intimacy, the indecency, of being out here alone with Finn Murray. She had not thought beyond his survival. But she had become aware of it the moment she had stepped back into his cottage and found him in bed. Had been aware of it as she had sat at the table in the thick stillness of night, listening to his heavy breathing. And she is acutely, painfully aware of it now.

She uncorks the jar. Hesitates for a moment. She reaches for the washcloth sitting in the basin and dips the corner into the ointment. She edges closer to Finn, fingers tight around the cloth. He swoops a hand out suddenly and snatches the jar. "Let me do it." His voice is husky.

Eva nods and backs away.

Finn doesn't look at her as he tentatively applies the ointment with his fingers. His shoulders round, as though he is trying to close in on himself. He turns away from her slightly, as if he too is feeling exposed.

He rips another strip of linen from the torn shirt hanging on the end of the bed. Ties it around his calf and pulls down the leg of his slops.

Eva hovers by the table. "I'm sorry," she says.

"For what?"

"It was all my fault."

He sets the jar on the floor beside the bed. "It was Martin Macauley's fault."

"You would not have been there if it weren't for me." She glances down at his wound. "Did you pull the ball out yourself?"

"The ball passed through. I told you, it's just a scratch."

She raises her eyebrows. "I think we both know that to be a lie."

One corner of his lips turns upwards into a hint of a smile. It takes Eva by surprise. "Well. I'm sure I will survive."

She catches his eye. "I am not leaving until I know that for certain."

CHAPTER FOURTEEN

"*Please,* Papa." Theodora is standing as close as possible to the doorway without actually being inside the bedroom. It's this room, his brother Oliver's room, that Nathan cannot bear to have his daughter in. He has just begun tearing up the stained and timeworn floorboards that are in desperate need of replacing. Already, he can't wait for the task to be over.

"Can I please have the doll? It's so beautiful, you just have to see it. It looks like an *actual* person. She has real, honest eyelashes."

Nathan looks over his shoulder at her. "Theodora, I've told you before—"

"I'm not *in* the room, Papa. I'm just outside it. Look where my toes are."

He can't hold back a smile.

"Auntie Harriet says the lady in the shop is keeping the doll for me and I just have to convince you to buy it."

Nathan raises his eyebrows. "Does she now?"

"Just this one doll, please. Then I'll never, ever come into the rooms you're working in again."

He comes towards her, blocking the doorway and ushering her from the room. Instinctively, she takes a step back, to avoid making contact with him. The gesture fills him with regret.

Physical contact—even with his daughter—has always been hard for him. An intense discomfort bordering on fear. It's a crawling beneath his skin. A hot swirling in his belly. When someone touches him without consent, he feels the ghost of the contact lingering for days.

Somehow, with Sarah, it had been easy. Nathan had always assumed he would never be a husband; never be a father. Had assumed he would live out his life in his self-imposed isolation—a strange, peopled loneliness. But when he had met Sarah, he had felt something inside him shift. For the first time in his life, he had craved her. Craved the feel of her hair beneath his fingers, her hand intertwined with his. Longed to have her body pressed against his own. She had been endlessly patient as he navigated his way through his fear, one graze of the fingers at a time. Sitting motionless as he explored her almost experimentally. A finger traced around her jawline. A hand pressed to her arm. And then, finally, slowly, a kiss; his skin to hers; his body moving inside her.

When Sarah had passed away three years ago, there had been another sensation alongside the grief. A sense of him closing up, stepping back into the shell of solitude he had existed in for so much of his life. A need to keep everyone—even his child—at a distance.

He knows, of course, what that distance could do to Theodora, especially after the loss of her mother. And so, he tries. Tries for Thea, and for everyone else around him. Tries to be as warm and affable as possible, to prove the distance he is keeping is nothing to do with them.

He hates how acutely aware Theodora is of his fear. Hates that his affectionate daughter changes her behaviour to appease him.

He gives her his brightest smile to make up for it. "You'll never come into the rooms I'm working in again? That does sound like a fine deal."

"It is," she tells him solemnly. "It's a very fine deal."

He laughs. "Very well. The deal is made. Just let me tidy myself." He locks the door behind him and shoves the ring of keys into his pocket.

"And at this house," Theodora says as they walk towards the village half an hour later, "there are two sheep. I call them Peter and Pigsy, but I don't know what their real names are."

Nathan chuckles. "Pigsy is a rather strange name for a sheep, don't you think?"

Theodora shrugs. "Not really. I think it suits him." She runs ahead towards the alley that leads to the back of the Macauleys' farm. "And I saw a beautiful big horse in here once."

Nathan calls her back hurriedly. "Don't go down there, my love."

She gives him knowing eyes. "The man who lives there is not very friendly."

"Something like that, yes."

Theodora skips away from the alley. She turns to look back at Nathan, stray pieces of blonde hair blowing over her eyes. Sometimes he adores how much she looks like her mother. Other times, he can't bear the ache of it. "On the way home," she says, "can we go and look for mermaids in the rockpools again? I wonder if they were all hiding last time because they saw us coming."

Nathan smiles. "You like it here, don't you." He is surprised. Had not imagined his city-born child would ever feel at home with earth-caked shoes and her hair blown wild with sea. Perhaps a little of his concern about her is unwarranted.

"Of course I do. I wish you had brought me with you when you first came."

He feels a pang of guilt. "You did not like being in London with Auntie Eva?"

Theodora balances across a log next to the road, her arms held out to the side. "Well, yes. But I'd rather be here with you." She leaps off the log and shoves open the door of the curiosity shop, making the bell above the door jangle.

Nathan follows her inside. He looks around the cluttered shop with a mixture of interest and horror. It feels as though the overloaded shelves might come crashing down at any moment and pin him and Theodora beneath them. At least that would be a memorable ending.

"Good day, there."

Nathan recognises the copper-haired shopkeeper from church. Julia Mitchell, Harriet tells him. She must know who he is—everyone here does—but her smile is warm and bright. It seems to light the dingy corners of the shop. He finds himself smiling in response.

"My daughter saw a doll in here last week. I hear you put it aside for her."

"In a green dress," Theodora puts in. "With eyelashes."

"Of course." Julia bends down behind the counter and

reappears with the doll in her hands. Theodora's eyes light as she hands it over.

"Thea," murmurs Nathan. "What do you say?"

"Thank you," she gushes, turning the doll around carefully and smoothing its creased skirts. "Look, Papa. Eyelashes."

"So I see."

Julia watches her with a smile, before looking back at Nathan. "So you're the famous Mr Blake."

He lets out a laugh he doesn't really feel. "I would have thought infamous was more fitting."

Her green eyes are apologetic. "I'm sorry you haven't been made to feel so welcome. Like I said to your sister, the people here can be rather stuck in their ways."

"Well. I don't suppose I can blame them for that. Especially not at a time like this."

She tilts her head. "I don't suppose you can. Trust is rather hard to come by these days, with war on the horizon."

Nathan jumps at the feel of something downy brushing past his ankle. He looks down to see a ginger cat sidling past, tail in the air.

Julia gives a short laugh. "She likes you. Usually she'll not go near strangers."

Nathan's smile twists into a grimace. He hates cats with a passion bordering on the unnatural. "The doll," he says throatily. "How much do you want for it?"

"It's yours," Julia tells him. "Consider it a welcome gift. I'm sure you could use one."

The gesture brings an unexpected rush of emotion to Nathan's chest. He swallows heavily. Shakes his head and pulls out his coin pouch. "I couldn't." The last thing he wants is a reputation of accepting charity.

Julia's lips part, and for a moment of horror, he wonders if he has offended her. "A shilling, then," she says finally.

Nathan shakes the money from the pouch and places it on the counter.

Julia sweeps up the coins in one swift movement and tucks them in the pocket of her apron. "If you find any treasures in that old house of yours that need a new home, this is the place to come. I'll give you a good price for them."

Nathan nods. "I shall keep that in mind." Warmth returns to Julia's smile, making him realise how much he had missed it. "Thank you, Mrs Mitchell," he says, bobbing his head to her.

"It's Miss. I've never been married."

"Oh," Nathan splutters. "Forgive me. I thought Harriet mentioned you had a son."

"I do, aye. His father didn't even stay around til the morning. Bobby and I are better off without him." Her bluntness makes Nathan's cheeks colour with something he can't quite identify. He garbles out a flustered response, then flies out the door, praying Theodora is following.

Eva pulls a basket of sorry-looking vegetables out from the bottom cupboard of the sideboard. Potatoes are growing sprouts, the onions are curling, and the carrots have the consistency of twine. Still, she is sure Finn will benefit from eating something more than bread and cheese—never mind that the bread is finished and she has no thought of how to make more.

She rifles through the chaos of the sideboard in search of

anything else to throw into her soup. If there is any kind of order to the cupboards, she cannot make it out; jars of potted meat are crammed in beside old ink pots and chapbooks, an enormous sack of flour shares space with fresh candlesticks. Shoved in a drawer beside the pepper mill, she finds a large leather-bound book.

Peeking over her shoulder to check Finn is still asleep, she opens it curiously. Page after page is filled with scrawled dates and times and notes; a logbook, she realises, tracking the tides and the weather, the sunrise and sunset, ships that have passed the island.

She turns back through the pages, following the dates. How long has Finn been out here? Has he been alone all this time? She has so many questions, and she feels quite certain none of them will be welcome.

The bed creaks and she shoves the book back in the drawer, retrieving the pepper mill and dumping it on the table with the vegetables.

"You're cooking?"

Eva whirls around. "Why?" she demands. "Did you not think me capable?"

An amused smile flickers on Finn's lips as he sits up in bed. "Your words. Not mine." He squints in the early-afternoon sunlight pouring in through the window.

Eva's cheeks flush. She hates how easily she is rattled by him. "How are you feeling?"

"All right." He rubs his eyes, rakes fingers through his dishevelled brown hair. "You can read the log," he says. "I don't mind. Although I don't imagine you'll find anything too thrilling in there."

The burning in her cheeks intensifies. She says nothing.

Just goes to the table and begins to slice the vegetables. She can count on one hand the number of times she has cooked in the past—and those were just childish games in which she had helped their family's cook by mixing dough and peeling potatoes. Without instruction, she feels completely lost.

Not that she has any intention of letting Finn Murray know that.

The soup, predictably, is terrible. Far too much pepper, and too little of anything else. Eva forces down a few mouthfuls at the table, while Finn sits up in bed, bringing reluctant spoonfuls to his mouth.

"You ought to check the lobster pots tomorrow," he says after a moment. "By the jetty. If there's anything in there, I'll show you how to cook them."

Eva smiles faintly. She had been expecting a far blunter assessment of her cooking skills. Buoyed by his attempt at conversation, she asks, "How long have you—"

"There's a box of cards somewhere," Finn cuts in. "Top drawer maybe. Do you play?"

"Do *you*? You seem to be rather lacking in opponents."

He chuckles. "Well, there's the ghosts of the old lightkeepers, of course."

Eva smiles. She forces down the last of her soup and rifles through the drawer for the box of cards. She hands them to Finn and pulls a chair up towards the bed.

"Cribbage?" he asks, pulling them from the box and beginning to shuffle.

Eva nods. Her curiosity and questions, she supposes, will have to wait. But she is glad they will not spend the day in silence.

There he is. The figure in the garden. The sight of him sends a bolt of shock through Harriet's body, though she does not know why she is surprised. For days she has been watching out the window of her workroom, waiting for him to appear.

What does he want with her family's house?

Spies. The thought is so ridiculous she almost laughs. What does she care who sits on the throne?

Perhaps, she thinks suddenly, recklessly, she will go out there and confront this intruder, and tell him just that. Demand to know what he thinks he is doing, trying to scare her family from their home like this.

Somewhere in the back of her mind, she is dimly aware that she ought to be afraid. Since they have arrived on this island, danger and death have seemed far too close at hand. But she can't quite make herself feel that fear. These days, she struggles to feel anything beyond a dull hollowness.

Is this man truly trying to scare her family from the island? If so, he is doing a rather terrible job of it. As far as Harriet knows, she is the only one who is aware of his presence. Surely if he intended to scare them, he would have come creeping about the shadows much closer to supper time.

The realisation makes her even more curious. And even more determined to confront him.

She hurries out of her workroom and glides towards the front door. When she pulls it open, a cool, salty breeze touches her skin. There's a faraway, haunting sound on the wind that could be seals howling, or could be imagination.

She steps outside. Rounds the house towards its ocean side, where she had seen the figure outside her workroom. Through the thin curtains, she can still see the faint glow of her candle.

But there is nothing else. No movement, no figure, no hint that anyone has been here. For a second, Harriet's mind goes to ghosts and otherworlds. But another part of her fights this explanation. Perhaps, many years ago, she would have believed the man a ghost. But now the world feels too cold and rigid for this to be the explanation, even out here on Holy Island with sea mist closing in.

Pulling her robe and nightshift up to her calves, she strides through the darkness and circles the building. Highfield House feels monstrous, with row after row of lightless windows staring down on her. The shed and unused stables behind the manor loom in the dark. Fine places to be hiding, if they weren't padlocked tight. For a second, she thinks to call out. Demand whoever is there show themselves. But she cannot be so bold, not when she is standing here unarmed and unaccompanied, in nothing but her nightshift and shawl. Not that there is any point in calling out. She knows for certain that no one will answer. The emptiness feels almost tangible. And doubtful of ghosts or not, Harriet can't deny the fact she is now alone.

CHAPTER FIFTEEN

The worst part of all this, Finn thinks, is that he likes having her around.

She has been here a week, and though he thinks himself capable of managing the skiff, he has not yet made the offer to take her back to Holy Island. Nor has she asked to be taken.

It's foolish. He had told himself he would get her off Longstone the moment he could make it into the boat. But he is yet to tell her she is leaving. He doesn't know why. All he knows is it's far too dangerous to be keeping her here.

All week she has been a vicious gatekeeper, refusing to let him leave the bed for anything more than a hurried piss. Now his fever has broken, she seems satisfied he is not going to die quite yet, and has been content to let him hobble about the place, leaning on the fire poker as a makeshift cane. The fresh air outside is a welcome relief after the stifling days and nights in the cottage, the prospect of death hanging a little too close at hand.

It's almost dark now, with slate-coloured clouds clogging the horizon, and the chill of autumn on the wind. Finn smells the rain before he feels it, and when the sky opens, he lifts his face upwards, enjoying the coolness of the water in his beard.

Eva appears from behind the cottage, lugging the trough she has filled from the rainwater barrels behind the house. Finn reaches out a hand to help her, but she pulls away.

"I can manage." Water slops down the front of her skirts as she climbs the steps. "Ought to have just left the trough out here to catch the rain." She shoulders open the door. "It almost feels like winter."

Finn smiles crookedly. "There's nought of a summer out here."

The night Eva had appeared on his island, terrified out of her mind, she had barely said a word beyond frantic, incoherent stammering. But with each day of her stay, she has become more chatty. There are stories about brothers and sisters and nieces and nephews, and a long carriage journey from London in a week and a half of rain. She seems oblivious to his forced coldness—or at least determined to ignore it.

He had told himself the best way through this was to remain tight-lipped. Offer her little more than a terse good morning and goodnight, and instructions where necessary.

But that is turning out to be much harder than he imagined. *Look at all these beautiful birds*, says Eva Blake, and he finds himself telling her about nesting patterns and mating calls, and asking her if she's seen the nightingales on Lindisfarne yet. Because against every grain of sense in his body, he is curious about her, eager to know more. And that curiosity is far too risky.

Finn limps up the stairs and pulls the door closed behind him. Eva is standing at the window watching streams of water roll down the glass. The trough sits on the floor beside the table, and she has left a trail of wet footprints in her wake.

The cottage is cleaner than it has ever been. Finn has never bothered much for tidiness, but since his injury, the place had seen a new kind of chaos. Eva has spent the last week bringing some order to the sideboard and mantel, dusting and scrubbing surfaces that have not been attended to in years. Jars of jam and potted meat are now tucked away in the cupboards, instead of being spread out across the table, and he can actually see through the windows. He can't deny there's much to be said for being able to stumble around the place without fear of tripping over a stray washbin or a greatcoat fallen to the floor.

"I suppose there's to be no beacon in weather like this." Eva sounds despondent.

Finn takes a jar of potted meat from the sideboard and uncorks it. "We can try. The fuel is dry at the minute, so if the rain eases a little we may have a chance, as long as we keep the fire fed. It's on nights like this that the sailors need the beacon the most."

"Of course." There is a seriousness in her eyes as she turns to look at him. "Then we will try."

Her words make something shift in his chest. When was this last a task for *we*? Not since he was a child, and his parents had kept the light together. He can't deny there is something achingly pleasant about it. But this cannot be a task for *we*, not when the second person is a member of the Blake family.

He feels suddenly restless, like he wants to walk the whole island. Of course, that's impossible. All he can do is stay here in the cottage, trapped like a bear in a cage of Martin Macauley's making.

"A big fire, then. Make sure it's burning well on the ground before raising the brazier." As she instructs herself, Eva goes to the hearth and pulls on the wet shoes she had only moments ago discarded.

"I can manage," says Finn. "I—"

"No. You need to rest. You've already been on your feet far too long today."

He has learnt there is little point in arguing. Eva Blake, he has also learnt, has something to prove. To herself or him, he is not quite sure. Perhaps both.

This well-mannered lady of the manor has immersed herself in the role of lightkeeper. Each night she is studious in watching the beacon; keeping flames reaching skyward, and watching the purple shapes of the shore in case a wayward vessel should come careening towards them.

She has fallen into a meticulous routine, of retiring to bed a few hours before dusk, and rousing herself in time to light the basket. Each time she appears in the living area, her expression business-like and serious, Finn feels a tug in his chest. There is a part of him that dreads the sight of her. And there's a part of him that craves it.

He tells himself there is no need for the dread. Out here on this thread of rock, there is no past and no future. Soon Eva will leave, and will be none the wiser to the things he has done. Why does that thought make him feel so hollow?

He digs his fingers into the jar of meat and swallows down a piece, then pulls on his coat and follows Eva outside. He shuffles to the beacon and lowers the brazier, while she hurries to the shed to gather the fuel. Rain swirls and whips against his cheeks, pelting hard against his greatcoat.

Eva dumps a pile of wood at his feet, then hurries back to the shed for a shovelful of coal. Finn resists the urge to take over. Instead, he hovers over the basket, shielding it as best he can from the rain, while Eva shovels out the last of yesterday's ash and carefully stacks the fuel.

"Build it a little higher tonight," he tells her, turning up the collar of his coat against the wind. "The more established we can make the fire, the more of a chance it will have against the weather."

She snaps the tinderbox, cupping the fragile flame with her hand until it begins to take. Finn huddles close to the fire, protecting the basket from the wind and rain. He takes Eva's elbow, tugging her forward to do the same.

"Stand close. Use your body to shield the flames. We need to let the fire take." Smoke coils upwards, meeting rain and a spray of sea. "Now bank up the fire with as much coal as you can."

The fire is a roar when Eva tugs on the chain and sends it into the sky, but the fierce rain attacks it in seconds. Steam hisses and curls. Finn catches the look of disappointment on her face. Hair whips around her cheeks as she stares at the dwindling flames. He puts a hand to her shoulder, urging her back inside.

Condensation is clouding the windows, and the cottage smells of woodsmoke and the misshapen bread loaf Eva had made that afternoon. She leaves a trail of water in her wake as she disappears into the bedroom, pulling the door closed behind her. She returns moments later in her dry blue skirts and shawl, her wet things over her arms and her damp hair dark and thready as it falls down her back. She slings her sodden skirts over the fire rail and hangs the kettle on its rusty hook. Lines her wet shoes up on the hearth.

As he lowers himself into a chair, Finn can't help but follow her with his eyes. He tells himself it's the strangeness of having another person here, inhabiting his space. But he knows it's more than that. There's a warmth to her, an inherent kindness. When Eva had first crashed onto his island, she had felt like an imposition. Now, padding around his cottage in her stockinged feet, her clothes dangling over his fire guard, she feels strangely like a comfort.

She pours the boiling water into the teapot, the rich, smoky smell of tea seeping out the cracked spout. She fills the tin mug she has made her own, and carries it back to the fire.

Finn pulls his chair a little closer to the hearth. A little closer to her. For the warmth, he tells himself. To bring life back to his frozen fingers. Nothing more.

He watches her sip from the cup. He doesn't know why he told her he doesn't like tea. It's far too inoffensive a drink to dislike. He supposes he had just been trying to rile her; to warn her not to make herself comfortable in this solitary life he has made for himself.

He eyes the teapot. He's longing for a cup, but doesn't want to embarrass himself by asking for one. He knows he's been a bastard to Eva, and she has every right to hurl the same sharpness straight back at him. "Your tea smells good," he says finally.

She gives him a lopsided smile. A smile that says she knows she has won. "Would you like a cup?" There's a mocking sweetness in her words, one Finn knows he deserves.

"Maybe just a small one."

Eva doesn't bother to hide her gloating smile as she takes a second cup from the sideboard and wipes it out with the cloth. She fills it and passes it to Finn.

"Careful. It's hot." Her fingers brush his as she hands him the cup. The feel of her bare skin sends a jolt through him he was not expecting.

Once the cup is firmly in his hand, she pulls away quickly and returns to her seat in front of the fire. He can feel her eyes on him, watching as he brings the cup to his lips.

"Well?" she asks.

"It's all right. I suppose."

She laughs, and the sound of it fills the room. When, Finn thinks distantly, was the last time this cottage heard laughter?

Eva doesn't speak, just sips from her own cup again, not taking her eyes from him.

Wind hurls itself against the house, sucking the last of the flames from the firebasket. The cottage fills suddenly with shadows, lit only by the dim flicker in the hearth. Eva gets to her feet instinctively.

"Don't bother," says Finn. He knows this wind, this rain; they can do no more than what they've done already. "There's no point." He reaches into the darkness and lights the lamp.

Eva nods faintly and sits back down, her face half-lit in the firelight. Is she closer to him now? Perhaps it's just his imagination.

He feels utterly trapped. He knows he needs to keep his distance from her, and yet he is craving her nearness with every inch of his being. Can feel energy coursing through him where his fingertips touched hers.

He gets suddenly to his feet, slopping tea across his breeches as he stumbles on his injured leg. He curses, dumps the cup on the table.

Eva looks up in surprise. "What's the matter?"

"Go to bed," he says shortly. "The light will stay dark tonight. I don't need you here." He turns his back to her, unable to bear the look of shock on her face. He's not so removed from the rest of the world that he can't see how his words might sting her. But he cannot let himself get close to her. Not any closer than he has already. And so he says, "I don't want you here."

He hears the rustle of her skirts as she stands, but she doesn't leave the room. His knuckles whiten as he grips the top of the chair.

There's a moment of silence. A horrible, deep silence in which he can feel Eva's eyes spearing him, demanding an explanation for this sudden cruelty. But when he hears the floorboards creak and the bedroom door thump closed, he knows he will have the solitude he has demanded. And that solitude has never made him feel more wretched.

CHAPTER SIXTEEN

Eva is still asleep when he wakes the next morning; at least, she is still locked away in his childhood bedroom. He doesn't blame her. He'd keep away from himself too if he had a choice in the matter.

The rain has blown over and the air smells fresh and clean. Lobsters are squirming in the pots beside the jetty. Finn leans heavily on the fire poker, testing the strength in his leg. After his foolish behaviour last night, it feels crucial that he gets Eva back to Holy Island and puts a large amount of sea between them.

The tide is low, and this morning Longstone feels vast and expansive. If he had it in his legs, he could walk to the southern tip of the island, a spit of rock so often under the veil of the tide, and look out towards the mainland.

He does not have it in his legs, of course. But he starts to walk in that direction anyway. Because there's a ship on the horizon. A three-masted barque, bigger than the fishing vessels he usually sees in these waters. Smaller than the passenger ships that shift silently by on their way to Edinburgh. Rebels from down south, perhaps, sailing to Auld Reekie to join the Earl of Mar's Jacobite army.

Finn shades his eyes from the morning sun. He squints at the hazy shape of the ship. As it glides past his island, he tries to make out the shape of the figurehead. From this distance, it looks to be an eagle with wide wooden wings.

His stomach twists.

Impossible.

What would the *Eagle* be doing in these waters?

He limps back to the cottage and grabs the spying glass from the mantel. And out he goes across the island, south, and south again, over plains of moss-streaked rock. The wound in his calf screams at him to stop, but he knows he can do no such thing. He needs a good look at that ship.

Impossible, he tells himself again. But he knows he can try and convince himself all he wishes, but that does not make it any less plausible that this ship might have returned to Northumbria. The *Eagle's* captain is a native of these parts.

Then again, he's surprised to see the ship at all. The last he knew, the *Eagle* was a licensed privateer, set against the French. But there has been a tentative peace with France for some months, and the Jacobite Rising is yet to begin.

He is out at the tip of the island now, with sea licking his boots. From here, the cottage and shed look like twin fortresses, buttressed against the sea.

His calf is throbbing in time with his heart. Birds are lined up along the green-tinged rocks out here, in this place so rarely intruded upon by humans. Finn skirts the colony, careful not to disrupt them.

The wind has picked up, and he sees it swell the sails of

the vessel. With a silent prayer that he might be wrong about the ship, he raises the spying glass.

He is not wrong. There is the barque he knows too well, with its eagle figurehead, silent and graceful on the sea. Moving north towards Holy Island, and then, with any luck, up into Scotland with no thought to the tiny spit of Longstone.

Finn tries to tell himself he is well hidden. No one will find him all the way out here. But he can't quite believe it. Not when he sets a fire blazing on his shore each night, showing the world the island is inhabited. Still, the *Eagle* is from a past that is distant enough to be forgotten. Distant enough for her captain to sail right on by the Farnes, with no thought to who might be lighting that beacon.

But he can't quite believe that either. Because with Eva Blake sleeping in his childhood bedroom and scrubbing the grime from his windows, that past is feeling less distant every day.

Nathan throws his weight against the pry bar, forcing up another floorboard in Oliver's room. Rotting wood splinters at his feet, exhaling a cloud of century-old dust.

He hates this room, with its hiding place within the wall.

The priest hole, Nathan's mother had told them, had been built into the house in the late sixteenth century when religious persecution was at its peak. Those were the days, she said, before the Catholic faith had been bred out of their family through fear and hasty marriages.

In spite of himself, Nathan's curiosity gets the better of

him. He puts down the pry bar and pushes against the wooden panel on the wall beside the fireplace. It pivots open, revealing the tiny brick enclosure behind. It has been more than twenty years since he has last seen it. It's a horrible cramped and dusty place. He cannot imagine the horror of being forced to hide in there with a priest hunter on your tail. He has no thought of whether it had ever been used to save a Catholic priest from being burned alive by the Protestants.

Nathan has vivid memories of playing in the priest hole with Oliver.

"Come out and face your maker." He can still hear Oliver's voice in his head, cracking and growling on the cusp of adulthood.

Nathan closes the priest hole hurriedly and shoves the pry bar beneath the floorboards again. The old wood splinters with a satisfying crack.

So much of this house feels on the verge of collapse. Boards hang loose and windows rattle, stairs groan as though they are about to spill open. Perhaps it really would be best for everyone if he let it crumble. Let the dunes swallow the place. He wishes he had that option.

He hears a bright peel of laughter float up the staircase. The sound catches him off guard. Laughter is not something this house has heard a lot of, of late, at least beyond the childish giggles of Thomas and Thea. He opens the door a crack; finds himself listening.

He recognises the bell-like voice of Julia Mitchell. She is chatting with Harriet in the entrance hall. Julia's laughter is oddly jarring against the coldness, the sadness, this room around him carries.

Harriet looks up the staircase, catching him poking his

head out of Oliver's bedroom. "You can come out and say good morning, Nathan," she scolds lightly, "instead of hovering there like some creeper."

He feels colour rush to his cheeks, but Julia catches his eye and gives him a smile that looks almost conspiratorial.

He quickly wipes his dirty hands on the cloth tucked into his breeches and wrangles stray curls behind his ears. He knows he looks a sight, and he does not like the thought of guests seeing him in such a state. But something makes him walk down the staircase anyway. There is something about Julia Mitchell's warmth that he finds himself craving.

"Come to scour the house for treasures?" he asks her. "I'm afraid you'll leave wanting. I can confirm there's nothing here except rotting wood."

Julia laughs. "Nothing like that. Harriet invited me for tea, is all. I've been longing to see what you've been doing to the place." She runs her hand along the intricately carved rosettes on the newel post. "Although I do think you're wrong about there being nothing of value in here. The paintings in the foyer are stunning. And these carvings are wonderful."

He nods towards the newel post. "It's not an original feature. Our father carved the post to suit the rest of the house," he tells her with a smile. "A hundred years too late for his work to be worth much."

"Well. It's beautiful in any case."

He looks again at the delicate woodwork, its finer features worn away by time. Perhaps it is beautiful. It's been a long time since he looked at things with such an eye. Life has felt too rushed and desperate for such a luxury.

"Nathan," Harriet says, sickly sweet. He had forgotten she was there. "Would you like to join us for tea?"

"Oh no," he says quickly. "I'd hate to impose. I only came down to wish Miss Mitchell a good morning."

"Is that so?" says Harriet, in her infuriatingly haughty way. He can hear the implication in her voice; the suggestion that he might have come downstairs with a little more in mind. That he might see more in Julia Mitchell than a visitor passing through. It's a foolish notion of course; these days, he can barely hold his daughter's hand without his stomach tying itself in knots. Building any kind of connection with a woman is completely out of the question. That part of him had died with Sarah.

He offers his sister a smile as forced and syrupy as her own. "Yes, Harriet, that is so." He turns back to Julia. "If you'll excuse me, Miss Mitchell, I'd best get back to work. This house seems to grow bigger every day."

He curses himself for his inane comment, but Julia laughs anyway. "Good luck," she tells him, as Harriet waves her towards the parlour.

Nathan is distracted as he returns to his work, pulling away the boards, sifting through the layers of the past and peering at what hides beneath. He can still hear Oliver's words in his head. It has been years since he had given his brother more than a passing thought, but here in Highfield House, Oliver seems to hide in every corner.

He is still working on the floorboards when he hears Harriet walk Julia to the door sometime later. He finds himself balancing across the exposed beams of the floor towards the window, watching as they embrace on the front doorstep. Watching as Julia begins to walk back across the dunes. She stops for a second and looks back up at the house, and for a moment Nathan worries he has been seen. But her gaze is beyond him, looking up at the peak of the roof, as though she is trying to see beyond the clouds.

CHAPTER SEVENTEEN

Eva stares up at the rugged wooden beams across the ceiling and listens to waves throw themselves against the edges of the island. A pale thread of sunlight shines through the gaps in the shutters and she turns her back to it, closing her eyes and pulling her knees to her chest. She has been lying awake in this lumpy old bed for what feels like hours, but can't bring herself to leave the safety of the bedroom.

Of all the unmooring, clouded parts of life on Longstone, navigating Finn Murray is the most difficult thing of all.

This life of firelight and tides is so different from the life she had lived in London; the life she thought she would live as Matthew Walton's wife. A few weeks ago, she would never have imagined herself with callused palms or coal-streaked hands. But a part of her feels oddly drawn to the hectic simplicity of lightkeeping on Longstone. The physicality of this life is completely foreign to her, and yet she welcomes the ache in her arms and legs each night. Welcomes the feel of rain in her hair and the smell of woodsmoke that has seeped deep into her clothes.

But then there is Finn and his painful changeability. His words last night had stung her deeply. She cannot begin to make sense of it. They had been getting on better than they ever had before he had turned on her like a rabid dog.

Eva tugs the blanket to her chin. Wounded leg or not, Finn can make his own damn breakfast this morning.

It's foolish, she knows, to let a near stranger make her feel so worthless. But Finn's coldness, his mockery, his fickle-mindedness, only reminds her of how unwanted she is. Reminds her of the way Matthew Walton had thrown her from his townhouse and declared her unworthy of being his wife.

Eva had found out early in her betrothal that Walton had wanted Harriet instead. Had overheard a conversation between him and her brother when they had assumed her out of the house. It had come as no surprise—Harriet was the princess and she was the lady-in-waiting. But by the time Walton had made his intentions clear, Harriet was already promised to Edwin.

Eva knew she was something of a consolation prize; how could she be anything else beside Harriet's impossible beauty? But she had done her best to show her betrothed she would make a fine wife nonetheless—a well-mannered, educated lady who would always put her husband's needs before her own.

It had not been enough. Eva had not appreciated the intensity of Matthew Walton's feelings for her sister. Had assumed they went no deeper than infatuation. But when Walton had sat her down in his office, he had spoken carefully and ashamedly about his unrequited love for Harriet and how, with further consideration, it made marrying Eva an impossible thing. And yes, Eva saw that too. How could she sit with her husband at a family dinner and know he was pining after her sister? She had not tried to argue, or convince him otherwise. She had just smoothed her skirts and packed her things, and requested enough money to see her and Thea to Holy Island.

Eva tries not to blame Harriet. She knows none of it is her fault. But sometimes she is unable to hold back her bitterness. At just nineteen, Harriet's life is in fine order: a handsome, wealthy husband, and a beautiful, healthy son. Meanwhile, Eva is shovelling coal with no prospects, despite being almost five years older.

She sits up in bed. The cottage is still oddly quiet. Since his fever burnt away, Finn has returned to his old fractured sleeping pattern, and she knows he would have retired late, despite the burned-out light. Nonetheless, she is surprised not to hear him clattering around the cottage by now.

She dresses, and, drawing in her courage, steps out of the bedroom.

Finn's bed is empty, his coat and boots gone. A half-eaten slice of bread sits abandoned on the table. She will not go after him, she tells herself. She will not chase him like some devoted puppy, determined to prove her worth.

She sits at the table beside the burnt-out fire and eats the remains of Finn's breakfast. Today, she will ask him how much longer he imagines he will need her. She will make it clear that she does not wish to be here any more than he wishes to have her. Perhaps up until last night that was not true. But it certainly is now.

She swallows the last of the bread, unable to shake the

irritating voice in the back of her head, nudging her to find out where Finn is, what he is doing. It's a flicker of worry, in spite of herself. She hates that it is there.

She goes outside and lifts a hand to shield her eyes from the sun. The tide is rising beneath a fierce blue sky, and licking at the edges of the island. Seals flit through the shallows and rock pools glitter in new places.

She hears him call her name.

She squints. And she sees the tiny figure of him out towards the southern end of the island. She hurries towards him, but her path is blocked by a blue-grey ribbon of sea. Finn is hobbling over the rocks, face contorted in pain. Has the fool been walking all morning?

"What do you think you're doing?" she demands. "The tide's far too high to be out here!"

Across the water, he gives her a sardonic smile. "It wasn't too high when I got here." He hunches, leaning on the fire poker and catching his breath. "I need your help, Eva. I shouldn't have come out this far."

Eva folds her arms, half wishing she had the nerve to leave him to his own devices. He'd deserve such a thing, she tells herself. Both for his callousness last night, and for being stupid enough to go off on this one-legged jaunt around the island.

"What do you need me to do?" she snaps.

Finn nods towards the river of seawater blocking his path. "It's shallow here at the edge," he says. "Come across. I need you to help me get back."

In case he hadn't registered her displeasure, Eva narrows her eyes and yanks off her shoes and stockings. She dumps them out of reach of the rising tide, then knots her skirts above her knees and steps into the water. The cold steals her breath and she bites back a curse.

"You'd best have a good reason for being out here," she snaps, balancing across the slippery rock beneath her feet. When she stumbles onto dry land, inches from Finn, an infuriating half-smile appears on his lips. "Did you do this on purpose?" she demands. "To see if I'd be mad enough to come after you?"

His smile disappears. "Of course not. I…"

"You what?" She glances at the spying glass in his fist. "What were you doing out there?"

"Nothing. I just saw a vessel passing and wanted a closer look. Seems I'm not quite as well healed as I'd hoped."

Eva glances down, glimpsing a fresh bloom of blood on the strapping around his calf. "You're a fool," she snaps.

"So it would seem."

She plants her hands on her hips. "Take your damn boots off then. And quickly. I don't fancy getting any wetter than I am already."

"My boots are already soaked. It's no matter. Just help me get across, aye?"

Eva grips his arm with both hands, digging her fingers into his flesh a little tighter than necessary. She doesn't miss his sharp intake of breath.

She helps him into the shallow pool. Finn swallows a curse as the seawater covers his wound. Step by step, they stumble through the water and back to the cottage.

Finn sinks onto the bed, pulling off his wet boots and dumping the spying glass on the mattress beside him. He leans against the wall, looking at Eva as she yanks her stockings back on.

"Let me see the wound," she says. "You've obviously done some damage to it, walking as far as you did." She snatches the jar of figwort from the mantel. Has half a mind to douse his calf in whisky instead. That would teach him to be so careless and hurtful.

She steps close to the bed, expecting Finn to protest. He stays motionless, waiting. And Eva's anger shifts, replaced with nerves. Nerves at his sudden nearness. And nerves over the task at hand. Slowly, carefully, she unbinds the wet strapping, tinged pink with blood and water. She is relieved to see that, though the wound has opened again in several places, it seems to be healing well. She dips the washcloth into the bowl and gently wipes away the blood. Then she dips the dry end of the cloth into the figwort ointment and touches it to the wound. Finn flinches.

"I'm sorry," she murmurs, her other hand sliding instinctively over his bare shin to keep him from moving again. She applies a little more ointment.

She can feel his eyes on her as she works, and it makes her feel intensely exposed. Vulnerable. She hates that he has the power to make her feel this way. Hates that all she can think about is how he had told her to leave last night.

"You don't think much of me, do you," she says after a moment.

He catches her glance, and there's a sincerity in his eyes she has not seen before. "I'm sorry if I gave you that impression."

Eva swallows heavily. An answer she was not expecting. She presses the lid back on the jar. "I know you want me out of your way. But how could I not help you? You got in the way of a bullet intended for me." Finn reaches for the torn shirt that hangs on the edge of the bed. He yanks off another strip of fabric and hands it to her. She wraps it around his calf and knots it tightly.

Finn tugs the hem of his slops down below his knee. "Martin Macauley wasn't shooting at you, Eva," he says. "He was shooting at me."

Her lips part. "What? Why would he shoot at you?"

He shakes his head. "It doesn't matter. It's nothing."

"Truly? Nothing? He could have killed you. He could have killed both of us."

Finn looks a little taken aback by her outburst. His fingers graze her elbow. "Will you hang the kettle?"

Eva finds herself giving him a half-smile. "Tea?"

He returns the gesture. "Aye. I like your tea."

Eva sets the jar of figwort on the mantel and hangs the kettle on the hook, tossing a log onto the fire and jabbing it to life with the poker. Finn reaches for her arm, tugging her back down to sit on the edge of the bed.

He is close to her now, less than a foot between them. She can see the golden flecks in his eyes. Can smell the woodsmoke and sea on his skin. And the look her gives her, it is not one of annoyance, or pity, but something else entirely. Something she can't quite read. There is something almost apologetic in his eyes, as though he is aware of how much his changeability has stung her.

"I stole some coal from the Macauleys," he says simply. "For the firebasket. Actually, I've stolen coal from them more than once."

"Why am I not surprised to learn you're a thief?" But there is no heat to her words. She supposes there's something almost noble about stealing coal to keep the firebasket burning. Almost. "They shot you for a little coal?"

He shrugs. "They're bastards." He gives a short chuckle. "Also, it was quite a lot of coal. Martin came out here a few months ago, seeking to take some of it back. I caught him before he got his hands to it. That's why I thought you were him when I heard you in the coal shed that night. My family has been feuding with the Macauleys since before I was born." He snorts. "Me and Martin are just carrying on a fine tradition started by our fathers."

So Martin Macauley had not been firing at her. He did not know she had knocked his father into the sea. The knowledge ought to settle her. But it doesn't. Perhaps it is because the thought of Martin shooting at Finn is no less unnerving than him shooting at her.

Or perhaps it's because none of this changes the fact that she is hiding the truth about what happened to Martin's father. And nothing will change the fact that she has killed a man.

"It was very brazen of him to shoot at you out in the open like that," she says.

Finn shrugs. "Who would notice if I disappeared?"

Eva shifts uncomfortably at the truth of it. How easily Martin would have escaped justice if his ball had hit Finn's chest. His crime would have been hidden away at the wild top end of Holy Island, no one to miss the unsociable man from Longstone. And the only witness a suspected government spy. A perfect crime, at least until a ship rammed into the unlit Farne Islands.

"In any case," Finn says, too easily, "I don't think he meant to kill me. Just give me a bit of a scare."

Eva shakes her head, unsure if his blasé attitude is real, or just a cover for how much the incident had shaken him. "And you will just let him get away with it?" She knows the answer before she finishes the question. Why would Finn draw attention to his own crimes by going to the authorities?

He doesn't bother to respond. "Why did you think Martin was shooting at you?" he asks. "I thought you would have assumed I was the target."

His question feels pointed. It reminds Eva that nothing she can tell Finn is worse than what he already knows her to have done. But something stops her from admitting it was Donald Macauley's body she had sent tumbling into the ocean. She has already told him far too much.

"We're unwanted on Lindisfarne," she says. "There are Jacobites on the island who suspect us of being government spies."

"But you're not."

"No."

Finn nods faintly, and she can tell he believes her.

"So that's where the coal comes from," says Eva. "The Macauleys' sheds."

"Some of it, aye. But most of it was paid for honestly, believe it or not."

"How do you pay for it?"

He chuckles. "I have money. I've not been here my entire life, you know. Despite what people like to say about me. I do a few days' farm work here and there when I need to. There are a few farmers on the mainland who hire me during the harvest and planting seasons. Sometimes they pay me with peat from their land. My da built up a nice collection too. Some of the fuel has been there for years."

"You've sacrificed a lot," says Eva. "To run the light. It

shouldn't be your responsibility."

"Aye, well Trinity House couldn't get the funds together to pay a proper keeper. And this is a dangerous patch of sea. My father lost two brothers out here on the Knavestone reef. Da was among the men who petitioned to have the light on Inner Farne built. When he realised they didn't have the money to light it, he built the beacon out here himself. And the cottage." He chuckles. "He liked to harp on about all the trouble he went to getting the stone out here."

"I can only imagine."

Finn shrugs. "We're only a few miles from shore. Plenty of people are willing to sail goods out here if you pay them enough. Mind you, my da never thought to tell no one he was building the place. When the church found out, they were wild about it. Da managed to talk them round. Made them see he was doing a good thing."

Eva smiles, surprised by his openness. It feels almost like he has forgotten himself, and the wall he is trying to maintain between them.

"That's why you do this?" she asks. "Because your uncles drowned out here?"

"That's why my da did it. I'm just doing as he would have wanted." There's a sudden thinness to his words, and he shifts back on the bed, as though regretting his brief moment of candidness.

Eva stands, putting space back between them. She takes the teapot from the mantel and begins to fill it with tea leaves.

"Shall I take you back tomorrow morning?" asks Finn. "I think I can manage the skiff."

Eva puts down the spoon, feeling a jolt in her chest. "Is that what you want?" She forces herself to look at him.

He holds her gaze. "I asked you first."

She hesitates. Draws in a breath. "No," she says. "That's not what I want. I want to stay until you're healed."

He nods. "All right." Looks away. "Good."

Eva hides her smile. It feels like a small victory. Or perhaps even a large one. She takes a step towards him, planting a hand on her hip. "If you want me to stay," she says, emboldened by his unexpected admission, "perhaps you ought to show a little gratitude."

"What?"

She looks down at him challengingly. "You've never thanked me. Not once. Not for coming to make sure you were all right, or for helping you keep the light. Not even for a damn cup of tea."

Finn stands, suddenly towering over her. He takes a step closer, his warm breath tickling her nose. Eva feels something twist in her stomach. "You've never thanked me either."

She swallows, but doesn't look away. "For what?"

"For taking you back to Lindisfarne after you washed up on my doorstep. And for not telling anyone you knocked a man into the sea."

He is right, of course. And the reminder of what she has done releases a fresh wave of guilt. But she refuses to show it. Refuses to back down. "Well," she says, challenge in her eyes, "who are you going to tell?"

CHAPTER EIGHTEEN

"There are baby seals, Papa." Theodora trots past the churchyard, and Nathan has to quicken his stride to keep up with her. "I can't wait for you to see them." Her cheeks are pink, her blonde hair spidery beneath her bonnet. And Nathan sees something in her eyes; a brightness, a glow of aliveness that has not been there since her mother's death. Holy Island has brought an energy to her she had not had in London. Since she has arrived, her nightmares have been almost non-existent. It will be harder than he had first imagined to take her back to the city when all this is done. He is glad at least one positive thing has come out of this whole debacle.

"Listen." She stops abruptly, bumping into his hip and darting away. "Can you hear them?"

The honking of the seals makes him smile. "I loved coming to see them when I was your age too," he tells Theodora. He winks at her. "Your Auntie Eva was terrified of them."

Theodora giggles. "Why would you be afraid of seals?" Skirts in her fist, she races down the hill towards the tiny outcrop of Saint Cuthbert's Island. In the low tide, the islet is linked to Lindisfarne by a chain of flat rocks and shingle.

They are not alone on the beach. Nathan stops at the edge of the embankment, recognising Julia Mitchell on the edge of the mudflats. She is teetering over the rocks with a dark-haired boy he assumes is her son. She is not wearing a bonnet or cap, and her fiery hair is coming loose from its knot, blowing wildly around her pale cheeks.

She looks up, flashing him a smile. Nathan approaches with a hint of reluctance. Harriet's behaviour the other morning had been far from subtle, and he does not want Julia to be misled. As appealing as he finds her, he would hate her to think he is offering more than he is capable of. Not, he is sure, that she would have any interest in someone as awkward and clumsy as him.

He smiles at Thea, who is already tearing across the beach with Julia's son. If only it were as easy to make new acquaintances as an adult as it was during childhood.

"Your son looks around the same age as Theodora," he says to Julia, cursing himself for the abrupt entrance into the conversation.

"Bobby is eight," Julia tells him easily. "Although sometimes I think him more like eighteen. He can be rather protective."

Nathan smiles. "A good man to have around."

"He is, aye." She brushes her hair from her eyes. "How is the restoration coming along?"

"Slowly," Nathan admits. "There's much to do. I'm thankful for my brother-in-law's expertise."

She nods. "Why did you decide to restore the house without outside help?"

"Because I couldn't trust anyone else to do it." The moment the words are out, Nathan can't believe he has spoken them. He barely knows this woman. How could he have admitted to such a thing? What must she think of him? "I'm sorry," he blurts. "I did not mean to suggest that the people here are not trustworthy..." His thoughts flash to Donald Macauley forcing Eva into his boat. Raising his musket on her. Perhaps he is right to be distrusting of the islanders. But in the back of his mind is the dull knowledge that he has likely offended Julia Mitchell again.

She gives a faint nod, but doesn't speak. Ought he take that as confirmation that the islanders are not to be trusted? Or is he reading too much into things?

Julia gestures to the beach where Bobby and Theodora are clambering over the wet rocks towards Saint Cuthbert's Island. Nathan hears Thea's giggles rising up in the cool air.

"You daughter seems to be enjoying herself here, at least."

Nathan smiles. "She is, yes." In another life, perhaps, he and Thea could be happy on Lindisfarne. But far too much has happened here for him to feel any sense of peace.

"You ought to send her to the dame school," says Julia. "With Bobby. The woman who takes the lessons is wonderful. A dear friend of mine. And a fine teacher at that."

Nathan hums noncommittally. He can't deny that, with Eva away, Theodora's lessons have fallen somewhat by the wayside. But settling her into school feels like far too permanent an arrangement.

"I don't know," he tells Julia. "I'm not sure how long we will be here. I would hate to put Thea into school only to take her back to London the moment she has settled in."

Julia eyes him. "That's a shame," she says, and he can't tell if she is referring to the school, or his plans to return to London. Heat prickles the back of his neck.

"I remember you, you know," she says suddenly. "From when you were a lad."

Nathan raises his eyebrows. "You do?"

"Of course. Every knew who you were; the family from the big house on the head."

He doesn't reply. What did people think of the Blakes back then, before they became Londoners? He suspects they were always something of outsiders, bundled away in their manor at the top of the island.

She eyes him. "You don't remember me, do you."

He hesitates. He wishes he did. Wishes he knew what this sunny woman was like as a child. He wonders how he might have missed her explosion of red curls running around the island.

She laughs at his lack of response. "Didn't think so. We're forgettable, us penniless types."

There is light in her voice and Nathan knows she is playing with him. Nonetheless, he says, "I'm sorry."

She shakes her head dismissively. "Truth be told, I remember more of your brother than you."

Nathan smiles wryly to himself. This is no surprise. Oliver was a far more memorable child; tall and lanky, with a shock of bright blond hair and tongue that could slice a grown man to pieces.

"He was always hovering about the harbour," says Julia, "watching over the fishermen's catches."

Nathan snorts. Stealing from them, more likely. "Have

you been on the island all this time?" he asks, keen to change the subject.

"Lived here my entire life," says Julia. "Never once thought to leave. I'm sure there's not a place on earth as beautiful as this."

"And the rest of your family?"

"After Bobby arrived, my father wanted nothing to do with me. Couldn't handle the shame of me having a child outside of wedlock. Made a life for himself over in Bamburgh. Barely knew my ma. And my brothers are off training with the rebels in the West Country."

Nathan raises his eyebrows, caught off guard at her brazen admission. Though a new Rising seems to be gaining momentum by the day, there are few people who speak so openly about supporting the Jacobites, even in this part of the country.

"Careful now," he says lightly. "Have you not heard we're a pack of government spies?"

Julia laughs. "I have heard that, aye. And what a load of rubbish it is too. If you were, I hardly think you'd be so obvious as to set yourselves up in the biggest house on the island."

"I wish the rest of the village had your sense."

Julia's gaze drifts past him and Nathan turns to see a small army of men appearing over the hill above the beach. Martin Macauley is among them. He catches sight of Nathan, and gestures to the others to change course towards him. Nathan's heart thuds, but he holds his ground. He darts a frantic look over his shoulder at Theodora. She and Bobby are splashing about in ankle-deep water. He doesn't wave her in. Wet shoes are far preferable to her being in earshot of these men.

Martin nods at Julia in greeting, then turns hard eyes to Nathan. "We're going out looking for my father."

"I see."

"We could use another pair of eyes."

Nathan blinks, caught off guard. What is this? A threat? A challenge? Or is Martin simply after all the help he can get?

Either way, he has only one option. "Of course," he says. Refuse and he will raise further suspicion.

Martin nods towards the harbour, where the fishing boats are bobbing on the rising tide. "Can you sail?"

"I can follow instructions."

Nathan feels Julia's eyes on him; a look of concern he cannot bring himself to acknowledge. He needs to believe these men don't want to harm him, or he will never climb into that boat. He glances at Theodora, then back at Julia. "Will you—"

"I'll see her home safely." She looks at him pointedly. "You be careful."

He nods. The thought of leaving Thea in the hands of a near stranger is almost as unsettling as sailing under Martin Macauley. But he realises he trusts Julia Mitchell. And he also knows he has little choice but to help the men with their search. He is following them towards the harbour before he can change his mind.

The sea is choppy, grey. Fine weather, Nathan thinks, for tossing a man overboard. He forces the thought away. Think guilty and he will look guilty.

Or at least, look as though he is hiding a secret for his guilty sister.

Nathan is sailing with Martin Macauley and Joseph Holland, from the fishing fleet. Martin had been deliberate in directing Nathan onto the same boat as himself. It is hard not to imagine he knows what he is hiding. After all, Martin had been there the moment Eva had returned to Holy Island after knocking his father into the sea. Surely he has his suspicions.

Three fishing boats have left the harbour. One is moving towards the mainland, another out towards open water. Holland's boat heads towards the Farnes.

Nathan feels the urge to speak; to convince Martin he and his family are not working for the government. But he stops himself. Donald had told his suspicions to Eva moments before he had ended up in the water. There is no way Nathan ought to know about them. He has no choice but to keep quiet. To let Martin and the other villagers sit with their suspicions, with his family in their firing line.

For far too long, there is silence, broken only by the rhythmic hiss of sea against the fishing boat's hull. The two other boats are tiny shapes on the horizon. Nathan hears his heart thudding in his ears. His stomach turns over at the constant roll of the sea and he prays he can keep his breakfast down. He despises boats at the best of times.

Holland glances at Nathan; at his white-knuckled fingers gripping the gunwale. He chuckles. "Not got your sea legs then, Blake?"

Nathan forces a smile. "Far from it."

"Typical Londoners."

While Holland's words are predictable, there's warmth in his tone. Is it designed to lull him into a false sense of security? Or is he seeing conflict where there is none to be found? His dealings with Joseph Holland so far have been civil; friendly even. When he had visited the man to borrow the frame saw, they had spent much of the evening chatting over whisky glasses, while Theodora chased Holland's dog around his house. Nathan would almost consider him a friend. But Martin Macauley's presence makes him nervous.

"I'm afraid you're right," Nathan says to Holland. If the man truly is attempting a little geniality, he does not want to destroy it with suspicion. "Us city folk have plenty to learn about island life."

"Did you tell that to your sister when she got caught out by the tide?" asks Martin.

Nathan's stomach dives. "Indeed. Though I suspect she has learnt her lesson."

"Heard about that, Joseph?" Martin keeps his eyes on the sea. "Miss Blake stranding herself on the mainland for the night? Same night Da disappeared."

The back of Nathan's neck prickles. Joseph Holland stands suddenly; points. "Up ahead. What's that?"

Nathan squints. There's a small shape ahead, bobbing on the water. From this distance, he cannot make out what it is.

Martin leans on the tiller. "We need to get closer."

Nathan's heart quickens. He is not sure why. He already knows of Donald Macauley's fate. And surely nothing they find out here is going to implicate Eva. How could it? All the villagers can possibly have on her is suspicion.

None of them speak as the fishing boat skims over the water. It's a small dinghy ahead of them, Nathan realises. Its oars lie in the bottom of the boat.

"This belong to Donald?" asks Holland.

Martin nods, not speaking.

At the sight of the boat, Nathan thinks of Donald

Macauley forcing Eva aboard. Taking her out to sea and raising his musket. He swallows down a swell of rage. He is not sorry Donald Macauley is gone.

But when he glances sideways at Martin, he sees the man's face twisted in grief.

"I'm sorry," he finds himself saying. And he means it. He knows the pain of losing a father, and he would not wish it upon anyone—even if that father is Donald Macauley. He hates the weight of this secret, this guilt he is helping Eva carry. Hates the weight of this silence he has insisted upon.

Will it happen now, he wonders? Will Martin Macauley, in the throes of grief, hurl Nathan from his boat, to sink to the bottom as his father has clearly done? He hears his own breath coming hard and fast, a counterpoint to the rhythmic clapping of the sea against the two boats.

"Tie the dinghy to us," Martin says finally. "We'll take it back to shore."

CHAPTER NINETEEN

Donald Macauley's memorial service is predictably awful. What seems to be the entire village crams into the churchyard to pray over the wooden cross erected in his memory. Nathan bats away poisonous looks and accusing eyes—real or imagined, he cannot tell. He stands stoically beside Edwin on the edge of the gathering, the two of them twin figures in their grey coats and breeches, as though doing their best to disappear into the morning mist.

Harriet had made her excuses in the name of mothering, though Nathan supposes it had far more to do with a need to paint—or sleep. In any case, one sister's absence seems to sufficiently explain the other's, or perhaps the gossip of Eva's journey to Longstone has already filtered through the village. Either way, Nathan is not asked questions about her whereabouts. And he is more than a little grateful.

The sky opens as the crowd begins to file out of the churchyard. Great sacks of cloud hang over the ruins of the monastery, raindrops bouncing off the headstones.

As he steps out of the gate, Nathan sees Julia on the edge of his vision. "Go on ahead," he tells Edwin impulsively. "I shall catch you up."

Edwin gives him a curious half-smile, but thankfully, says nothing.

Nathan falls into step beside Julia. Bright curls are escaping out her bonnet, a stark contrast to the gloom that has swallowed the rest of the village.

"Good of you to come," she tells him.

Nathan allows himself a wry smile. Not for a second had it felt like a choice. "Well. We are a part of the village now. Ought to pay our respects."

"I see Harriet has no such concerns."

"Well. Harriet is a special case."

Julia laughs. "She is indeed." She stops outside the door of her curiosity shop. "Will you come in out of the rain? I can make us some tea?"

"Oh…" Nathan falters. "I would hate for people to think badly of you. If they were to see us alone together, I mean."

She laughs. "Don't concern yourself with that. This village made their mind up about my decency years ago." She gives him a pointed smile. "And I'd say they've made their mind up about you too."

Rain runs down the back of Nathan's neck. "Yes," he admits. "I suspect they have."

He steps into the shop. It is stuffy inside, holding the warmth of the smoking logs in the grate. Rain patters softly against the windows.

"Wait here if you like," says Julia. "I'll bring some tea down."

As she disappears up the staircase, Nathan lets out a

breath he had not realised he was holding. This is easier, of course, floating around here in the wilds of the curiosity shop, than the uncomfortable intimacy of venturing into Julia's living quarters. This way he can tell himself he is nothing more than a customer; can remind himself there is nothing of note between the two of them. And how could there be? Everything of note is an impossibility.

Nathan wanders through the shop, neatly avoiding the cat, who is curled up asleep on the hearth. In the far corner, he spots a telescope sitting on a wrought iron stand. He inspects it curiously, running a hand along the shaft. It's an old six-draw piece, with a tarnished brass barrel and wood at one end. Much like the telescope his father had given him when he was a child. Nathan hunches, holding his eye to the lens. He sees nothing but a blur, of course, with the glass pointed into the corner of the shop, but there is some odd comfort in the action itself. Something that reminds him of simpler times.

"Where do all your wares come from?" he asks Julia when she reappears in the doorway. She has a teapot in one hand and two mismatched porcelain cups in the other. She sets them on the counter and drags two chairs out from the corner of the shop.

"I collected things at first," she says. "Went around the village gathering up the treasures that people no longer wanted. Bought cheap pieces from curiosity shops on the mainland." She lets out a private laugh. "Before I opened the shop, Bobby and I were living with my brother. He was not all that happy when I started filling his kitchen with my treasures."

Nathan smiles.

"Most of the things I have now come from my customers.

They bring me their unwanted pieces and I give them a few pennies for them." She nods towards a large brass candleholder on the top of the nearest shelf. "That one belonged to Donald Macauley. He weren't impressed when I only gave him a shilling for it. Told me it was worth two pounds at least. He always was a bit mad, the poor old fellow." She fills the cups and slides one across the counter to Nathan. "Still, I imagine he would have liked to know there was so much mystery around his passing. Suspicious old bastard that he was."

Nathan swallows heavily. "Did you know him well?"

"He was a good friend of my da's. He always had a liking for me. At least, he was less grumpy around me than he was around most." She smiles crookedly. "I suppose he liked that we had a similar alliance."

"Are you not afraid to speak of your Jacobite alliance so openly?" asks Nathan, sipping his tea.

"I'm not speaking of it openly. I'm only speaking of it to you. I trust it will not go further than this room."

Her words are light, but Nathan feels the gravity of them. He is painfully aware of all he is keeping from Julia. It feels like the greatest abuse of her trust.

"In any case," she says, "I'm doing my best to stay out of the Jacobite cause. My brothers wished me to be more involved. Running messages and the like. I told them I'd not do it. My and Bobby's safety is far too important."

"Very wise of you," says Nathan. "If you were caught running messages, you'd be arrested at once." He is not sure why the thought of Julia being involved in the Jacobite cause makes him feel so unsettled. Is it the thought that she might put herself in danger? Or the uncomfortable notion that, if forced to choose sides, they would clearly not be allies?

"Do you miss London?" she asks suddenly. "As Harriet does?"

"No," says Nathan. His thoughtless response catches him off guard. London is home—a place to be returned to once Highfield House is finally off his hands. But: "There's little to miss, really." And he finds himself telling her about the dire business decisions he had made of late; of the clients who, one by one, had taken their money elsewhere. Tells her of the shame he had felt at being forced to sell the family's London home.

"I am sorry to hear it," Julia says. Her eyes are warm. "Your wife?" she asks tentatively.

"Sarah passed three years ago," he says. "Influenza." He cannot remember the last time he spoke aloud about Sarah, even to his daughter. Speaking her name has become a forgotten thing, and doing so makes something warm in his chest.

"It sounds as though you've had a difficult few years." Julia tops up the teacups. "I'm sure such things are not so easy to speak of." She looks up, fixing him with vivid green eyes. "Thank you for being so open with me."

Guilt seizes him. Because he has not been open with her. Not at all. She had clearly cared for Donald Macauley, and here he is hiding the truth of his death. The secrets he is carrying have never felt more weighted.

"I ought to go," he says suddenly, despite the freshly filled teacup. He will offend her again, of course, but what does that matter? What point is there in staying here, when all he can offer are secrets and lies? He gets to his feet before she can protest.

CHAPTER TWENTY

"I need to go to the mainland," says Finn. He is digging last night's ash from the firebasket and depositing it into a bucket for Eva to dump into the sea. "For food. And peat." He glances at her. "You've no problem digging up a little peat, have you? Carting it back to the boat?"

A look of horror flashes across her eyes, but she blinks it away quickly. "Oh… Yes… I mean, no… I'm sure…"

Finn chuckles and her face flushes scarlet. Sometimes this is too easy.

"We've enough fuel to keep us going for a while longer," he says with a grin. "But I appreciate your commitment." He dumps another shovelful into the bucket, sending a grey cloud rising into the air. "There's no need for you to come ashore. I can manage on my own."

Eva looks at him with raised eyebrows. He supposes he can't blame her. His little misadventure with the tide a week and a half ago certainly suggests otherwise.

As does the fact that he has not yet asked her to leave.

"I'm coming with you," she says, her tone leaving no room for argument. "I know you don't like it, but you need my help. At least for a little while longer. I'll not let you traipse around the market with blood running into your boots."

I know you don't like it. She has it wrong, of course. Not that he can blame her for thinking such things. A part of him wants to tell her everything, every piece of it. Tell her he likes it too much, and that that is far too dangerous. Tell her the thought of taking her back to Lindisfarne leaves him hollow. But he just taps the bucket with the shovel. "It's full. Dump it over by the jetty."

"How often do you leave Longstone?" Eva asks as they make their way to the skiff in the early afternoon. She brushes a streak of ash from her skirts.

The fire poker Finn is leaning on crunches against the rocky ground. "Once a fortnight, perhaps. Sometimes more often, when there's work on the farms."

"Do you not get lonely out here? Do you not miss human interaction?"

He considers the questions. "Sometimes." He has acquaintances. Men he works with on the farms, takes a drink with at the end of the workday. Familiar faces around the markets of Bamburgh. But it has been a long time since he has had someone he could call a friend. Someone with whom he can be open and honest and say what is on his mind. He reminds himself hurriedly that he does not have that luxury with Eva either. "But what's to miss really?" he says instead. "Most humans are bastards."

Eva shifts the basket she is carrying to her other arm. "Is that so?"

"Most humans, aye." He glances sideways at her. "Is that not your impression too?"

He sees a small smile. Wonders what she is thinking. "Perhaps not most humans," she says. "But some, yes." She eyes the skiff. "Can you get into boat?" she asks, a frown creasing the bridge of her nose.

Finn gives her a half-smile; a look that tells her she is worrying too much. "I'll be fine." He nods to the boat. "Get in."

Eva gathers her skirts and steps onto the jetty, then into the boat with a single step. She stumbles as the skiff rocks on the water, and lurches forward to grab the gunwale. He sees her eyes drift over the wine-dark blood staining the bottom of the boat. He climbs in quickly, nudging her towards the bench seat in an attempt to distract her. He grits his teeth at a jolt of pain, then unloops the moorings and sits. The skiff seesaws over the swell as he pulls away from the jetty.

Once they have cleared the island, he nods towards the furled sail. "Open it up," he tells Eva. "It's a fine day for sailing."

She looks at him in alarm. "You want me to sail the boat?"

"You're here to help me, aren't you?"

She presses her lips together. She knows he is testing her, surely, finding out how far she will go before admitting she is incapable. And he can tell that, above all things, she does not want to be incapable.

She gets tentatively to her feet and approaches the furled sail as though it's a wild animal she does not want to provoke. Finn chuckles. "Untie it. It won't bite."

Eva flashes him a look, then turns back to the knotted bindings, frowning in concentration as she unties them. The sail spills open, thwacking against the wind.

Finn pats the seat beside him. "Now sit down and take up the halyard."

Eva stumbles back towards the bench. He takes her arm to steady her; helps her sit. He hands her the rope and she pulls. Her eyes light as the sail comes to life.

Finn helps her secure the line. He tears his gaze from her to guide the boat past the edges of the archipelago. "Let me get free of the islands, then you can take the tiller."

Eva lifts her face to the sky. Wind tousles the spidery strands of hair poking loose from her bonnet. Her blue eyes are glowing. "It's very beautiful here," she says.

Finn looks out across the water, and for a moment it is as though he is seeing the place for the first time. Clouds are banking steadily, and the ocean is a patchwork of colour; green on the fringes of the island and blackening in its depths. Castles of rock reach up out of the water, guarded by armies of birds. As they pass Inner Farne, he looks up to see the crumbling walls of St Cuthbert's Chapel. A reminder of the holy men who had once made these islands home. He feels like the most unholy of replacements.

But Eva is right; there's an eerie beauty here; bleak and windblown with barely a speck of human scarring. A beauty he forgets all too often to see.

Bamburgh village is swarming. People jostle through the narrow streets, and Eva can hear shouting coming from within the cobbled alleyways. The beach is dotted with dinghies pushed high up on the sand, and there are several larger vessels in the deeper water beyond the shore.

"Is it always so busy?" asks Eva. She had not expected the place to be such a wash of activity. The air feels restless and charged.

"No." A frown darkens Finn's face. "It's not."

Eva glances at him. She guesses it a decent walk from the beach to the market, and she does not want a repeat of the tide incident. "I can go to the market alone," she tells him. "There's no need for you to come traipsing around the village."

He shakes his head. "It's best I come with you. Something is going on." He takes a step towards her, closing the space between them.

Since running into trouble, he has clearly resigned himself to her company. But it does not seem to be reluctantly. This morning, as they had sat at the table drinking their tea together, there was a look in his eyes she would almost describe as warmth, if she had not learnt better. Whatever it is, it is a welcome relief. If more than a little disorienting.

The crowd, Eva realises, is gathering close to the castle, and funnelling into the narrow streets. Most are men, several dressed in tartans, though she sees a few women among them. Many of them are waving flags, and among them she sees both the Stuart coat of arms and the White Horse of Hanover, signalling support for King George. Many in the crowd have the white cockade of the Jacobites pinned to their cloaks and bonnets. Men are pushing through the crowd, shoving tracts into the hands of passers-by.

"A protest?" she asks Finn.

"Looks that way. Let's get what we need and leave."

Eva doesn't take her eyes from the crowd. "Do they not

know of the new riot act?"

Finn chuckles. "I'm sure they'll find out about it soon enough."

"Is it likely to get violent?"

"There's a chance of it, aye."

Eva glances at him. "Do you support them? The Jacobites?"

"Nah." He wraps his hand around her bare forearm, tugging her close. "Not that I support the German. I just don't want to see this country at war again."

Eva walks with her shoulder pressed to Finn's. Though England has been at war for most of her life, conflict has never felt as close as it does here, with Donald Macauley's death on her shoulders and the shouts of protesters echoing through the streets.

The noise of the riot dims as they get further from the castle. "Do the Jacobites truly imagine they have a chance this time?" she says, keeping her voice low. "The last time they tried to rise, they were defeated before their troops even managed to land."

"Things are different for them now," Finn reasons. "They feel they've more of a chance with a foreigner on the throne."

Eva nods. In London, too, displeasure at the new king had been widespread. Ever since Queen Anne's death last year, pamphleteers and protests had been rife throughout the capital. Up here, so close to Scotland, the energy of the riots is magnified. "Still," she says, "what chance do these rebels have against the army?"

"Perhaps nought," says Finn. "But they believe God put the Stuarts on the throne. And they will fight for that to the death."

Eva glances back at the crowd of protesters. She cannot think of anything she would risk her own life for. Cannot think of anything she would even bother protesting over.

She suddenly feels empty. With her life laid out in front of her for long, with her townhouse mentally decorated and her children pre-emptively named, there had seemed little else to put her mind to. Yes, she has always kept up with the turnings of the world around her, but this had come from a need to maintain the intellect she had sold herself to Matthew Walton with, rather than a desire to bring about any sense of change.

But look at those men and women beyond the castle, putting themselves in the path of the redcoats out of love for their exiled king. Look at Finn Murray, resigning himself to a lonely life on Longstone so the firebasket might come to life each night. Even Harriet, when she stands in front of her easel, comes alive with a passion that Eva craves. She has never known anything worth fighting for. Nothing that is worth challenging the neatly ordered life that is expected of her.

Finn does not release his grip on her arm until they reach the market. They make their way from stall to stall, filling the basket—carrots and potatoes, flour and apples. A seed cake, and a bottle of whisky from a still in the back of a wagon.

The staccato rap of horse hooves echoes through the marketplace and a raft of soldiers thunders past. Eva feels the air shift against her cheek. A shout goes up as they clash with the rioters at the end of the street. Gunfire splinters the sky.

Finn puts a hand to her shoulder, guiding her quickly towards the tavern at the end of the alley. "Let's get out of the street. Hopefully they'll bore themselves soon enough."

Eva stops walking. "In the tavern?" she says. "No, Finn, I

can't."

"Why not?"

"Because it is not the done thing. I'm an unmarried woman. I cannot be seen alone with you in such a place."

He grins. "I promise I'll be the most decent gentleman you ever did see." He nudges her towards the doorway. "Come on, now. It's dangerous out here. You'll just have to find a way to resist my charms."

Eva hesitates. She glances back over her shoulder as gunfire breaks over the castle. And she steps through the door that Finn is holding open for her.

The air inside the tavern is thick with pipe smoke and drink. Sunlight struggles through grimy windows, is drowned by dark stone walls. The pale light from a single lantern spills from the beamed roof. Eva glances around, wary of being recognised. She is glad to find the place quiet. A few men lean up against the bar and another sleeps on a bench in front of an unlit grate, but it seems most of Bamburgh is out in the street.

Finn gestures to a table in the back corner of the tavern. "Here. Sit down. Hopefully we'll not be here long."

Eva slides onto a stool and takes off her bonnet and cloak. She sits her hat in her lap and winds its ribbons around her hands edgily. What if word gets back to Nathan that she is prancing around a tavern in the company of a man? Still, she can't deny she feels safer inside solid walls than she had in the midst of the protest.

Finn shuffles to the bar and Eva turns to look out the window. Fat drops of rain are pocking the glass. Though she can't see much through the grimy pane, she can hear shouting in the street. Can hear the dull clatter of wood striking wood.

The sharp echo of gunfire.

Finn returns with two tankards and sets one in front of Eva. She takes a sip, not caring what's inside. Lukewarm ale slides down her throat.

Finn sits opposite her. "All right?" he asks.

She nods. Takes another mouthful. A little of the tension begins to ease from her body. "Has it been like this for long up here?" she asks. "So unsettled, I mean."

Finn sips his drink. "Aye. A while. Riots and the like, since the German took the throne. Big protests on Restoration Day, of course. And on the anniversary of Geordie coming to power."

"In London, there was talk of the king fleeing," says Eva. "Can you imagine it?" She shakes her head. "And then my family appears on the island among all this unrest... It is no surprise they distrust us. We are outsiders."

"It's not just because you're outsiders," says Finn. "It's because you own Highfield House."

Eva frowns. "What do you mean?"

"Before you lot turned up, it was used as a meeting place for the Jacobites on Lindisfarne. I daresay they weren't happy when they found out your family'd returned. They'll be back to holding their meetings in cellars and cart houses again now."

"Why would the Jacobites need to hide away in Highfield House? The islanders are sympathetic to them."

"Some of them," Finn agrees. "But not all. Word is there really are government spies on Holy Island."

"Who are they?"

He smiles. "I've no idea."

She tilts her head, taking him in. A strand of hair has come loose from its queue and hangs across his eye. "How do you know all this when you spend all your time on Longstone?"

"I don't spend all my time on Longstone. I told you, I come to the mainland at least once a fortnight. And I make it a point to go to Lindisfarne from time to time too. Keep an eye on things there." He gives a short chuckle. "Not that that worked out so grand for me last time."

"Everyone there seems to know who you are," Eva tells him. "Is that because you're so light-fingered?"

He returns her half-smile. "Probably. I've not made too many friends over there. But I need to keep an eye on the place. It may feel isolated out on Longstone, but I'd like to know about it if we're to go to war again."

"Is that what you believe will happen?" Eva asks. "War?"

Finn runs a finger along his bristly chin. "Only a matter of time before the Rising kicks off proper, I'd say."

Eva turns her tankard around. If the Jacobites do take up arms again, she hopes her family will be back in London. Holy Island feels far too exposed, a stone's throw from Scotland, with escape at the mercy of the tides.

"What is so special about Highfield House?" she asks. "Why were the Jacobites using it? Holy Island is full of places to hide away."

"It's hidden in the dunes," says Finn. "Private. Hard to see from the land. And it has easy access to and from the sea. Easy to make an escape."

Eva takes a long mouthful of ale. Twenty years ago, her mother had made an escape from Holy Island. And she cannot make sense of why.

She sits back in her chair, cradling her tankard. Rain is pelting against the windows now, and much of the daylight has been obscured by cloud. In the half light of the tavern, it feels as though nightfall is approaching, though she knows it can be no later than four or five.

Finn looks up suddenly and curses under his breath. A man is striding towards them; Eva recognises him as one of the Lindisfarne fisherman. She grapples for his name. Cordwell, perhaps? He's a bear of a man, with a long white beard and broad, meaty shoulders. From Finn's reaction she can only gather they know each other, and do not get along. She wonders if Finn has been stealing from him too.

Cordwell hovers over their table, arms folded across his thick chest. His greatcoat smells sour, like old salt and herrings. His eyes shift between Eva and Finn.

"Aren't you too much of a lady to be gallivanting around the place with this scoundrel, Miss Blake?"

Eva feels her cheeks flush, hiding her tankard of ale beneath the table. She prays Cordwell does not tell Nathan about having seen her. "Leave us be," she says tightly.

The fisherman turns to Finn. "You been out Donald Macauley's way lately, Murray?"

Eva's heart quickens.

"Nah." Finn gives him a thin smile. "I've enough coal to see me through til winter."

Cordwell snorts. "We ought to send the constable after you."

"You should," Finn agrees. "But then you'd have no one to keep you from getting wrecked when you go out after those herrings so late at night."

A muscle ticks in Cordwell's jaw. "Maybe we ought to be asking you about Donald's disappearance."

Finn's lips part beneath his beard. "Donald Macauley is

missing?"

"Aye. No one's seen him in almost a month. Everyone's saying he's dead. They found his boat floating out your way. You know anything about that?"

Eva feels a jolt in her chest. Her heart is thumping so loudly she is sure the men can hear it.

Finn stares Cordwell down. "Why would I know anything about that?" He shakes his head. "Leave us alone, man. You know I had nothing to do with poor old Macauley."

Cordwell hesitates for a moment, then makes his way across the tavern without looking at them again.

Finn glances at Eva; a pointed look, full of questions. But he says nothing.

The door creaks open, letting in an explosion of noise. Rioters bluster into the tavern, dripping trails of rainwater. One has a sodden Jacobite flag slung over his shoulder. The downpour blows in through the open doorway.

"Out of here, you lot," the barkeep calls, pointing a fat finger towards the door. "Don't want none of this trouble in my tavern."

"Looks as though the redcoats have broken up the protest," says Finn. "Hopefully they'll—" He stops abruptly, his eyes following a man who steps into the tavern behind the Jacobites. He is tall and broad-shouldered, fair hair tied back in a long queue. He removes his cocked hat and shakes the rain from it, then makes his way towards the bar, weaving neatly through the protesters.

Eva frowns. "Who is that?"

Finn pulls his eyes away. "No one. I thought I knew the man. But I was mistaken." He tosses back the last of his drink and gets awkwardly to his feet. "Let's go. It's getting madder in here than it was outside."

Though the riots around the castle have broken up, the narrow streets are still teeming with people. Two men are dragged past the tavern by soldiers and shoved into a wagon at the end of the lane. Rain is bouncing off the cobbles and wind tears through the alleys. Eva tucks the food basket under her cloak in an attempt to keep it dry. Her heart is still hard and fast with the knowledge that Donald Macauley's boat has been found. Do people suspect her involvement, given she had been missing from the island the night of Macauley's disappearance? Cordwell's questions had suggested not, but she cannot find much comfort in them—especially since his suspicions were squarely aimed at Finn.

She glances sideways at him. Now they are alone, she is certain he is going to ask. Because surely now he has come to suspect that Donald Macauley was the man she had sent to the bottom of the sea.

They emerge from the tangle of streets to find a wild grey ocean folding out ahead of them. Waves are stirring the beach, tugging at the dinghies lined up along the sand. The Farnes have vanished behind a thick wall of cloud. A few hundred yards from shore, a larger vessel rocks at anchor, the wings of its large eagle figurehead tilting in the rain.

Eva hears Finn curse under his breath. "This weather's only going to get worse," he says. "We never should have stayed this long." Water drips from the ends of his hair. "It's a bad idea to try and get back to Longstone tonight."

Eva pulls her wet cloak tight around her body. Water has soaked through her shoes, and she can barely feel her toes. She longs to curl up in front of the fire in the cottage on

Longstone. But she trusts Finn's knowledge of the sea. "What about the firebasket?" she asks.

He rubs a hand over his jaw. "It'll do no one any good if we drown trying to get back out there."

Eva nods. Shivers. "Is there an inn here in town?"

"Aye. Of course." He leads her back into the village, a hand pressed lightly to her shoulder. The feel of him goes someway to steadying her unease.

The lodging house is a sorry-looking building not far from the tavern, with a crooked front door and sagging wooden awnings. But Eva can see the glow of a fire through the windows; can smell cooking spices. She marches towards the door. Finn holds her back.

"I think…" He swallows. Tries again. "I think we ought to take a room together. It doesn't feel safe here tonight." He rubs the back of his neck. "I don't mean… Rather, I'd keep my distance… I…"

Eva can't help a slight smile.

A part of her wants to agree to his suggestion. But the thought feels suddenly overwhelming. It's foolish, she knows, to be feeling this way. She and Finn have spent three weeks keeping the light together. She has spent nights hunched over his bed, a damp cloth held to his forehead as he slept. Has tended his wound like the most devoted of physicians. There is no reason why she ought to be so unmoored by this suggestion. But something about this feels different.

Something about *him* feels different.

With the world rioting around them, Finn is caring and protective. Unable, or unwilling, to keep her at a distance.

And that new warmth is a little terrifying. Because it has made Eva strikingly aware of the way his closeness has her heart thumping in her chest. Strikingly aware of how much she wants to be near him. And strikingly aware of how impossible that might be. No doubt Nathan is already knee-deep in another plan to secure her a husband. And she feels quite certain that plan does not involve the thieving lightkeeper from Longstone.

She pulls a handful of coins from her pouch and strides inside out of the rain. "I will be quite all right in the dormitories."

CHAPTER TWENTY-ONE

Nathan has far too much to do to be sitting here at his desk staring blankly at his inkpot. There are business proposals to compose, in an attempt to rebuild his enterprise after the disastrous decisions he had made last year. And then there is the letter to Matthew Walton he has been putting off for far too long. It ought to be a strongly worded letter, of course. One in which he professes his utter dissatisfaction at the way his friend had treated both Eva and the family as a whole. But strongly worded letters have never been his strength. He can't quite find space for it.

Really, what he wants is to sleep. To curl up beneath his blankets and listen to the weather throwing itself against the house. But his thoughts are charging far too rapidly for that.

He fears that, at any moment, Martin Macauley might appear on his doorstep to string him up for his lies. To hunt down Eva for her role in his father's death.

Nathan uncorks a bottle of gin and refills the empty glass beside his inkpot. He wishes Eva was here. He has always enjoyed his sister's company, and tonight, he could use her level-headedness to keep his thoughts from venturing into dark places. Not that he supposes her own thoughts might be any less troubled. Still, perhaps they could steady each other somewhat, remind each other that, though they are teetering, nothing has toppled yet.

Since Sarah's death, Nathan has come to value Eva's place in his life even more. The two of them are strikingly similar, with a bone-deep hatred of conflict and a need to see everything in its rightful place. Logical and undistinguished middle children, against the terrifying brilliance of Oliver and the flightiness of Harriet.

He thinks of her out on that tiny speck of rock. Fleeing to Longstone is not the kind of impulsive thing he has ever known her to do. When Harriet had told him of Eva's leaving, he had had half a mind to go after her and demand she do nothing so reckless and improper. But he knows Eva, and he knows she is doing it for the right reasons. Knows how heavily her conscience must be weighing on her heart.

He can also only imagine how inordinately dreadful a boat trip out to Longstone would be. And he'll quite willingly leave his sister to her own devices if it means avoiding such a horror.

Thunder stirs out over the ocean and he finds himself glancing out the half-open curtains. Most nights, he can see the shipping beacon on Longstone winking in the darkness. Tonight, though, the horizon is black. Of course, there can be no firelight in weather such as this.

Nathan brings his glass to his lips, listening to the storm rattling the shutters. He has given up on the idea of writing tonight, but he knows that sleep is still far away. In the wild wind, the house shifts around him, not quite alive, and not quite still. He can hear footsteps in the passage downstairs, no doubt belonging to Harriet. The ceiling creaks loudly above his head.

If he is honest with himself, it is not the letters, or Eva's absence, or even Donald Macauley's death that has him so rattled tonight. It is thoughts of Oliver and the bedroom with the priest hole tucked into its walls.

Nathan had looked up to his older brother. Revered him, been blind to his flaws. His cruelty. All too often, Oliver had shunned his brother's company, preferring to explore the island alone, or lock himself away in his bedroom, doing heaven only knew what. Anytime he could grab a scrap of his older brother's attention, Nathan took it.

Come out and face your maker.

Oliver had always been obsessed with the dark history of Holy Island. The stories of the Viking raids had fascinated him. He would walk the ruins of the priory, telling Nathan tales of monks murdered in their monastery by the wild men from across the seas; stories of the villagers slaughtered in their homes.

They had been walking the rocks around St Cuthbert's Island when Oliver had pulled the knife from the water. Barely six inches long, it was tarnished with time, but its blade was still sharp enough to inflict plenty of damage.

"A Viking knife," Oliver had told him. "From the raids."

At seven years old, Nathan had believed him.

Oliver had taken the knife home, tucked into his pocket to hide it from their mother. "Let's play a game."

Nathan had agreed at once. A game, yes. When was the last time Oliver had sought his company?

Go and hide in the house. Don't make a sound. Imagine the Vikings are coming for you.

And Nathan would run, thrilled and terrified, craving his brother's attention and fearing it too. He knew, of course, to hide out of sight of his mother, and the housekeepers, and anyone else who might catch sight of what they were doing. Knew to hide in the cupboards and wardrobes and under the beds where no one would find them.

His brother, three years older, was sharper, stronger, wiser. Would uncover Nathan's hiding places in minutes.

Come out and face your maker. Always spoken in the same low, taunting voice, letting Nathan know he had been found.

And Nathan would find himself frozen in place, terrified of facing his brother and the punishment he would suffer for having his hiding place uncovered. Hands around his ankles or wrists, Oliver would drag him from the cupboard, the wardrobe, from the beneath the bed. Hold the knife to his throat.

And now you will die like the monks did.

Hard enough to cause a murmur of pain. Hard enough to fear the knife would break the skin.

Once, Nathan had hidden in the priest hole. Oliver had not appeared within minutes to drag him from his hiding place, and at first Nathan had been proud of himself for tricking his brother. He sat there in the tiny darkness with his heart thumping hard, half exhilarated, half terrified as he waited for that moment when the priest hole would flood with light again. That moment when his brother would drag him out into the bedroom and press the knife to his throat.

More time passed. Minutes—or was it hours? Perhaps Oliver was not coming. Perhaps the hiding place was too good. Nathan could not bear much longer in this airless, lightless space. He shoved against the panel that opened out into the bedroom. It did not move. And he knew at once that he had not tricked his brother at all. Because there was no tricking Oliver. His mind was too sharp. Too wicked. Nathan did not know what his brother had pushed in front of the priest hole to prevent it from opening. All he knew was that, once again, he was at his older brother's mercy.

Nathan had no idea how long he stayed prisoner in the hole. Time was distorted by the dark, and by fear of that moment when Oliver would come for him. He did not cry out. Did not call for his mother. He knew that would only make things worse.

Finally, he heard the scrape of wood on wood as Oliver shoved—*what?* His bed? Wardrobe?—away from the door of the priest hole. "Come out and meet your maker."

Nathan's muscles stiffened as his brother reached for him, yanking him out into the light. His legs ached from being held to his chest for so long, and he could do little more than spill out across the floor. Oliver loomed over him, obscuring his vision of the tree-trunk beams across the ceiling. "Show a little imagination next time, Nathan. I think you need to be punished for choosing such a dreadful hiding place."

Nathan tried to scramble away from his brother's grip, but Oliver held him down. And then the knife. His chest. His stomach. His throat. The pain intensified and he felt a thin line of blood run onto his collar.

Nathan cannot say for certain that Oliver's game had led to his fear of human touch. He cannot determine when such a thing had begun. All he knows is that he does not remember having such a fear in the days before his brother had found the knife in the ocean.

"There are rats in the roof, Nathan," says Harriet, appearing in the doorway of the study. Paint is streaked along one cheek, and her blonde curls are spilling loose over her shoulders. Though it is well past midnight, she is still dressed in her pale blue day dress, as though she has no intention of sleeping. "I can hear them moving around up there. Big ones. I can hear them over all this rain. Can smell them too. The filthy beasts." Lightning jags, filling the room with sudden white light.

"What would you like me to do?" Nathan asks. "Climb up to the attic and kill them all?"

"That would be nice," she says. "It's dreadfully hard to concentrate with all that scrabbling."

Nathan bites back a retort. He knows Harriet is only trying to get a reaction out of him. "What does Edwin think about you staying up so late?"

"Edwin is fast asleep," she says. "As he is most nights. He probably assumes I'm asleep too." She pins Nathan with hard eyes. "Do not even think of telling him."

He hesitates. "He is your husband, Harriet. I think he ought to know what you're up to."

"Do not even think of it," she repeats, jabbing a long finger in his direction. "It's your fault we're up here in this dreadful wilderness. My painting is all that's keeping me sane."

Nathan sighs. He'll not think of telling Edwin, no. As far as he is concerned, Harriet's theatrics are for her husband to deal with now, and he has no desire to get involved. The rats, however, are a different story.

He leaves his study and makes his way down the passage.

He looks upward, listening. Perhaps there is a rustling. And definitely a foul smell. Little wonder. After twenty years of abandonment, the place is probably crawling with far more than rats. But as far as he knows, the space inside the roof is inaccessible. He has no thought of how he might find his way inside.

As he is pondering that unpleasant prospect, a shriek comes from his bedroom.

He rushes down the passage and throws open the door to find Theodora huddled on the floor next to her truckle bed. He drops to his knees beside her. "What's happened, my love?"

She replies only with a loud sob. Nathan grits his teeth and scoops her from the floor. She throws her arms around his neck and clings to him as he carries her to his bed. His heart hammers against his ribs at the feel of her little body wrapped around his.

"Were you sleepwalking again?" he asks gently. "Did you have a bad dream?"

Her reply is muffled against his neck.

Nathan smooths her hair. Feels sweat prickling his skin. His instincts war with each other; half desperate to comfort his daughter, half desperate to put space between their bodies. He forces himself to breathe. To keep a hold of her.

"Men in the walls," Theodora manages.

He eases her back so he can see her face in the lamplight spilling in from the passage. "What?"

"Men in the walls," she says again.

"Where?"

She bursts into a fresh rush of tears. Buries her head in his shoulder. Nathan eases her under the covers, forcing himself to keep his fingers tucked around hers. *Just a dream*, he hears himself say. Can't make sense of why he is finding it so hard to believe his own words.

CHAPTER TWENTY-TWO

Something wakes Eva from a broken sleep. The dark is thick, and for a moment, she is disoriented, until she makes out the outlines of the dormitory's five other beds. The smell of roast meat and cold grease drifts in from the nearby kitchen, joining the fug of wet clothes and shoes. Rain is still loud against the windows, punctuated by a rattle of thunder.

Eva hears yelling in the street. The words are thick with a Scottish drawl and she can't make them out. But the pistol shot that follows is clear enough.

She sits up, heart jolting.

"Bloody animals," says the older woman in the next bed. "Thought the redcoats cleared this place out." She slides out from under her blanket and goes to the window. She pulls back the curtain, letting a spear of light from the streetlamps into the room. Through the wash of rain on the glass, Eva can just make out the shapes of men brawling in the street. She hears drink on their voices. Knots of shouted Gaelic.

The barrel of a musket comes flying through the window.

Glass sprays out between the curtains and the older woman lets out a shriek. Eva scrambles out of bed and hurries to her side. On the other side of the room, someone lights a lamp.

"Are you all right?"

The woman looks down at her arms and hands, inspecting them for damage. "I think so." The curtains bloom in the wind and rain blows in through the broken window, along with a gust of cold, sea-scented air.

There is a pounding on the door. Eva hears Finn calling her name. She hurries across the room and pulls open the door, poking her head into the passage to obscure his view into the dormitory. He is dressed in only his breeches and shirtsleeves, the neck of his shirt hanging open, revealing sparse curls of hair.

"What are you doing?" Eva hisses. "You can't be in here."

The older woman shoves her way past them, shoes in one hand and shawl in the other. She disappears down the passage.

"There's a fight in the street," says Finn. "I thought I heard glass breaking." He peers over her shoulder to the shattered window. When he looks back at her, there's an intensity to his eyes that she hasn't seen before. "Please, Eva. Come upstairs with me. I just want to make sure you're safe. I'll sleep outside the door if you wish it. But I don't want you in here."

And it's bare instinct that makes her nod. She wraps her arms around herself, suddenly aware of the thinness of her shift. "Just give me a moment to dress."

What in hell is he doing? The *Eagle* is moored in the harbour, his former captain is here in Bamburgh, and now Eva Blake is about to curl up to sleep in his room. Having her in such close quarters would be a brainless idea at the best of times, but having caught sight of the captain in the tavern earlier—and having glimpsed his barque anchored off the beach—only emphasises the stupidity of this. The impossibility of his desire for Eva. She cannot know any of it, of course. Not of the *Eagle*, or his past with Captain Ward. He wonders if she had believed him when he had fibbed about recognising Ward in the tavern. He had hated the lie. But what is one tiny fib amongst everything else he is keeping from her?

The wooden stairs of the inn creak beneath his weight. He did not for a second imagine Eva might agree to this. But he hears her steady footsteps behind him and his heart is thunder in his ears. This is clearly inviting trouble. But what else can he do? Letting her stay in the women's dormitory is not an option, not with bullets flying across the street and men brawling outside the window. He knows Eva can look after herself in many ways—but he also feels fairly certain that her life in London has not thrown her in too many situations like this one.

He tries not to let her nearness rattle him. After all, he has spent almost a month in her company. But something about this feels different. Is it the fact that tonight, when he sleeps, there will be no wall between them? Or because, in his concern for her safety, he has let her glimpse the way he really feels about her?

He turns the key in the lock and steps aside, gesturing to her to enter. She turns to look back at him. "Are you not coming in?"

He shakes his head stiffly. It's a bad idea. "Just bring me my coat. I'll stay out here."

"Finn. Don't be foolish. You're still hurt. I'd rather go back to the dormitories than have you sleeping in the hallway on account of me." She meets his eyes. "No one need know of this. No one will judge us. Besides, we've been sharing the cottage for weeks." It sounds as though she is trying to convince herself more than him.

Reluctantly, he steps inside. Locks the door behind him. The glow of a street lamp fills the room and Finn pulls the curtain closed. Now Eva is safely with him, he has no desire to watch what's going on out there. Though he can still hear voices in the street, mingled with the steady slap of rain, the violence seems to have eased. A single candle flickers on the side table, and a fire simmers steadily in the grate, making shadows dance across the walls. His wet coat and vest hang drying on a chair beside it.

Eva hovers on the opposite side of the room, her cloak and bonnet clutched to her chest. Her hair hangs over one shoulder in a dishevelled brown plait, the ends curling slightly.

Finn nods towards the basket sitting on the table, filled with the food they had bought from the market. "Are you hungry?" His voice comes out stiff and strained.

Eva goes to the table and rifles through the basket. She considers the loaf of bread and the seedcake, then pulls out an apple. Her eyes drift towards the narrow bed pressed up against one wall, its blankets undisturbed. "Have you slept?" she asks. Smiles faintly. "I suppose not."

"I'll sleep when we get back tomorrow morning."

He can hear the faint sigh of the sea beneath the storm. Thinks of waves breaking on the Knavestone reef. And tonight, the firebasket will not be lit. Still, he knows he has made the right decision. Trying to get back to Longstone in this weather would have been far too treacherous. After all, he never has a beacon to guide himself home. Tonight, he knows, the waves will break against the walls of the cottage. He has not closed the shutters over the windows, and he hopes he will not return to broken glass and a flooded home.

But there is little point dwelling on that dark firebasket. He just has to hope that tonight, no wayward ships will be passing the Farne Islands.

Finn takes the poker and stirs the fire. Clears his throat. "You ought to try and sleep. Take the bed."

"I'm far too awake to sleep any more. Those men firing their pistols outside my window made sure of that." She takes a bite of the apple that echoes in the stillness of the room. The sound shatters the tension and makes Finn laugh.

"So you decided you'd wake the rest of the inn too?"

Eva jabs him in the ribs with her elbow. She takes another thunderous bite, and gives him a defiant smile.

With his wet clothes occupying the only chair, Finn lowers himself awkwardly to the floor. Eva sits beside him.

"Do you think you will do it forever?" she asks, once she's swallowed down the last of her food. "Keep the light, all on your own?" She tosses the apple core into the fire.

Finn shrugs. Usually, he tries not to think too far into the future. There does not seem to be much in it except the Longstone light. "Someone needs to do it," he says. "So I suppose I will be out there until Trinity House puts up a real beacon in the Farnes."

"They never thought to pay you?"

He shifts his injured leg, trying to dull the ache of it. "The church that owns the islands is letting me live out here without paying a penny."

Eva catches his eye. "They're getting a fine deal. It is not a job for one man."

"Good thing I've got you then, aye?" The comment comes out sounding far more intimate than he intended. Eva looks down at her clasped hands. Doesn't speak.

Longstone had been Finn's first home. His uncles had drowned on the Knavestone more than a decade before he was born, and his father had petitioned heavily for the beacon to be raised on Inner Farne. When that proposed light had remained dark, the Newcastle merchants unwilling to pay for its upkeep, he had taken it upon himself to change that. Near single-handedly, he had gone about building the cottage and the firebasket on the island closest to the reef that had taken his brothers' lives.

Finn's childhood had been spent fishing and sailing, and learning to light the firebasket, taking turns with his parents to keep watch over the light.

But he and his father had never got along. Had never seen eye to eye. Finn was eight when his mother passed, and after that, the island had felt particularly stifling.

But it wasn't just his relationship with his father that made him want to leave the place. As a child, that inkblot of rock was just not enough. Each night, as he helped his father light the basket, he would look out to sea and watch the lights of passing ships. Imagine where they might be heading; where they might have come from. He longed to see more of the world than this stifling, sea-drenched corner. For the first decade of his life, his world was unbearably tiny, made up only of Longstone and the small mainland villages nearby that kept them fed.

He felt resentment towards his father too. Didn't understand his need to make the firebasket his life. Why did his da feel the need to do what no one else was willing to do? The Farne Islands had been dark for centuries. Why should it be their job to change that?

Yes, his father's brothers had succumbed to the sea. But sacrificing his life like this would not bring his brothers back. It would only worsen his already strained relationship with his son.

Finn was nine years old when he met Henry Ward. He had taken the skiff over to the mainland, leaving his father with no way off Longstone except the leaky dinghy they saved for emergencies. He'd fought with his father the night before; can't remember why—barely a night went by without them bickering about the watch or the supper, or anything else as inconsequential. They had both flown into a rage, as usual, and had spent the night in silence.

When he had arrived in Beadle Bay, he had found Ward's barque in the middle of the harbour, effortlessly attracting attention. The ship was beautiful, its intricate eagle figurehead looking out over the water and daring passers-by to ask questions. Finn rarely saw vessels like that here—usually the harbour was cluttered with fishing ketches and the barnacled hulls of single-masted dories. Curious, he circled the ship in his skiff, eyes on the barque as he leant on the tiller. He guessed it too small to be a ship of the line. A merchant, perhaps? Privateer? Perhaps even a pirate. What would it be like to climb aboard a ship like that and see the world?

Finn had not expected anyone to be aboard, but Henry Ward appeared on deck and called down to him.

"You like the ship, lad?"

He nodded, squinting into the sun. "Aye, sir. It's a beauty."

Ward watched him ease the skiff around the bow. "You look as though you can handle a vessel. How old are you?"

"Nine years, sir."

Ward raised his eyebrows. "You're big for your age. Would you like to come aboard a moment? Have yourself a look at my ship?"

That moment aboard the *Eagle* had led to the invitation Finn could not refuse. He needed a cabin boy, said Henry Ward, to ferry messages across the ship and run the captain's errands as they fired broadsides at the French, under the title of legal privateers. A letter of marque signed by the king himself.

A life as a cabin boy fighting the French was far more than Finn could have imagined. Far more excitement, more fear, more exhilaration. A life far more expansive than he had lived so far.

For two years, he had sailed with Ward and the *Eagle,* prowling the Channel, tracing the seas of Europe, in search of French prey. Two years of hammocks and hardtack and smoke in his lungs.

Henry Ward was a good captain. Strict but fair, with a constant eye out for his cabin boy. Finn ate his meals in the officers' wardroom. Learned to scramble up the rigging in seconds to trim the sails. Ran messages across the ship while gunfire roared around his ears.

But everything had changed in an instant. A single

moment, a single mistake. Two years after he had first climbed aboard the *Eagle,* Finn had had no choice but to run from Henry Ward and his crew.

For years he roamed the country, a moving target in case Ward saw fit to come after him for the crime he had committed. Fishing and farming in whichever part of England the work led him. Sometimes even up into Scotland, hauling ancient wooden ploughs through muddy fields. Anything to put pennies in his pocket and keep him from thinking about his time on the *Eagle.*

Finally, seventeen years after he had left Longstone, guilt brought him back. Guilt and a long-buried need to be a decent son. It had taken adulthood for Finn to see the odd nobility in what his father had made his life; made him see the utter decency in keeping the light and protecting strangers' lives at the cost of his own freedom. And it had taken adulthood for him to realise just how terribly he had treated his father. How much worry and regret the man must have felt for him, out there alone on his island.

When Finn had stepped back onto Longstone for the first time, an odd stillness had hung over the place. It had always been a place of unsilent silence. But now it felt different. Otherworldly. The firebasket swung in the wind, old, cold ash skittering over the surface of the rock pools. The candles in the cottage had burnt down to stumps. A loaf of bread sat in the middle of the table, gathering mould.

He found the body the next morning when the tide fell. Dark and swollen, a mat of grey hair half-obscuring the face. Finn stared at it for a long time. He tried to imagine what his father's last moments had been like. Had his heart seized and taken him suddenly? Or had he suffered slowly, unable to move from the grasp of the rising tide? The grotesque, discoloured body was impossible to look away from. Barely recognisable as his father. It seemed to highlight all the terrible mistakes Finn had made.

He wrapped his father's remains in sailcloth and rowed out into deeper sea. Slipped the body into the water, murmuring a prayer cobbled together from distant childhood memories. Eighteen years ago, he and his father had buried his mother out here like this too. At least his parents would be together now, at the bottom of the lightless sea.

Regret hung heavy on his shoulders as he rowed back to Longstone. He and his father were all each other had had in the world. And Finn had left him to die a lonely death; left his body to disappear beneath the tide.

He is only dimly aware of having spoken aloud to Eva. Of having told her of his return to Longstone, and the discovery of his father's body. Of course, he had said nothing to her of the barque with the eagle figurehead.

I'm sorry, say her eyes, but she doesn't speak. He is glad of it. Speaking will not change anything. And he does not want her pity.

He knows he should not have told her. Knows no good can come of getting close to her, of allowing these feelings he has for her to turn into anything at all. Because what he does not tell her, is how, from the moment he returned to Longstone, he has always been aware of that vast house on the edge of Holy Island, a stone's throw across the water.

The silence between them is weighted. She is leaning forward slightly, as if waiting for him to speak again. No. There will be no more. There can be no more. It would send her running into the street to be caught up in the remnants of the protest.

"You are doing a good thing, Finn," she says finally. "I am sorry people don't see that."

"Well, I've stolen from people on Holy Island. Other places too. I can hardly expect them to look past that." And his mind goes to a vanished man, a vanished boat; to the accusation Tom Cordwell had made against him in the tavern. He looks at Eva. He wants to ask; can't ask. But what what what was she doing at sea with Donald Macauley? Because surely this vanished man is now lying at the bottom of the German Ocean.

He and the Macauleys have never gotten along. He and Martin had been born into a feud between their fathers, a petty thing over some long-forgotten dispute that he'd foolishly felt the need to continue. Stormy years, he thinks. The years of his father; of Donald Macauley; of Eva's mother. Kind and foolish Abigail Blake. He tries not to follow that thought too far.

He glances at Eva again, willing her to speak unprompted of Macauley's drowning. She won't, of course. She has kept that information close to her chest for three weeks. Finally, he says, "Why were you at sea with Donald Macauley?"

Eva stares into the fire for a long time, glassy-eyed. She does not look surprised at his question. No doubt she has been waiting for him to ask ever since Cordwell planted the idea at his feet.

She draws in a long breath. "He believed I witnessed an exchange of information between him and a Jacobite messenger. He thought to be rid of me before I could report back to the government. He forced me into his boat, and when we were far enough out to sea, he raised his musket. I swung the oar at him before I even knew what I was doing."

"So you were defending yourself."

"I don't think his son will see it like that, do you?"

"No," Finn says finally. "Probably not."

Eva covers her eyes with her hands. "Martin deserves to know what happened to his father. I cannot just keep the truth from him. I need to tell him."

Finn presses an impulsive hand to her knee, forcing her to look at him. Her skirts are still damp beneath his fingers. "If you do that, they'll string you up. If they truly believe you a spy, they'll be looking for a reason to be rid of you. They'll see you on the scaffold for murder."

Eva sucks in a breath, and for a moment, Finn regrets his harshness. But she needs to know where truth-telling will lead her.

She gets to her feet suddenly and begins to pace across the room. "How can I ever go back to Holy Island?" she is saying. "Knowing what I know? How can I pass Martin Macauley in the street, or sit by him in church?"

He can hear the guilt rearing up inside her. Guilt she has clearly been pushing down for weeks. He stands, ignoring the sharp pain that shoots up his leg. He catches her arm as she paces past. Pulls her to a gentle halt. "The man was trying to kill you," he says. "What were you to have done? Let him shoot you?"

Eva says nothing. She closes her eyes and her tears spill. As though on impulse, she wraps her arms around his waist. Finn pulls her close. Swallows hard. He is dimly aware of just how hard his heart is pounding.

He wants this. Desperately. Wants to be the one to hold Eva Blake, to comfort her when she falls apart. But how can that ever be when his past has the power to break her?

He runs his palm over her damp hair. Feels her shiver slightly. After a moment, she steps back and wipes her eyes with the heel of her hand. In the coppery lamplight, Finn can see the faint sprinkle of freckles across her nose. Sees the dark flecks in her blue eyes. Before he can stop himself, his hand rises to cup her cheek. And she lifts her hand to cover his.

"You won't...tell anyone, will you? About Donald Macauley?" She lets out her breath. "No," she says, before he can speak. "Of course you won't." Her fingers slide between his, erasing any chance he had of pulling away. She looks into his eyes, and his other hand slides to the back of her neck. Before he can think, can stop himself, his lips find hers. She tenses for a moment, then her mouth opens beneath his, seeking more. He feels her sink against him. Grips a fistful of her hair as he deepens the kiss.

It is intoxicating, seamless. And the most dazzling of mistakes.

He pulls away suddenly. "I'm sorry," he mumbles. "I'm sorry." He turns so he cannot see her. Steps back, forcing himself to put space between them. "You take the bed," he says throatily. His boots thud dully, unrhythmic, as he goes for the chair in the corner. "You ought to try and sleep."

CHAPTER TWENTY-THREE

Eva manages a far more broken sleep than if she was keeping the light out on Longstone. She stares into the blackness, feeling Finn's kiss on her lips, and sensing the coldness that had fallen over the room the minute he had pulled away. She cannot make sense of it. Cannot make sense of his regret. His changeability. Cannot make sense of anything more than the hollow, sinking feeling in the pit of her stomach.

All she knows is that it is time for her to leave him.

She is glad when blue morning light finally pushes through the curtains. The room is chilly and thick with the smell of cold ash and tallow. She can hear the faint patter of rain against the glass, but the wind has calmed and the storm blown over.

She hears the chair creak and dares to glance at Finn. He is already pulling his vest and coat on. Eva slides out from under the blankets and reaches for her shoes.

"I'm going back to Holy Island," she says brusquely.

Some foolish part of her wants him to protest. Instead, he just nods. "I'll take you."

"No." She gathers her cloak from the table. It is still slightly damp, but she slings it over her shoulders anyway. "I don't want you anywhere near the place. Not after what happened last time." Her voice is clipped. "I can make my own way there."

"Don't be daft. It will take you hours."

"I have the time."

Finn sighs. "At least let me walk with you. I can manage."

Eva lets out a cold laugh. "Can you now?" She shakes her head. "I can manage just fine without you." She hopes he knows she is referring to far more than just the walk to Holy Island.

He reaches for her suddenly, his coarse fingers wrapping around her bare forearm. The sudden feel of him makes her breath catch. "Eva." She looks up at him, expectant. His lips part but he doesn't speak. He gives her wrist an almost imperceptible squeeze, then shakes his head. Lets his hand fall. "I'm sorry."

So it is to be like this. Is he not even to offer an explanation? Perhaps it's best this way. She does not need an explanation. Everything in Finn's eyes tells her that last night was a mistake. It will do her no good to hear the words spoken.

She yanks on her bonnet and marches out of the lodging house, not waiting for him to follow.

He manages to catch up with her in the street outside the inn. The cobbles are littered with footprinted banners and sodden tracts, smeared with running ink.

"Let me at least walk with you as far as the beach."

"For what purpose, Finn?" She feels her anger rising. "You've made it very clear that what happened between us was a mistake. This morning you can barely even look at me. How am I supposed to take that?"

He scrubs a hand over his face. "I know. I should never have…"

"You ought to have slept outside the door," she snaps.

"Aye. I should have."

He turns suddenly, looking past her. There is man they had seen in the tavern yesterday, the man who had caught Finn's attention. He is striding purposefully towards the beach, hands dug into the pockets of his greatcoat. Three other men are following a few paces behind.

"Who is that?" Eva asks tautly.

"No one. It's no one. It doesn't matter."

She shakes her head. Let him be tight-lipped with his secrets. They are no business of hers. "You're right," she says. "It doesn't matter."

She turns and strides away from him without another word.

The walk, of course, is utter stupidity. Ten miles at least. It will take her most of the day. But she had stuffed half of the bread they had bought in her cloak pocket and she is sure it will be sustenance enough to see her home. Hours of walking is preferable to climbing back in that boat with Finn.

The air smells of rain, but blue sky is beginning to break through the clouds, suggesting summer might linger a little longer yet. The golden light feels like a stark contrast to her mood.

Eva blinks back tears as she walks. Every inch of her body

feels weighted with sadness. Nothing about this makes sense. Not Finn's abrupt coldness, or his evasiveness, or his hungry kiss.

She hates that she can still conjure up the feeling of his lips against hers. Hates that she craves it. Hates the way her body longs for his in a way she could never have imagined wanting Matthew Walton.

The miles pass slowly. Exhaustion tugs at her legs, and her feet begin to rub inside her shoes. But she doesn't care. It gives her something to focus on beyond the hollow ache inside her. She knows, of course, that there is no more foolish thing she could have done than allow herself to grow feelings for Finn Murray.

The tide is still draining when she reaches the sands that lead across to Lindisfarne. A thin pane of sea blocks her way onto the island. She ought to wait until the path is dry, of course, but all she wants is to be back home. She takes off her shoes and stockings and steps into the shallow water.

The sea is glassy, the deep stillness both welcome and disconcerting after the chaos of last night. Water licks at her ankles and she bundles her skirts up in her free hand. What must she look like, striding barefooted through the water like this? Before her time on Longstone, she would never have considered doing such a thing. Now, it almost feels normal.

The sea is breathtakingly cold against her aching feet, but the chill brings with it a sense of clarity. She reaches down and splashes her face with seawater, washing away the last of her tears. She tells herself she has cried all she is going to cry for Finn Murray. He is worth no more than that.

CHAPTER TWENTY-FOUR

"I'm glad you're home," says Nathan. "And I'm glad you're safe. Although I do wish you had waited for the tide before crossing back."

Eva gives him a pale smile and brings her teacup to her lips. She looks exhausted, her eyes underlined with shadow and her body sinking against the settle. Her cheeks are pink from sun, and if he didn't know her better, he would have said she had been crying. Her dark hair hangs loose over her shoulders, and though she has changed out of the damp clothes she arrived in—into one of Harriet's dresses, he thinks—she still looks like a windblown islander. Alarmingly out of character for the sister he knows.

"How have you been faring here?" she asks. "I heard Donald Macauley's boat was found..."

Nathan nods. He tells her, succinct and undetailed, about the discovery of the dinghy; about the memorial cross that now stands behind St Mary's.

For long moments, Eva doesn't speak. She stares blankly

ahead, toying with the lacing on her bodice. "Does anyone suspect…"

"No," says Nathan. But he is not convinced. He cannot help but feel as though Martin Macauley is biding his time, searching for proof, waiting for the right time to confront them.

"Heard about that, Joseph? Miss Blake stranding herself on the mainland for the night? Same night Da disappeared…"

But this he will keep to himself.

Eva's gaze drifts out the window as she takes another sip of tea. "There was a Jacobite protest in Bamburgh yesterday," she says after a moment. "I was there helping Mr Murray buy food. It turned rather violent."

Nathan nods. "I can't say I'm surprised. The Rising is gaining momentum. Sounds as though the new riot act is having little effect."

"They were using this place, you know," says Eva. "The Jacobites. They used to meet here, out of sight of the authorities."

Nathan raises his eyebrows. "Well. I suppose we cannot be surprised. Given how long the house has been empty." The thought is more than a little unsettling. For not the first time, he regrets leaving Highfield House unguarded for so long. He sips his tea. "You weren't in danger, I hope? In Bamburgh?"

Eva keeps her eyes down. "I was safe."

"And this Mr Murray. I trust he behaved in a gentlemanly manner while you were taking care of him?"

Eva wraps her arms around herself. Her jaw tightens. "He did nothing untoward," she says tautly. "If that is what you're asking."

Nathan frowns. She is not usually one to show her emotions so openly. "Eva? Is there something else?"

"No," she says. "Nothing else."

Nathan lets the silence settle for a moment, hoping to nudge her into speaking further. But she just sips her tea with a faraway expression.

"I mean to write to Matthew Walton today," he says.

Eva looks up, finally drawn away from the contents of her teacup. "You've still not written him?"

"I know I ought to have done it sooner. But I was rather upset by his behaviour. I feared my words might come across too harshly."

She scoffs. "Do you not think he deserves a little harshness?"

Nathan bristles. She is right, of course. But he still has faint hope of rescuing the betrothal, and he knows harshness will not help the situation.

"It would do you good to be angry every now and then, Nathan," Eva tells him, before he can speak. "Surely it cannot be healthy to be so agreeable all the time."

"I'm an agreeable person," he says. "Is there something so wrong with that?"

Eva lets out a harsh breath, but does not bother dignifying his question with a response. "There's little point writing to Walton," she says instead. "Especially now, after so long. What can it possibly achieve?"

"Well. At the very least, he owes me an explanation."

"What were you expecting would happen?" she demands. "You betrothed me to a man who preferred my sister over me."

Her words catch him off guard. "You knew of that?"

She nods. "I overheard the two of you speaking of it."

Nathan lets out a breath, hit with a pang of regret. He and Matthew had spoken of Harriet twice: once when Walton had expressed his initial interest in her, and a second time…when? At the rented house in Islington, he realises. Matthew had come to him airing his concern over marrying Eva when he had such feelings for her sister. Nathan had had no idea Eva had been in the house at the time. He had gone on to list her many positive qualities. Had convinced Matthew she would be a far more suitable wife than prickly, quick-tempered Harriet. He had left the conversation certain Matthew was more than happy to become Eva's husband.

"Is that why he changed his mind about marrying you?" he asks.

Eva nods, her cheeks colouring slightly. The glassiness in her eyes seems to have magnified, and Nathan regrets raising the issue.

"I'm sorry," he says. "I wish you had not overheard that conversation. But when I told Matthew you would make a fine wife in Harriet's place, I truly believed it. He would have been immensely lucky to have you."

After supper, he writes the letter.

It is brief and curt. Hurried words expressing his displeasure at the breaking of their agreement, and his treatment of Eva. And then a carefully worded urging to him to reconsider. He doubts it will make any difference. And he knows it is probably for the best. But now, on top of all the stresses of the house, he must set out to find Eva a more suitable match. A near impossible thing to do from Holy Island, of course. He knows there is little hope of them returning to London by year's end. But hopefully by the spring, this whole sorry episode will be behind them and Eva will be happily married. He finds it hard to remain optimistic. To be a woman of almost twenty-five and without prospects is hardly an enviable position. Nathan knows he ought to have pushed Matthew to marry her sooner. Their drawn-out engagement has done no one any favours.

Nathan slides the pounce pot into the drawer and peers through the window into the night. A thin moon is tossing its light off the water.

He has always had a fascination with the sky, at times even bordering on obsession. As a child, he had spent countless hours poring over star maps and tracking glittering trails of light across the night sky. The vastness of the universe has always calmed him; always made his problems seem a little less pressing. But with adulthood, that fascination had faded away, as life's challenges had refused to be relegated to unimportance. The telescope his father had given him had sat unused for years, and he had sold it before coming to Holy Island. It had not even crossed his mind to bring it with him. Nonetheless, leaving his curtains open for the starlight to spill inside is a habit he has not attempted to shake.

Sarah had always encouraged him to go back to astronomy, his childhood love. She had claimed it would be good for him, and he knows she was probably right. But without her nudging him in that direction, he feels even less likely to do so.

He had been more open-minded before Sarah had died. More willing to spend time in the stars, to see the magic in the everyday. It had been easy to do in the presence of his ethereal, blue-eyed wife. But with Sarah gone, the world feels far more stern and rigid. A difficult place to navigate with his ethereal, blue-eyed daughter.

Men in the walls.

Theodora has always been an imaginative child, prone to sleepwalking and nightmares. But something about this chills him. Perhaps it's because he remembers people in the walls in this place too. Remembers them all too vividly.

I think you need to be punished for choosing such a dreadful hiding place.

There is no way Theodora ought to know about the priest hole. Nathan has been painfully deliberate in keeping her out of Oliver's old room. Indeed, that room had been one of the main reasons he had not wanted her in the house in the first place. And he is certain none of the others know of the priest hole's existence. Still, Theodora is no angel. If she has sneaked into Oliver's room for a little exploration, it would certainly not be the first time she had deliberately disobeyed him.

He takes the ring of keys from his desk drawer and the lamp from the mantel. Heads out into the hallway. Faint light is glowing under the door of Eva's bedroom. They are becoming a family of nocturnal creatures. Nathan is careful not to make a sound as he passes. He does not want his sister to catch him. Does not want to admit he is going looking for the shadows from Thea's nightmares.

He rattles the door of Oliver's room, finding it locked tight, as he had left it. Would Theodora have stolen the keys from his desk drawer? He does not want to believe it. But he can't deny it's a possibility. He unlocks the door and steps inside.

He shines the lamp around the room, golden light arcing

over the walls. Everything is just as he had left it, with half the floorboards replaced, and a large gap in the floor by the window, revealing the beams beneath.

He presses on the panel to open the priest hole. With a pounding heart, he shines his lamp inside. Empty, of course. Was he truly expecting otherwise?

He shakes his head, trying to expel his racing imagination. What is he thinking? Of course Thea has not ventured in here. *Men in the walls* is nothing more than a nightmare—and hunting through the house in the dark like this is no way to allay his daughter's nocturnal fears.

He leaves the room, locking the door behind him, cursing the house for upturning his ordered thoughts.

Eva lies on her back, staring up at the ceiling. It feels like hours since she had blown out her lamp, but sleep continues to evade her. She supposes she can't be surprised. Three weeks of lightkeeping have wreaked havoc on her sleeping habits.

In spite of herself, she slips out of bed and goes to the window. She sees the faint flicker on the horizon; the glow of the Longstone light. She lets the curtain fall.

She hates that there is something comforting about the sight of the firebasket. It assures her of Finn's safety—and she hates that she cares so much. Hates that she can't push him from her mind like she ought to.

She grabs her shawl from the end of the bed and makes her way down into the kitchen. The lamp in her hand lights a faint path in front of her. A mouse scuttles past her feet and disappears down the staircase. Eva pushes open the kitchen door, finding her sister taking a cup from the shelf.

Harriet whirls around. "Evie. You scared me. What are you doing awake?"

"I couldn't sleep. Are you working?"

"I am." She hands Eva the cup and takes down another.

"I don't suppose you'd like a little company?"

Harriet makes her way out of the kitchen, nodding for Eva to join her. "I've a bottle of Edwin's whisky in my workroom. Sneaked it in there when no one was looking."

Eva follows her into the workroom. Despite the lamp blazing on the side table, a chill has settled into the walls. Harriet has come prepared, she notices, dressed in thick winter skirts and a heavy green shawl. She takes a blanket from the chair in the corner and tosses it to Eva, then uncorks the bottle.

Eva accepts a cup and wraps the blanket around her shoulders. She tilts her head to inspect Harriet's painting. Pale streaks of sunlight pour across the sea, its light reflected in a row of waves. Shadowed forest crams the edges of the foreground.

"It's beautiful," she says.

Harriet's nose wrinkles. "Is it? I can't tell anymore. I've been staring at it so long it's ceased to make sense to me. Perhaps I ought to just return to still-lifes. But they just feel so empty. I need to go further than that. Although I'm starting to feel as though I don't have the skill to do so." It sounds as though she is speaking to herself.

"I see." Eva feels completely adrift. Completely devoid of culture and beauty. She sinks into the chair in the corner and takes a gulp of whisky.

Harriet stays at the easel, examining her painting as she sips from her cup. "It's too bleak," she says finally. "The trees are almost indistinguishable from the water. That is not the effect I was trying for at all. It's all wrong." She laughs humourlessly. "Perhaps that will teach me to paint by lamplight in the middle of the night."

"Is that how you're feeling?" Eva asks curiously. "Bleak?"

Harriet shrugs. She looks surprised by the question. "Sometimes, I suppose."

Eva turns her cup around in her hands. Her encounter with Finn Murray has left her feeling utterly colourless too, but over the years, she has learnt better than to drop her problems at Harriet's feet. Her sister has a way of making things all about her.

"Do you truly hate it here so?" she asks instead. "I think the island is beautiful."

Harriet snorts. "Isn't it. Impossibly, disgustingly beautiful." She sips her drink, leaning back against the table. "It's the quiet I don't like. Too much space to think. In London, I've my circle of other artists, and I don't have to pause and look too closely at the way of things."

"What do you mean? What things?"

Harriet stares towards the window, though the drawn curtains prevent her from looking out. "Do you ever feel as though you were made for entirely the wrong thing?"

"I'm not sure what I was made for. I seem to be of little use to anyone." The moment she has spoken the words, Eva regrets her self-indulgence. Harriet glides right past it.

"I'm a terrible wife. A terrible mother. And yet those are the things the world sees me as."

"You are not a terrible mother," says Eva.

Harriet lets out a cold laugh. She tosses back the last of the liquor and refills her glass. "I thought when Thomas was born, I would be drawn to him," she says. "But I wasn't. I'm not. He feels like someone else's child. Like a stranger. Edwin too, sometimes." Too lightly, she says, "It's terribly lonely."

Eva hesitates. Harriet is rarely so open with her, and she knows she cannot let the moment pass without comment. But what can she offer beyond empty platitudes and consolation? She knows nothing of being a wife. Nothing of being a mother. And nothing of being as capricious and flighty as Harriet.

Before she can open her mouth, faint footfalls sound outside the house.

Harriet darts to the window. She peeks through the curtain and gasps. "He's here."

"Who's here?" Eva is on her feet, jostling her sister at the window. Through the glass, she sees nothing but darkness.

"The prowler," says Harriet. "He's been coming for weeks now." She sounds oddly close to excitement. "I've gone out to try and catch him once or twice, but he always manages to disappear. It's the strangest thing."

Eva's eyes widen. "Are you mad? There has been a prowler coming to the house for weeks? Did you not think to tell anyone?"

Harriet rolls her eyes. "Don't be so dramatic."

Eva snatches her arm as she darts towards the door. "You can't go out there. We have no idea who they are, or how dangerous they might be." She shakes her head, hardly able to believe her sister's apathy. Does she truly not understand the danger this family is in? She squeezes her wrist. "Please, Harriet."

As though catching hold of the seriousness in her eyes, Harriet gives a resigned nod. "Very well. I'll fetch Edwin. Tell him to bring his pistol."

CHAPTER TWENTY-FIVE

Nathan has just climbed into bed when he hears the thud of footsteps down the passage. He hears Harriet open the door across the hall and hiss her husband's name.

"Come quickly," says Eva.

Nathan slides out of bed and snatches his breeches from the chair in the corner of the room. He steps out into the passage. "Is something the matter?" Eva is barefooted, with a blanket wrapped around her body and her dark hair hanging loose. Harriet is still dressed, a heavy shawl at her shoulders and a look of excitement in her eyes.

"There's a man outside the house," says Eva. "Creeping around in the dark."

Edwin emerges from the bedroom tugging on his jacket, his pistol in his hand.

The two men are out of the house in moments. The night is clear and still, an explosion of stars. The sea sighs steadily against the invisible beach.

Nathan looks back at his sisters, huddled in the doorway.

"Which way did he go?"

"Harriet saw him pass her workroom," says Eva. "I've no idea where he went after that."

He grips the pistol he had taken from the bottom drawer of his desk. A lantern sways in his other fist. The moon is bright, lighting the arc of the dunes. He moves around the house to the left; Edwin to the right. Nathan strides past Harriet's workroom. "Who's there?" he calls. "Show yourself." The knot in his stomach tightens.

Movement in the dunes, but the light catches only the fleeing shape of a deer. Nathan completes his circle of the house, meeting Edwin back at the front door. He shakes his head in response to the wordless question.

"Perhaps you were imagining things," Nathan tells Harriet.

She lets out her breath indignantly. "Is that really what you think?"

"It's not the first time she's seen him," Eva puts in.

"What?" Edwin demands.

Harriet glares at her sister. She sighs, folding her arms across her chest. "He's been coming regularly. Ever since we moved in."

"And you did not think to tell us earlier?"

"Perhaps we might save the lecture for later, Edwin? He must be around here somewhere. Perhaps you ought to find him."

The pool of light from Nathan's lantern skims across the dirt path in front of the house. It's flecked with footsteps; his and Edwin's yes, but perhaps another set as well. He follows the faint trail around the corner. It leads up to the wall of the house, he realises. No, not to the wall. To the drain leading out from the kitchen.

He crouches, pulling away the grate blocking the mouth of the drain. It's impossible. Although the drain is wide here, at its other end it is nothing but a narrow pipe leading out from the trough in the kitchen. Certainly not big enough for anyone to fit inside.

Edwin crouches beside him. Leans forward to shine his lamp into the hole. "This is big enough for someone to get inside, Nate," he says.

"No. It's just the drain. Leading down from the trough. No one could—"

"Just look."

And so he does. Kneels forward, eyes to the ground, hot light scorching his cheek as he shines the lamp into the dark opening. There is the narrow pipe leading up towards the kitchen. But branching off from it in the other direction is a wider tunnel, big enough for a man to fit through. Leading— where? Somewhere inside the house?

Nathan's stomach rolls. He thinks of his daughter, asleep upstairs with a prowler on the loose. His eyes drift upward. He is right beneath his bedroom window, he realises. Right below where Theodora is sleeping.

Men in the walls...

Had she seen the prowler slip in through the grate? Disappear into the walls of Highfield House?

"I'm going in," says Edwin. "Are you coming?"

The thought of it is horrifying, of course. It's every vile piece of Oliver's twisted games. But the alternative—doing nothing—is far worse.

He glances over his shoulder. His sisters have followed them to the grate. Eva wears a deep frown, while Harriet watches with a look of detached fascination.

"You go first," Nathan tells Edwin. "I'll follow."

On hands and knees, Nathan shuffles into the tunnel, clinging to his lamp as though it might save him from drowning in the darkness. The pistol in his pocket presses against his hip.

He sees at once that this tunnel is not new. Nor has it been hastily built by whoever has been creeping into their house these past weeks. Worn wood panelling shores the walls, interspersed with smooth stone to keep the earth at bay. It is a part of the house, he realises; has always been a part of the house. Built, perhaps, by whoever had created the priest hole.

Nathan shuffles deeper into the passage, loose earth grazing his palms. Is he under the ground? Or within the walls of the house? He is not sure which is more disconcerting. After what could be no more than ten or fifteen yards, Nathan hears:

"There's a ladder."

Ahead of him, he sees Edwin wriggle out of the tunnel, his feet disappearing upwards. The ladder is narrow, rough-hewn wood. It leads up between the outer stone wall of the house, and the wooden panelling of the internal walls. Nathan steps onto it tentatively, hearing it groan beneath his weight.

The ladder stops on the second storey. He and Edwin are crammed into a narrow space, with a stone wall on one side and wood panelling on three others. A sour stench thickens the air. Beneath their feet are the same worn floorboards Nathan recognises from Oliver's room. But this is not the priest hole. This space is tall enough to stand in. And even as a terrified child, Nathan knows he would have remembered seeing a ladder that led down into the walls of the house.

Edwin shines his lamp up to one of the internal walls. "Look at this." The panelling is slightly crooked. He pushes against it. The wall groans and shifts beneath his weight. And it swings open, revealing the priest hole beside it.

"A double-barrel priest hole," Nathan murmurs. He has heard of such things before; a hiding place within a hiding place; an extra layer of protection against the priest hunters. And in this elaborate system: a way to escape the confines of the house. He would almost be fascinated if he had not just followed a prowler up here.

Nathan crawls into the priest hole, then out into Oliver's room, fingers tightening around the pistol. He tries the door. Locked from the outside, as he had left it earlier that night.

"The prowler," he says, "he must be in this room. There's no way for him to get out into the house."

"He's not in that room, Nate," Edwin calls to him from within the hole. "He's up here."

He is shining the lamp up towards the thick beams of the attic. Faint footholds have been scraped into the stone wall, and in the pale light of the lantern, Nathan sees the loose boards in the ceiling, allowing access to the roof space.

He sets the lamp at his feet and grabs at the footholds. The stones are worn enough to give him purchase, and he hauls himself up towards the attic.

He realises then that he is not climbing into blackness. Not entirely. There is a faint, fragile light up here, as though from a single candle. And that smell; that acrid, animal stench he had sensed the night of the storm, it's more potent with every step.

He heaves his body through the gap in the roof, the splintered boards scraping his arms through his shirt. And as he spills out onto the floor, he freezes. Crammed into the attic space are two men. And one woman, her coils of red hair spilling out the side of the scarf tied around her head.

Julia Mitchell.

She is dressed in breeches and a man's greatcoat that hangs ridiculously from her narrow shoulders. Their prowler.

At the sight of Nathan, she backs away, as far from him as she can get, before the pitch of the roof prevents her from going further.

Nathan stares in disbelief. In the light of the candle spluttering in one corner, he sees two blankets laid out across the floor, a large waterskin and a loaf of bread beside them.

The two men have the same shock of red hair as Julia. Their beards are long and unkempt, and the stench of human waste rises from a wooden bucket in the corner.

Nathan looks from Julia to the men, then down to the food and water sitting between the blankets. She has been making regular visits, he realises, to keep her brothers fed and watered while they hide away in Highfield House. Anger stirs inside him. He feels utterly betrayed.

The boards creak as Edwin emerges into the attic. Nathan hears him curse under his breath.

"I'm so sorry, Mr Blake," Julia gushes. "Please let me explain."

Nathan swallows heavily. "How long...?"

"A few months," Julia says, her voice low. "My brothers, they're in trouble with the law. They needed somewhere to hide. When we first came here, the house was empty. We had no idea your family was coming back."

A few months...

"Leave," he grinds out. "This second."

"Please, Mr Blake," says one of her brothers, "we've nowhere to go."

Nathan laughs coldly. "Nowhere to go? Your sister has a fine shopfront on Church Lane that I'm sure she could cram you into."

"No," Julia says. "They can't. They—" She stops speaking suddenly, then gives a nod of resignation, half directed at Nathan, half at her brothers. The two men begin to gather up the waterskin and bread.

"Leave it all," hisses Nathan. "Just get the hell out of my house."

Neither man argues. With their blankets tucked under their arms, they head for the hole in the roof, stepping past Nathan with looks of wordless apology. Nathan watches them disappear into the blackness below. "Go after them," he tells Edwin. "See that they leave."

As though taken aback by Nathan's uncharacteristic sharpness, Edwin doesn't argue. He follows the two men to the hole in the roof and climbs back down into the tunnel.

When Nathan tears his gaze away, Julia is watching him with wide mournful eyes.

"I meant for you to leave too," he tells her sharply. His heart is thudding and his skin is hot with anger. To think he had let his guard down around her. And to think he had felt guilty over the secrets he is keeping from her. How laughable that seems now.

"The passage," he says tautly. "How did you know of it?"

"The Jacobites have been using the house as a meeting place for years," she murmurs. "We know every inch of it."

Nathan lets out a cold laugh. How fitting, he thinks, that the people of Holy Island might know this house better than he does. He doesn't look at her. "And your brothers?"

Julia lets out a breath. "They left for the West Country a few months ago to join the Duke of Ormonde's Jacobite army. I begged them not to go." She starts pacing across the attic, tugging at the hem of her oversized coat. "The fools barely made it out of Northumberland before they got themselves in trouble. Got into a fight with the redcoats at a protest in York. One of the soldiers was shot. My brothers only just got away."

Nathan's anger flares. Rage spills out; rage he has always forced himself to keep inside. It tears through him, making him unable to see straight. "How dare you? Do you have any idea… There are children in this house!" He snatches the waterskin from the floor and hurls it across the room. "Not only do you dare to bring violent men into my home, you have the audacity to befriend us in the process?" It's not just rage at Julia now, he realises. It's rage at the manufacturer who had deceived him; rage at damn Matthew Walton for the way he has treated this family; rage at God for taking his wife. He feels it pour off his body in waves. Letting it out feels oddly cathartic.

"My brothers would never hurt you!" Julia cries. "They are not violent men! They're just fools who got caught up in all this madness." Her tears spill suddenly and she shoves them away with the back of her hand. "They thought they were doing the right thing. They swear the soldier's death was an accident. They were just defending themselves. If they're caught, they'll hang. And you saw the way they look—they are hardly capable of blending into a crowd.

"The house was empty when we moved them in here," she says. "I never expected you and your family to come back.

You've been away from the place for twenty years." She begins to pace. "Do you truly think I liked creeping into your house night after night, bringing enough food to keep them alive? All the while, making friends with Harriet? And…coming to know you too?"

Nathan turns away uncomfortably. Her words just remind him of how much of a fool he has been. "Your brothers are easy targets here in the house," he snaps. "Anyone comes looking and they'll be found at once."

She looks at him pointedly. "It took you more than two months to find them."

Nathan smacks an angry hand against the wall. He hates that she is right. "If you want them to be safe, they need to get off Holy Island. It's far too small a place to hide. They'll be safer hidden away in London." There is no warmth in his voice. None of the compassion he is so used to forcing.

"Do you truly think I don't know that?" Julia wraps her arms around herself and stares at her muddy boots. "I have a third brother," she says, voice low. "Hugh. He was with Michael and Angus at the protest. In the fight. They got split up when the soldiers came after them. The two of them made it back to Holy Island. But they've no idea what happened to Hugh." She draws in a breath. "They refuse to go to London without him. Once they leave, I know we'll not be able to write each other. Not while things are so unsettled at least." Her voice wavers slightly. "It's too dangerous. If the letters were intercepted, my son and I would be in danger. Michael and Angus know that if they leave for London now, they'll likely never see Hugh again."

Nathan folds his arms. The story would be far more pitiable if she hadn't been deceiving him all this time. "They cannot stay here," he says firmly. "I'm sorry."

Julia looks up at him with pleading eyes. "Might they at least stay until I find somewhere else for them? I swear to you they'll do no harm to any of your family."

"Are you truly asking me such a thing?" Nathan demands. "After the way you deceived me? Deceived all of us?"

"I know it's wrong," she says. "I really do. But I'm desperate. Please, Mr Blake. I'm begging you."

For a moment, the rage falters. For a moment, he wavers. But no. He can't. Cannot let this woman take another inch. "I want you out of the house immediately."

CHAPTER TWENTY-SIX

Harriet lifts her face to the sky. It is a pleasure to be out of the house, away from Thomas's tears and Eva's sulkiness and the background dread that has settled over the place since they discovered Julia's brothers hiding in the attic.

Edwin had had firm words for her after learning she had kept the prowler's visits to herself for so long. And Nathan, well, he seems to be carrying around decades of repressed anger in his eyes, skulking around the place with barely more than a grunt for anyone. This morning he had yelled at Theodora for knocking over the milk jug. She had sat silent and tearful through the rest of breakfast, that eerie beast of a doll in her lap.

Harriet has been waiting for Edwin and Nathan to leave for the mainland all morning, so she might slip away to visit Julia at the curiosity shop.

She supposes she ought to be outraged at Julia too. But in truth, she had imagined far worse things for that prowler to be. Had imagined it might be Martin Macauley, or an armed

Jacobite, or—when she is at her most sleepless—a ghost vanishing into the dunes.

She pushes open the door of the shop. The bell tinkles and Julia looks up from behind the counter. When she sees Harriet, she flashes a desperately apologetic half-smile.

"Have you come here to tear me to pieces?" she asks. "I know I deserve it."

Harriet shrugs. "I've come for tea. If you're making it."

Surprise passes over Julia's face. "I can make tea. Will you watch the shop a moment? Just make sure no one comes in and pockets anything."

Harriet nods and Julia disappears upstairs into the living quarters. Harriet glides through the shop, scanning the cluttered shelves, without taking anything in. Julia's cat brushes against her legs and she bends down to scratch its ears.

Julia returns with a teacup in each hand. She sets them on the counter and pulls up the chairs.

"I saw you from my workroom," says Harriet. "I wondered if perhaps you were a ghost."

Julia gives a short laugh, then her eyes grow serious. "How angry is your family?" she asks, hands interlaced around her cup.

Harriet shrugs. "Nathan is steaming. But it will pass."

Julia nods, eyes down.

"Don't look so sad," says Harriet. "It could well be the best thing that's ever happened to him. Will do him good to get a little of that anger out of his blood."

Julia smiles half-heartedly. "Must be something right special about me to have been the one to get the anger out of him."

Harriet smiles to herself. Julia is right, of course. Nathan clearly does see something special in her. Not that he would ever admit it.

"What about your husband?" asks Julia. "Is he wild with rage too?"

"More at me than you," Harriet says. "And Eva, well, I think the only thing she has on her mind is that rogue from Longstone."

"Longstone?" Julia repeats. "Finn Murray?"

Harriet nods, rattling swiftly through the drama that is Eva's tryst with the lightkeeper. She is surprised Julia had not heard of it earlier.

Julia raises her eyebrows. "Interesting. From what I know of Mr Murray, I didn't imagine he'd welcome anyone onto his island."

Harriet drops her voice, though they are the only ones in the shop. "Are your brothers here with you?" She's had enough of Eva's woes of late; has no desire to rehash them with Julia.

"They're down in the cellar. But they can't stay here. It's not safe. We know there are spies on the island. But we've no idea who they are. If the wrong people were to find out Michael and Angus are here..." She trails off. "Their only choice may be to go to London. Lose themselves in the city."

"Nathan tells me they are waiting for your other brother to return."

She sighs heavily. "It's no good them waiting for Hugh if they're caught in the process." She picks at something beneath her fingernail. "And honestly, with every day that passes, I feel less and less confident that Hugh is going to return home at all. It's been months. I know there's a chance he may have gone on to the West Country alone. When he left, he was determined to fight with the rebels. But surely if that were the case, we would have heard from him by now. He would have written to let me know he is safe." Her voice wavers.

Harriet reaches over and squeezes her wrist. "Let me speak to Nathan. He——"

"No," Julia cuts in. "Please don't. It's far too much to ask."

"He's fond of you. I can tell."

Julia smiles wryly. "I doubt he is any longer."

They sit in silence for several moments. The cat leaps onto the counter and circles the teacups.

Julia sighs. "Harriet… I truly am sorry for what I did. I never meant to hurt you or your family."

Harriet shakes her head airily. "You did what you had to do."

"You're not angry with me?"

Somewhere in the back of her mind, Harriet knows she ought to be. Knows that, in many ways, what Julia has done could—should—be considered a betrayal. But she can't find the energy to be angry. Or really, to care.

Has she always felt like this? So empty and detached? She can't seem to make herself care about anything except her art these days, not even her child. Or strangers walking within the walls of her house. That will change, she tells herself. When she returns to London and her artist friends. When her life is bigger than this thread of an island and she leaves the house behind.

Longstone feels empty without her. Particularly now he knows she'll likely never set foot on this island again.

The duffel bag Eva had arrived with is still tucked away in a corner of the cottage. Her tin of tea is still on the mantel. Her skirts hanging over the end of her bed.

Every time he sees them, Finn is back at the inn in Bamburgh, feeling her lips against his own. Seeing the hurt in her eyes when he had pulled away.

Taking a room with her was bound to lead to trouble, of course. There had not been a second that he'd doubted that. But letting her stay in the dormitory had not felt like an option. Not with armed men brawling outside and a shattered window littering the floor.

He has never felt like this about anyone before. Why did it have to be a woman from that cursed house? That cursed family? Fate certainly has a way of playing tricks.

The daylight is beginning to drain away. He can hear seals barking on a nearby island. He trudges outside to light the firebasket. Tonight, it feels like a chore. Tonight, he is feeling the weight of the responsibility he has shouldered. Tonight, he would rather be anywhere else.

The shovel in his hand, he glances out to sea, then looks away quickly. He keeps his back to the water as he builds the fire in the basket and strikes the tinderbox.

It's not just Eva that is making him so unsettled. It's the knowledge that Henry Ward is back in Northumbria, sailing the *Eagle* far too close to Longstone. For reasons that Finn does not dare think about.

There has always been a part of him that has been afraid of Ward returning. Afraid of being dealt a long-overdue punishment for the mistakes he had made as a young and foolish cabin boy.

A big part of him wants nothing more than to leave Longstone. Climb into his skiff and disappear to some place where Henry Ward won't find him. But he can't do that.

Thanks to him, his father had died alone. Had not even had the dignity of a real burial. Lighting the firebasket feels like the least he can do for the father he had abandoned. The least he can do to make up for the time he had spent under Ward's tutelage. And for the terrible mistakes it had led to.

Finn heaves on the firebasket chain, sending the spitting brazier into the sky. He keeps his eyes on the flames, avoids looking out to sea.

What is Ward doing in these parts? Yes, he had always had an affinity with Holy Island, but that was back when Abigail Blake had owned Highfield House. Finn had been surprised to see him still sailing the *Eagle*. The fragile peace against the French means there is little cause for privateers in these waters. Perhaps it's the Rising that has brought him north; perhaps he imagines there will be a place for privateers if the Jacobite army takes up arms.

Finn's logical side knows, of course, that Ward is not here looking for him. It does not make sense for him to do that after so many years. Besides, there is no way, surely, that his old captain would have recognised him in the tavern, or in the street in Bamburgh. Finn had been a child the last time they had seen each other. He tells himself again, trying to make himself believe it. Because that morning at the beach, he had seen a glimmer in Ward's eye that had looked far too close to recognition.

He looks out to sea, daring to scan the horizon for the *Eagle*.

There is no sign of Ward's ship. But the ocean is not empty. A small fishing dory is headed directly for Longstone, as if drawn towards the light.

For a brief, foolish moment, his heart leaps at the possibility. Eva. He quashes it quickly. Even if Eva did have any desire to see him, which he is sure she does not, she would never find someone willing to undertake this treacherous sailing so close to dark.

He stands on the jetty with his arms folded, watching the boat approach. Two men and a woman. Not Eva.

One of the men brings the vessel up alongside the jetty. The woman gathers her skirts and leaps out, without waiting for assistance. Her face is pink with cold, and loose red curls blow around her cheeks.

"I'm a friend of the Blakes," she says. "And my brothers need a place to hide."

CHAPTER TWENTY-SEVEN

Eva narrows her eyes at her reflection as she runs a comb through her hair. In the morning light, the shadows under her eyes are horribly pronounced. She tells herself her sleeplessness is simply her body readjusting after three weeks of nocturnal life. But she knows it has more to do with the thoughts of Finn Murray that have been circling around her head without pause since she returned from Longstone. She does not like who this ordeal has turned her into. Since when is she the kind of woman who lets herself be so upturned by a man?

Had she looked into this mirror as a child too? Stood on the bed to see her tiny self, sharp-eyed and serious beyond her years? And had she had stood at the window and looked out towards the Farne Islands? Watched that flame come to life on the horizon as the sun slid into the water?

She tries to shake the thought away, but it lingers. She flings the comb onto her bed and marches across the room to yank closed the curtains. Can't help but pause there for a second, squinting into the hazy light. The crack in the window seems to have widened, and the view of the Farnes feels oddly distorted.

"I must say, Evie," says Harriet, appearing in the doorway, "you've been spending an awful lot of time at that window."

Eva lets the curtain fall hurriedly, her cheeks colouring. She turns to face Harriet's smug expression. Eva opens her mouth to speak, but decides against it. She has no desire to explain herself to her little sister. She feels like enough of a fool as it is.

"The lightkeeper?" says Harriet with a smirk. "Truly?" She is still dressed in her robe and nightgown.

Eva plants her hands on her hips. "And what do you know of him, Harriet?" she snaps.

Harriet's self-satisfied expression doesn't falter. "I know that Nathan will never allow it."

Eva looks down. "There's nothing to allow. Believe me."

Harriet perches on the edge of the bed, placing the discarded comb on the nightstand. "You ought to have gone over there with Julia. Paid him a visit."

Eva frowns. "What do you mean?"

"I thought you knew," Harriet says airily, in a tone that suggests she knew Eva was completely unaware. "I told her of your little dalliance with the lightkeeper, and she decided Longstone was the perfect place for her brothers to hide while they wait for Hugh to show himself."

As she races into the village, Eva's anger burns away her hatred of conflict. She will confront Julia Mitchell for her deviousness, and she will demand she go back to Longstone to collect her brothers, and she will do it all without getting so damn shaky and flustered.

Eva has had a crawling sensation under her skin ever they had discovered Julia's brothers hiding in the attic. The thought of those men creeping around their house had been bad enough. And now Julia has the nerve to foist them onto Longstone?

"Ah," says Julia, when Eva blusters through the front door of the curiosity shop. "I suppose Harriet told you of my plans. And I suppose you don't approve of them." Her eyes are lowered with shame, but somehow that makes it worse. As though she is well aware of the damage she is doing, but has decided to do it anyway.

"Plans?" Eva spits. "It sounds as though they're already well in motion."

Julia comes out from behind the counter and looks up to meet Eva's eyes. "I'm sorry. Truly."

Eva folds her arms. "Is that how you always operate? Do as you wish, then beg forgiveness afterwards?"

Julia glances over Eva's shoulder, as if to check there are no customers approaching. "I had no choice but to take my brothers to Longstone." Her voice is a murmur. "They are in grave danger."

"Yes," Eva hisses. "I gathered that when we found them hiding in our roof." She feels her skin growing hot. Ignores it. "What if the authorities had found them in the house? We would have been implicated. You put my family in danger. And now you're putting Mr Murray in danger too."

Julia nods. "You're right, of course. And I truly am sorry. But would you not do the same for your brother and sister?"

Eva grits her teeth. She has no idea what she would do if she were in such a situation. But she knows it is of little consequence. "Do you know how to sail?" she asks Julia instead.

"Yes, but—"

"Take me to Longstone," she demands. "I need to see Finn."

CHAPTER TWENTY-EIGHT

Julia doesn't argue. At Eva's demand, she locks up the shop and heads wordlessly for the harbour.

Eva's heart is quick as she follows close behind. She is nervous about seeing Finn. They had parted on such bitter terms, and her anger at him has not faded. Nor has her desire for him. But that is not what this is about, she reminds herself. Somehow, Finn has got caught up in business that was not his; business that could put him in danger. She needs to apologise; on Julia's behalf, and on her own. And she needs to convince Julia and her brothers to get the hell away from Longstone. She knows it is only because of her dealings with Finn that Julia even thought to dump her brothers on his island. Once again, she feels horribly responsible for the danger he is in.

When they reach the water, Julia nods to a tiny dinghy tied up to the jetty. "Get in. My brothers' fishing boat is out there." She points to a small sailboat in the middle of the anchorage.

She rows them out to it and ropes the dinghy to the stern. She knots her skirts at her calves, then climbs expertly onto the larger boat. Eva clambers up the ladder, ignoring Julia's offer of assistance.

They don't speak again until Longstone is in sight.

"I asked his permission, you know," says Julia, handing in the sail as they approach the island. "I did not just dump them there."

Eva doesn't respond. She has no idea whether Julia is telling the truth. Her eyes are fixed to the thin silhouette of the unlit firebasket and she is hit with a pang of longing. Perhaps coming here was a mistake. She knows she has little chance of convincing the Mitchells to leave the island. In the back of her mind, she knows it is her desperately missing Finn that has brought her here. And her hollow hope that things might be different. That this time he might beg her forgiveness and ask her to stay. She shoves the thoughts away.

They have not come unnoticed. As Julia eases the boat towards the jetty, Finn is already striding towards them, reminding Eva that little that happens here escapes his notice. But he halts in his step as he gets closer, perhaps noticing her for the first time. His pale brown hair is loose on his shoulders and blows across his cheek in the wind.

Eva swallows heavily. Tries to ignore the way her stomach flips at the sight of him. She climbs out of the boat and strides deliberately in his direction. "Julia Mitchell's brothers are here?" she asks.

A look of surprise flickers over Finn's face. "Aye. They're inside. Is that why you're here? I..." His face softens slightly, and she sees that same gentle look of concern she had seen the day of the riots in Bamburgh. Behind her, she hears Julia's footsteps disappearing towards the cottage. Eva is grateful for the privacy.

"I'm sorry, Finn," she says, her voice low. "I had no idea she was going to do this. But it's my fault. She only thought to come here because she knew I'd spent time with you."

Finn tilts his head, looking at her intently. "You blame yourself for a lot of things, Eva. Very few of them are your fault."

She feels his eyes on her, searching her face. She looks down, gaze fixed on her feet.

After a moment of silence, Finn says, "Don't worry yourself over the Mitchells. If they need to stay here a while to keep their necks unbroken, they can do so."

"What if the authorities come looking? You'll be seen to be harbouring Jacobite criminals."

"No one will come looking out here. Besides," he smiles crookedly, "I've got them taking the midnight watch while I'm sleeping away the night in your room." He falters. "The bedroom, rather."

Eva swallows hard. "Did she ask your permission at the very least?"

He shrugs. "In a way, I suppose. At least, she thanked me once they were here."

She lets out an angry breath. "That woman. I can hardly believe her insolence."

Finn chuckles. "Watch that vulgar tongue of yours, Miss Blake. It will get you into trouble."

Eva finds herself smiling slightly. In a strange sort of way, she has missed his mockery. "How are you?" she asks finally. "Has your wound healed?"

"Almost. The figwort is good for it. Turns out you were

right. Imagine that." Finn holds her gaze for a long second, and she feels her chest tighten. He shifts slightly; moves towards her, then stops, as though thinking better of it. "Take care, aye?" he says thickly. "Things are only going to get more unsettled. Especially in this part of the country."

She nods. Tugs her cloak around herself as cold wind whips up off the water. She glances at the cottage. Julia and her brothers are speaking in the doorway. "We ought to leave. That is, if you are all right with all this…"

Finn nods shortly. "Thank you. For everything. I know I've never said that before."

Eva closes her eyes. How can he show such kindness to her in one breath, and be so cold and dismissive the next? She swallows a lump in her throat. Turns and marches back to the boat so she doesn't have to respond.

Finn goes back to the cottage, unable to watch her leave. He can't shake the thought that he will never see her again. For the best, he tells himself. Even if there wasn't this great secret keeping them apart, he knows a man like him does not belong with a woman like her. Eva Blake is an educated, genteel lady; and him, well he's like something the tide dragged in.

The Mitchells have been into the whisky; have pulled three tin mugs from the sideboard that Finn hasn't seen in years. Michael fills a cup for him and nudges it across the table. "Drink up, man. You look as though you need it."

And yes, he does need it, because there on the floor beside the sideboard is Eva's duffel bag. He ought to have reminded her of it. What will he do with it now? He cannot throw her things away. But nor can he bear the sight of it. He tosses the whisky back in a single gulp. Holds the cup out to Michael for another.

When dusk falls over the island, he goes out to the firebasket and sets the beacon simmering. He sits on the rock beside it for a long time, staring out over the leathery water, feeling the warmth of the flames on the back of his neck.

He can hear dull chatter coming from inside the cottage. Can hear the clatter of dishes, the thud of the sideboard door. It's far too crowded in the house with these strangers.

He stays on the edge of the island until the dark is thick and stars are glittering between clouds. And there is more light, out on the water. Moving; another vessel, but bigger this time, than the fishing boat Eva and the Mitchells' sister had arrived in. Finn stands, squinting out at the light. It's close; too close. No vessels come this close to the Farnes unless they are in trouble.

Finn watches the wooden eagle emerge from the dark. His blood pumps hard, hot with whisky and dread. And he knows the time has arrived when he can no longer outrun the past.

CHAPTER TWENTY-NINE

It is long dark when the rap of the knocker echoes through Highfield House. Nathan hears Mrs Brodie's footsteps clicking down the passage.

Eva looks at him from where she is seated on the other side of the parlour. "Are you expecting someone?"

Nathan can see the apprehension in her eyes. He is also well aware that the book in her lap has been open to the same page for at least twenty minutes. "No," he says, getting to his feet. "I'm not expecting anyone."

He finds Joseph Holland at the door, hands dug into the pockets of his greatcoat and a woollen cap covering his bristled head. When she sees Nathan approach, Mrs Brodie bobs her head and disappears back towards her living quarters.

"May I come in?" asks Holland.

Nathan swallows. Tries for a friendly smile. "Of course." He steps back, allowing the man into the house.

Holland's eyes roam the foyer, taking in the faded

paintings with curiosity. "Is your sister here? Miss Eva?"

The knot in Nathan's stomach grows a little tighter. "She is. May I ask what you wish to speak with her about?"

"I imagine you know the answer to that question."

Nathan keeps his expression level. "No. I'm not sure I do." Has Holland come on Martin Macauley's bidding? What conclusions have they drawn? Sweat prickles his neck as he gestures down the hallway. "We can speak in the parlour."

Holland follows him down the passage, his boots clicking loudly on the flagstones. Nathan feels like a prisoner walking to the gallows. Deny everything, he thinks. Surely they have no proof of Eva's involvement in Donald Macauley's death. How could they?

When they arrive in the parlour, Eva is already on her feet. Her hands are knotted and her face is pale. She looks painfully guilty.

Nathan clears his throat. "Eva. This is Joseph Holland. I'm not sure the two of you have met."

Holland nods a greeting, and Nathan ushers him towards the armchair in the corner of the room. He ought to offer tea, of course, or whisky. But he just wants this man gone.

"I'll be frank, Mr Blake," Holland begins. "There are suspicions. Regarding your sister and the night of Donald Macauley's death."

Nathan glances at Eva. She is perched back on the edge of her armchair, her hands folded tightly in her lap. Her face is stony, but she does not speak. Nathan looks squarely at Holland, hoping he cannot hear how hard his heart is thudding.

"The night of Mr Macauley's death, Eva was in Beal, caught by the tide."

"Aye, I know the story." Holland slides forward in his chair and pulls a folded page from the pocket of his coat. He shifts his attention to Eva. "It is not up to me to judge you, Miss Blake. But the matter stands that Donald's son, and many of the other villagers, believe you had something to do with the man's disappearance."

Eva's knuckles whiten. "Is that so?"

Holland places the page on the tea table in front of them. Nathan frowns. "What is that?"

"It's a written statement from the innkeeper at the tavern in Beal, stating Miss Blake was indeed lodging at his tavern on the night in question. Along with a copy of his ledgers containing her name."

Eva flinches, catches Nathan's eye. This statement, it's a lie, of course. Is Holland aware of this?

Clearly aware of his confusion, Holland spears Nathan's gaze with his own. "The innkeeper in Beal is a staunch supporter of King George and the government," he says. "He is determined to quell another Jacobite Rising. As are many of us on this island."

Nathan raises his eyebrows. He had expected Holland's sympathies to align with Martin Macauley and the other Jacobites.

"I went to him and told him of the situation," Holland continues, "and he agreed to provide this document. A document which, if presented to the authorities—and Martin Macauley—will clear Miss Blake of all wrongdoing."

Nathan swaps glances with Eva. Why does this feel like a trap?

"What do you want for it?" Eva blurts.

Holland turns to her. He does not look surprised by her

outburst. "We want use of Highfield House," he says bluntly. "As a delivery point for messages between the government spies across Northumbria. We know Lindisfarne is an important site for the Jacobites. It's a fine vantage point to see vessels approaching from Scotland. We suspect they have eyes on the castle, and we need a secure rendezvous point on the island." He glances at Eva, before looking back at Nathan. "With the restoration of the house taking place, no one will be suspicious of people coming and going. The messengers can disguise themselves as workers."

Nathan's skin feels hot. The last thing he wants to do is get involved with the chaos that is beginning to sweep the country again. He has far too much to concern himself with, without entangling himself in these poisonous politics. But what choice do they have? The islanders have been suspicious of this family since they set foot back on Holy Island. He knows it is only a matter of time before the net closes completely around Eva. Agree to this and they will—rightly or wrongly—clear her name.

"This house is well known to the Jacobites," Nathan tells Holland. "They were using it for their own purposes until very recently." He does not dare speak Julia Mitchell's name. In spite of all she has done, he cannot risk putting her and her son in the line of enquiry of Holland and the other government spies.

"We are well aware of that," says Holland. "But I trust that activity ended when your family returned."

"Yes," Nathan says thinly. "Of course it did."

He sees the irony of this. It was the villagers' belief that his family were government spies that had led them to this position in the first place. And now here is an actual spy providing them with a way out. Or perhaps it is a way in—to a place Nathan never wanted to go.

He can feel Eva trying to catch his eye. She knows, of course, of the stress he has been carrying. Of the huge weight that has been pressing down on him since they arrived on Holy Island. No doubt she has been feeling no less strain herself. And no doubt she is aware of the extra pressure it will place on him to have Highfield House used by government spies. He knows there is every chance she will refuse this way out, for his benefit.

"Mr Holland," she begins.

"You may use the house as you wish," Nathan cuts in, before Eva can finish. He snatches the innkeeper's statement from the table, his fist tightening around it. If he cannot see his sister into a secure and comfortable marriage, he will at least keep her from the scaffold. No matter what it costs him. He does not dare think about what would happen if Martin Macauley and the other staunch Jacobites discovered he is about to open his door to government spies. He tells himself Holland will not let that happen. It is in his best interests, of course, to ensure the secret is kept.

Unbidden, Nathan finds himself thinking of Julia. What would she, an active Jacobite, think if she discovered what Highfield House was about to be used for?

And then Nathan wonders why he cares.

He stands, ushering Holland towards the door. "I assume I shall be hearing from you?"

Holland nods once, briskly. "You shall."

And as the door closes behind him, Nathan is overwhelmed by something that is either relief or dread.

Holland has barely been gone ten minutes when there is a second knock at the door. Eva's shoulders tense. She knows she ought to feel relief that she might have escaped punishment over Donald Macauley's death. But she knows the last thing in the world Nathan wanted to do was get caught in the riptide of the Rising. Using Highfield House as a rendezvous point will plant them firmly against the Macauleys and the other Jacobites on Holy Island.

Not that they weren't firmly planted against them already.

Nathan has not returned to the parlour since showing Holland out, and she hears his footsteps sound down the passage towards the door. Hears him murmur to whoever is on the other side. When he returns to the parlour, the frown on his face has deepened.

"Eva? Miss Mitchell's brothers are here. They need to speak with you. They say something has happened on Longstone."

CHAPTER THIRTY

Part of Henry Ward's game, Finn is sure, is to make him wait. Agonise. He must have been sitting here in the great cabin of the *Eagle* for at least an hour. Three of Ward's men had rowed their longboat up to the jetty on Longstone and ordered him aboard, pistols waving.

Ward's great cabin is painfully familiar, with its polished oak panelling and the ornate black lantern swaying above his head. A large wooden desk is tucked into a corner close to the curtained-off bed, books crammed into the shelf above. At the far end of the room, large windows look out over ink-black sea.

Ward's great cabin had always had a certain mystique about it—or perhaps that was the captain himself. In those days, Finn had seen him as a hero. He had sat beside Ward at this table many times, learning to decipher maps and navigate by starlight; smoothing his clumsy reading and writing into something more fluent. He was forever in awe of him. Always desperate to do his best; to prove to Ward he had done the right thing by making him a part of his crew. His captain had filled a gap left by the father Finn had abandoned.

Finally, the door clicks open.

Henry Ward is just as Finn remembers him: wolf-eyed, clean-shaven and impossibly neat. His black justacorps is trimmed with silver, a row of matching buttons down his chest. A white cravat is knotted at his throat, his greying hair tied back and powdered neatly. Though twenty years have passed since they last stood face to face, Ward barely seems to have aged.

Of course, Finn cannot say the same for himself. He had been a child of eleven when he'd last seen the captain, on that fateful night in Highfield House. He had not for a second imagined he might be recognised. Perhaps the panicked glance he'd sent Ward's way in the Bamburgh tavern had been his undoing.

Ward's boots click rhythmically as he makes his way across the cabin. He opens a cupboard beneath his desk and produces a bottle of claret and two tin cups. He carries them to the table and sits opposite Finn. Looks him up and down, curious, taking in his adult form. Finn shifts uncomfortably under his scrutiny. He knows that, to Henry Ward, he is a source of great disappointment.

"You don't look surprised to see me." Ward uncorks the bottle and fills the cups. His voice is deep, smooth, just as Finn remembers.

"Why should I be surprised? You've been following me for days."

"I've not been following you. I came to these parts for other reasons. Though I must say, I was surprised to find you still here. I thought you would have fled Northumberland long ago." He nudges Finn's cup towards him. "You always said keeping the Longstone light was not enough for you. Was that not why you came to me in the first place?"

"Aye," says Finn. "I was a fool."

The corner of Ward's lips turn up. "I'm glad there's something we can both agree upon."

Finn's eyes drift around the great cabin. How many times had he knocked on the door with a message for Ward from one of the other officers, waiting breathlessly to be invited inside? "I'm surprised this ship is still sailing," he says. "It's peacetime. Just. The king has no cause for privateers. I never imagined you as a merchant captain."

"There is no cause for privateers," Ward agrees. "But a man can make his own fortune if he is bold enough. Willing to bend the rules a little."

Finn snorts. "Piracy. I thought you had more decency than that." The knowledge is uncomfortable. It suggests Henry Ward has given up on a little of his morality. And Finn knows that does not bode well for him.

Ward tilts his head. "Sometimes a man has no choice but to do things he never imagined himself doing."

A knock at the door interrupts and Ward's steward enters, carrying two plates. He sets one down in front of Finn. It is loaded with roast beef and gravy-slathered vegetables. He looks up at Ward with raised eyebrows. "Am I truly to eat with you?"

Ward lifts his cup towards Finn's. "It's been many years. Perhaps for old time's sake?"

"Before you hang me from your yardarm? That's why I'm here, aye? So you can hand out the punishment you think I deserve?"

Ward takes a sip and sets his cup back down. "Even the worst of men deserve to go out with a good meal in their belly." He nods at the steaming food. "I'm sure this is far better than most of the swill you make for yourself on Longstone." He slices his meat and pops a piece in his mouth. "Or have you a wife out there? Children?"

Finn turns his eyes downward. "No." He slices into the meat, but doesn't eat. "What are you doing back in Northumberland?"

"That's no business of yours."

He gives a short laugh. "You're to kill me, aren't you? Surely you can at least tell me why you've come back. Who am I going to tell? The devil?"

A second knock at the door makes Ward turn. "I'm sorry to interrupt you, Captain," says the steward. "The lookout has sighted another vessel. Looks to be a small dory. Two or three people aboard."

Ward gets to his feet and strides from the cabin, abandoning his meal. Finn hurries after him, the steward at his shoulder. He follows Ward through the lamplit passages of the ship, trailing a hand along the bulwark to steady himself. They break onto deck. Several men are clustered at the gunwale.

"Watch him," Ward murmurs to them. One of the crewmen grabs Finn's arms, wrenching them behind his back.

He glances down into the dark sea. The skiff is close to Ward's ship now, its lantern casting a faint pool of light over the water. This is his boat, Finn realises, taken from the jetty at Longstone. The realisation turns his stomach. Because there are the two Mitchell brothers, each pulling hard on an oar. And there is Eva with her jaw clenched in fear, taking in the barque with the eagle figurehead. Henry Ward looks down on her with blatant interest in his eyes.

This, Eva has no doubt, is by far the most foolish thing she has ever done in her life.

When the Mitchells had come to Highfield House, they had only come seeking information.

The men in the ship. Do you know who they are?

And Eva thought at once of the vessel in Bamburgh harbour with the eagle figurehead. The man in the tavern that Finn had refused to speak of. She knew it had to be the ship the Mitchells were speaking of. But what other information could she offer? Whatever his connection to the ship, Finn had been determined to keep it to himself.

The Mitchells had made to leave, promising to search for him.

"I'm coming with you." Eva had had no intention of not being involved. Apart from anything else, she has no idea whether Michael and Angus Mitchell are any more trustworthy than their sister. She had run upstairs to grab her cloak, then slipped out the door before Nathan could ask questions.

The ship had been easy enough to find, lamps aglow just a few miles east of Holy Island. The sailor who had taken Finn clearly had no interest in hiding. Perhaps he imagined no one would care enough to come after Finn. Eva knows that, a few weeks ago, he would have been right.

She looks up at the ship now; at the shadowed faces of the men staring down at them. Their only flimsy plan had been to approach in the dark and somehow make it aboard without being noticed. With the brightly lit vessel looming over them and men lined up at the rail, Eva sees now how fragile and foolish such a plan was. But the sight of Finn, alive and unharmed, steadies her a little.

The man she had seen in Bamburgh watches with folded arms as their skiff approaches. Whatever manner of ship this is, he is clearly the captain. And from the way he had taken Finn against his will, she doubts he is operating legally.

"Eva!" Finn shouts down at her. "What in hell are you doing? Get away from here!" One of the crewmen shoves him away from the gunwale.

The captain's eyes shift to Finn, then back down to her. In the lamplight shining down from the mast, she sees curiosity in his eyes. "Eva? Eva Blake?"

Her heart thunders. How does he know her name?

She does not respond. But her silence seems to tell the captain everything he needs to know. He turns to speak to a crewmate beside him, then a rope ladder appears over the side of the ship.

"Come aboard, Miss Blake," he says smoothly.

"Row away, Eva," yells Finn. "Don't come anywhere near him!"

"Closer," Eva tells the Mitchells. "Let me get aboard."

"Are you certain?"

"Yes."

Michael and Angus pull through the water. The skiff knocks against the side of the ship, close enough for Eva to grapple with the ladder. Angus passes her his pistol and she tucks it into the pocket inside her cloak. She reaches for the first rung. Her skirts tangling around her legs, she climbs

243

carefully up the ladder. Feels it sway beneath her. She takes another step, feet grappling clumsily against the slippery hull of the ship. When she reaches the top, the captain holds out a hand to help her over the gunwale. Reluctantly, she takes it, scrambling onto the deck and hurriedly straightening her skirts.

Finn pins her with hard eyes. "I told you to leave," he says thickly. She meets his eyes, but doesn't speak.

The captain looks her up and down. "Eva Blake. You were a child last time I saw you." He takes a lamp from above the door of the forecastle and holds it to her face. The light is hot against her cheek. There's a faint smile on the captain's lips— an expression that almost seems warm. "You look just like your mother."

Eva darts a horrified glance at Finn, but his jaw is still set grimly, his face giving nothing away. She looks back at the captain. Up close he is painfully handsome, with a square, clean-shaven jaw and fierce blue eyes. There is something unsettling about his rugged, unnatural beauty. "How do you know my mother?" She hears the faint waver in her voice.

"Abigail was an acquaintance of mine. We met on Lindisfarne one day when she was in need of some assistance. I spent much time in these parts back when you were a lass." He gives her sympathetic eyes. "I was very sorry to hear of her passing."

"How do you know of that?"

"News travels." He glances over the gunwale at the Mitchells in the skiff, then turns to back to Eva. "Tell them to leave."

Her stomach tightens. They were her way back to safety. But the only other option is leaving Finn here alone. She cannot do that. Nor can she just walk away without learning what this man knows of her mother.

She leans over the gunwale. Calls down to the men, with instructions to leave. Yes, she is sure.

She turns away. Can't watch them go.

The captain nods to one of the crew, and without speaking, the man steps up to Eva and begins patting her down.

She stumbles back. "What do you think you're doing?"

"Calm yourself," says the captain. "No offense intended. It's merely a formality."

The crewman's roaming hands find the pistol in her cloak. He pulls it out, handing it to the captain.

"Why are you here, Miss Blake?" he asks, tucking the weapon into the pocket of his coat. "Surely you haven't come for Mr Murray."

Eva's eyes dart to Finn, then back to the captain. "What do you want with him?" She hears her voice rattle.

The captain gestures towards the forecastle. "We've a fine dinner on the table and it's getting cold. May I suggest we continue this conversation inside?" He puts a hand to the small of Eva's back, guiding her inside without waiting for a response. Finn follows close behind, a crewman at his shoulder.

The captain leads her down a lamplit passage towards the cabin in the stern of the ship. Filled wine glasses and two plates of food sit on the table in the centre of the room. They have barely been touched.

"Please." The captain gestures to the table. "Sit." His voice is warm. Unsettlingly so. He looks to his steward. "Have the cook bring a third plate." He turns back to Eva. "Forgive me.

Henry Ward." He offers her his hand.

Eva accepts it warily, her eyes darting between the two men. She slides onto the bench at one side of the table. Finn sits opposite, not taking his eyes from her.

Ward takes a third cup from a cupboard below his desk and fills it for Eva before taking his seat at the head of the table. He lifts his wine. "Well. To this unexpected pleasure."

Eva raises her glass uncertainly. She brings it to her lips and takes a miniscule sip. Finn's hand tightens around his cup. He doesn't drink.

"It's an honour to have you at my table, Miss Blake," says Ward. "The last time I saw you, you were a little lass running the hallways of Highfield House."

Eva hears her inhalation. "Why were you in my house?"

"Your mother invited me. Invited us."

"Us?" Eva coughs. Who is he referring to? Surely not to Finn. No, she tells herself. Impossible. She had left Highfield House at four years old; Finn could have hardly been older than ten or eleven. But when she looks back at Ward, and to the lowered, shameful eyes Finn is hiding, she sees all she needs to know. Her stomach rolls.

"Why?" she asks, her voice thin.

Ward sips his wine. "Abigail was a good woman. A kind woman. She was good enough to offer my crew hospitality whenever our voyages brought us back to Northumbria." He smiles. "She knew how much a sailor values a night on dry land every now and then. The comforts of a warm house."

Eva shakes her head. "My mother would not have let pirates into the house."

"I assure you, Miss Blake, the *Eagle* was operating completely legally. Under a letter of marque authorising us to attack the French. I'm sure Mr Murray will attest to that if you doubt me. He was a valuable member of my crew for a number of years." Ward smiles thinly. "I suppose I cannot be surprised that he has not told you any of this. I must say, I think your loyalty is somewhat misplaced, given you have come traipsing all the way out here to find him."

Finn looks at Ward, eyes blazing.

"Mr Murray is not one to speak of his past," Eva says thinly.

A plate of roast meat appears in front of her, making her stomach turn. Ward nods his thanks to the steward, then turns back to Eva. "Well. I'm sure his silence is understandable, given the circumstances of that night."

Eva's heart quickens. She hears her breathing come loud through her nose, disoriented by the captain's words, and the swaying light of the lantern above her head. She knows instinctively which night he is referring to. Can there be any other night than when her mother had pulled her children from their beds and they had gone tearing out across Holy Island?

But whatever Finn's role in their fleeing, she does not want to hear it from this self-important sea captain. She wants to hear it from Finn himself. And she wants him to look into her eyes as he tells her, so she knows he is telling her the truth.

"What do you want with me?" she asks the captain.

Ward smiles. "You came aboard my ship voluntarily, Miss Blake. I invited you here on account of our shared past. Our shared affection for your mother."

"So you will let me leave when I wish?"

"Of course."

"What about Finn?"

"That matter is more complicated."

"I see." Eva stares into her plate, trying to order her thoughts. She feels completely overwhelmed, unmoored by this new information. She cannot trust Ward; of that she is certain. As for Finn, she has no idea. She wants to trust him, desperately. But how can she do so when he has clearly been keeping so much from her?

"You were in Highfield House," she says to him, voice low. "With his crew."

Finn's knuckles whiten around his cup. "I was, aye."

She forces herself to breathe deeply. Glances between the two men. "Something made my mother flee the house. Did she leave that night?"

"That I do not know," says Ward. "All I can tell you is that after that night, I never saw Abigail again."

"Why?" Eva pushes. "What happened?"

Ward glances at Finn. When he gets no reaction, he says, "Your brother died rather violently in the house, Miss Blake. Oliver."

Eva frowns. "No. Oliver died of smallpox. That's what my mother always told me."

"Your mother was lying to you," says Ward. "To protect you, I suppose. That—"

"Stop," Finn says suddenly. "I need to be the one to tell her." His hands make fists, then he looks up at her squarely. "Your brother didn't die of smallpox, Eva. He died the night I was in the house with Ward's crew." He draws in a shaky breath. "He died by my hand."

CHAPTER THIRTY-ONE

Finn's words fall heavily into the silence, and for long moments, Eva doesn't speak.

He thinks of her tearing onto Longstone and confessing to her part in the death of Donald Macauley. He had not judged her then, and he does not judge her for it now. After all, how could he? He is carrying the same guilt on his shoulders.

Highfield House was like a myth. A fable Ward disappeared into from time to time, when there was no action to be had a sea. Warm beds, good food, fine wine, and even better company.

The house of Abigail Blake. Ward spoke her name almost reverently.

Sometimes, he would go to the house alone. Other times he would take his officers with him, loaded with liquor, and in their finest clothes. Even as a child, Finn wondered whether Ward was truly as welcome at Highfield House as he believed himself to be. Or perhaps that simply didn't matter to him.

And then the night Ward came to Finn and told him he was to join him at the house. Finn had been racked with a vicious head cold for more than a week, and couldn't be sure he wasn't imagining the invitation.

"You want me to join you, sir? At the house? At the gathering?"

Ward laughed. "At the gathering, no. You're too young for that yet, lad. But I'll see to it that you get a comfortable night's rest. Sleep off the last of your illness."

Highfield House was everything he imagined it to be. Vast and shadowed and elaborately beautiful, with a sense of the otherworldly, wrought by salt-splattered windows and candlelit halls. This place had always fascinated him. How many times had he stood on the deck of the *Eagle* while Ward was at the house, staring across the water at the forest of chimneys, wondering what might lie inside? He couldn't believe he was standing in its foyer.

The woman who had let them inside inspected the group with shrewd, narrowed eyes. She was fine-boned and slight, dwarfed by Henry Ward and the five other men he had brought with him. She had clearly dressed for the occasion, in a lace-trimmed blue gown, and jewels at her throat, her dark hair piled high on her head.

Her eyes fell to Finn. "He's one of yours?" Surprise in her voice.

"He is. A hardworking cabin boy, fighting the last of a fever. He's in need of a warm bed for the night."

The woman managed a smile, but it didn't reach her eyes. "Of course," she told Finn. "You can have my eldest son's room. He can share with his brother for the night. Wait down here a moment." She turned to Ward. Gave him a faint smile. "Make yourselves comfortable."

Ward gripped Finn's shoulder, told him to behave. Then the men were off deep into the house, bottles swinging in their fists.

Finn hovered awkwardly in the foyer. In the flickering lamplight, the paintings on the walls seemed to be shifting; the sea on the canvas rolling, the eyes of the portraits looking his way. He glanced up the wide wooden staircase that led to the second storey, the steps at the top swallowed by darkness.

Finally, the woman appeared from the gloom of the stairs. She walked halfway down, holding a lamp out to guide Finn's path. "This way."

He followed her upstairs and down the passage. The woman brought a finger to her lips, gesturing for silence, and Finn tiptoed, guessing there were sleeping children behind those doors.

She pushed open the door of a room at the end of the passage. An enormous black fireplace filled most of one wall, dark wood panels on either side of it. The bed in the centre of the room was piled with blankets, and even a pillow. Finn was not sure he had ever slept on something that looked so comfortable.

He thanked the woman. Waited until she had closed the door behind her before pulling off his boots and climbing into bed. He was on the edge of sleep when he heard the door groan open again. Heard footsteps sounding across the room. Saw a globe of lamplight through his closed eyelids.

Finn scrambled into sitting. Came face to face with a boy about his age. Tall and thin, with white-blond hair tickling his shoulders. His eyes glittered in the lamplight.

"Who are you?" asked Finn.

"This is my room," said the boy. "I'm Oliver Blake. And I ought to be asking you that question."

Eva is staring at him, eyes full of questions. But it is Ward she speaks to first. "Do you mean to kill Finn? As punishment? Is that why you brought him here?"

He looks at her squarely. "Do you not think that is what he deserves?"

Eva's lips part. Ward must know, surely, that she is in no place to answer such a question. Not with only the barest fragments of the story. Or maybe those fragments are enough to condemn him.

When Eva doesn't speak, Ward turns to Finn. "You were a member of my crew when Oliver Blake was killed. Therefore you are bound by the articles of the ship. Articles that claim a slaying outside of battle or duel is punishable by death."

"Ward, please." Finn scrubs a hand across his eyes. "Let's not have this discussion in front of Eva."

"No," she cuts in, looking at him squarely. "I wish to hear what you have to say."

Finn holds her gaze for a moment. What can he possibly say that will make this any less horrific? He knows nothing can save his relations with Eva. They were doomed before they even began. But perhaps he can find a way to save his own life. He knows punishment is what he deserves. Death, if that is what Ward has planned for him. But his survival instinct makes him speak: "Oliver's death did not happen on your ship."

The captain leans back. "No," he concedes. "It did not. Therefore I know it could be argued that you were not bound by the ship's articles at the time. If one was looking for a loophole. But is that really what you feel you ought to be doing, while you are sitting face to face with Oliver's sister?"

Henry Ward had always been a strict captain. Finn had watched men hanged from the yardarm, and keel-hauled beneath the hull of ship, for breaking the laws set out in the articles. He knows he deserves no less.

But he does not want to die. And he also knows that, killer or not, he has a valuable job to do. He likes to think that the light he has set burning almost every night for five years might have saved the lives of countless sailors. And perhaps, in some small way, that might begin to atone for Oliver Blake's death.

So perhaps he is looking for a loophole. But he is doing it because surely, he is worth more alive than dead.

"You'll not kill me," he tells Ward. "Because it's not your place to do so, and you know it. I did not kill Oliver aboard your ship. And you have always been fair and rigid when it comes to your ship's articles."

Ward doesn't speak. Finn knows he is considering his words. He stands and looks squarely at his former captain. Tries to invoke a confidence he doesn't feel. "Take me back to Longstone. I've to light the firebasket to make sure men like you don't end up at the bottom of the sea."

Ward reaches over and refills Finn's wine glass, though he has barely touched the first. "Sit down, lad. You're not going anywhere."

Finn clenches his jaw. He knows he has no choice. Even

if he were to shove his way past Ward and break out onto deck, his only option of escape would be to swim. Out here, the German Ocean would steal his breath in seconds. And he has no thought of how far he is from Longstone. Of course, none of that matters. Even if he could find his way off the ship, he cannot leave Eva here alone.

Can it truly be a coincidence that Ward has returned to Northumberland at the same time as Eva and her family? It does not feel like it. But he has no thought of what Ward might want with the Blakes.

He sits. Brings his cup to his lips to appease the captain, but he doesn't drink. He needs to keep as clear a head as possible.

"What?" laughs Ward. "You think I've laced it with nightshade? You know I've more decency than that. Or more creativity at least." He reaches over and spears a piece of meat from Finn's plate. Swallows it in one mouthful. "You ought to try a little. Good quality stuff. Fresh from shore."

Finn pushes his plate away. "I think this dinner is over, Ward." He turns. "Eva?" Dares to look at her.

She nods, her eyes unreadable.

"Very well." Ward tosses back the last of his wine and stands. He goes to the cabin door and calls for his steward. Murmurs to him with instructions, Finn is sure, to imprison him somewhere on the ship.

Ward turns to Eva. "I cannot let Mr Murray go. I'm sorry. What of you, Miss Blake? Do you wish to leave? If you do, I shall have one of my officers take you back to Holy Island."

Finn's stomach knots at the thought of Eva climbing into a longboat with a member of Ward's crew. But it is better than the alternative.

"No," she says. "I wish to stay."

Ward merely nods, as though expecting such an answer. "I shall have my crew find you comfortable quarters."

Finn grabs her arm before she can follow the steward down the passage. "She stays with me." He expects a protest from her. It doesn't come.

"Miss Blake?" says Ward. "Is that what you want?"

She glances at Finn. "Yes."

The steward leads Finn and Eva out of the great cabin and down the narrow, lamplit passage. He pulls a key from the pocket of his coat and unlocks a door at the far end of the corridor. Nods wordlessly for them to enter. The cabin is an airless tomb, thick with the stink of tallow and bodies. Two hammocks are strung across the bulkheads at the back of the room.

The crewman hangs the lamp on the hook beside the door. Then he steps back out into the passage, the lock clicking loudly in the stillness. His footsteps disappear. And they are alone.

CHAPTER THIRTY-TWO

Eva stands with her back to the door, but does not attempt to put space between the two of them. She is inches away from him, her eyes full of questions she doesn't ask.

Unable to bear the silence, Finn says, "Why are you here? Why didn't you leave?"

She lets out her breath. "How could I leave?"

"How could you have stayed?"

She closes her eyes; leans her head back against the door. "I need to hear it all, Finn. Every word."

Of course she does. The thing is brutal, but surely it can be no worse than whatever images are clattering around her head right now.

And so he tells her. Every piece of it, just as he remembers. Tells her of Abigail Blake opening her door to Ward and his crew; tells her of her mother being kind enough to offer him a bed for the night, to sleep off the last of his fever.

And he tells her about her eldest brother: blond-haired, sharp-eyed Oliver, who had pulled him from sleep with a spear of lamplight in his eyes.

"Why are you in my house?" Oliver asked. "Are you with them? The sailors?"

Finn slid from the bed, his bare feet soundless on the wooden floor. He said nothing. He had learnt by now that in situations like this, silence was best. For all Ward liked to play up the honour of what they did, Finn knew one wrong turn would lead them all to the hangman. The line between privateering and piracy was a flimsy one.

Oliver took a step towards him, holding the lamp close to his face. Finn was inches taller, and Oliver had to look up to meet his eyes. "Why won't you speak to me? Are you a half-wit? Or are you scared?"

"Leave me alone," said Finn. "I just want to sleep. Your mother gave me this room." His body was still aching from the remnants of his illness; his throat on fire. The door sighed open and a second boy slipped into the room. Smaller, with wide blue eyes and dark curls around his shoulders. He stood with his back pressed against the door, as though desperate to keep his distance, but too curious to stay away. Oliver glanced over his shoulder at him, then turned back to Finn. He lifted his hand, revealing a small tarnished blade that had been hidden by the sleeve of his nightshirt.

"Look at this," he said to Finn. "It's a Viking dagger. From the days when they raided this island."

Finn snorted. "A Viking dagger?" Was the boy trying to impress him? Intimidate him? "It is not."

Oliver's nostrils flared. "Are you calling me a liar?"

"You're lying, aye? Or are you just stupid?"

Oliver took a step towards him and Finn flinched, expecting retaliation. But he stopped coolly, turning the blade over in his fist. Finn felt the hair on the back of his neck prickle.

Oliver looked over his shoulder at his brother. "Tell him, Nathan. Tell him it's from the Viking raids."

They both turned to look at the younger boy. He hesitated, mouth hanging half open. Finally, he said, "I think it's just a fishing knife. But there's a real priest hole in this room. Behind the panel by the fireplace. Over here—"

Oliver shoved him away. "Get out."

Nathan looked up at his brother. Finn saw fear in his eyes. There was a part of him that was feeling it too. But he refused to let himself be intimidated by this boy. How could he be afraid of a child after he had stood on the deck of the *Eagle* and sailed into French gunfire? But there was something about Oliver Blake that made him wary. Made his fists clench instinctively. Made his heart quicken in readiness for a fight.

The door clicked closed again, leaving the two of them alone.

"Leave me be," Finn said again. "I'm not afraid of you." He wondered if the boy could tell he was lying.

A smile flickered in the corner of Oliver's lips. "Have you heard what the Vikings did to the monks on this island?"

Finn gritted his teeth, forcing away the urge to throw a fist into the side of Oliver's head. He could not fight this boy. Not Abigail Blake's son. Ward would never forgive him. And how many times had the captain lectured him about controlling his temper? About not flying into a rage at every provocation, like he had done with his father?

258

But Ward had also taught him not to let himself be pushed around.

What was this about, he wondered? Was Oliver Blake marking his territory? Or did he just like the power of inflicting fear? Surely this could not be a personal attack. Oliver Blake had no idea who he was.

"They cut them to pieces," said Oliver. "Ransacked the church and sliced their throats like they were pigs." He lifted the blade to Finn's neck. Instinctively, Finn shoved him away. Oliver stumbled backwards, his eyes widening in surprise for a moment, before a faint smile tilted his lips. He took another step towards Finn and pressed the tip of the blade into his stomach. "Left them all to die."

Finn's chest tightened. It was not fear he was feeling. Not anymore. Now it was anger; hot and sharp. Heart rapping against his ribs, skin prickling. This anger, he had felt it before, in those suffocating nights on Longstone when he and his father would spur each other into rage. Back then, he had let his anger out unbridled. But he knew his actions had to be calculated if he was to come out of this on top. He stood frozen against the silver tip of the knife. He had no idea what this boy was capable of. He only knew he had to act. Disarm him somehow. Run downstairs to find Ward. The other officers would mock him, of course. But he didn't care.

The floorboards in the hallway creaked.

"I can hear you out there, Nathan," said Oliver, not turning away from Finn. "Go to bed." There was silence in the passage. No movement. Oliver raised his voice slightly, turning back over his shoulder to speak to his brother. "Do you want to spend another night in the walls?"

Finn seized the distraction. He shoved Oliver backwards

and lurched towards the door. Oliver grabbed a fistful of Finn's shirt, yanking him back. Lashed at him with the knife. Finn saw the stripe of blood appear on his forearm before he registered the pain. He swung a fist. Hard—too hard—into the side of Oliver's head. He fell sideways, skull cracking against the foot of the bed. His body slid to the floorboards, almost silent but for the soft clatter of the knife against the floor. Cold blue eyes stared up at Finn, but there was no light behind them. A thick seam of blood crept out from beneath Oliver's head, edging towards the blade of the knife.

Finn's lungs seized. He gulped for air. His legs wavered beneath him and he grappled with the bed head, trying to stay upright. His vision swam and vomit rushed up his throat.

Outside the door, he heard the younger boy cry out. And then there were footsteps moving up the staircase. Steady, growing louder. He rushed to the window; shook wildly at the sash, but it refused to open. He looked around for something with which to smash the glass. He was two storeys off the ground, yes, but surely the fall would be better than whatever Henry Ward would do to him once he found out what he had done.

The footsteps came closer. Finn thought suddenly of the younger boy's words. A priest hole in the panelling beside the fireplace. It would be no escape, but it would be a place to hide. He raced to the far wall, throwing his weight against the worn wooden panels, searching for the hidden compartment. Finally, he felt it give way. The priest hole opened up before him and he dived inside. He yanked the panelling closed, enclosing himself in blackness.

He hugged his knees, pressing his face to his thigh to silence his breathing. He could feel the warm wetness of the blood on his forearm. The cut pulsed in time with his racing heart. He heard footsteps thunder into the room; heard the screams of the boys' mother. And muffled words he knew came from Henry Ward.

He heard the captain call his name.

Finn pressed his hands to the wall on either side of him. Above his head was the same heavy stone that made up the fireplace. It felt as though the tiny space was closing in on him, draining the last of the air. His breath came fast and loud. Loud enough to hear, surely, on the other side of the wall.

He shuffled backwards, his shoulder pressing hard against the corner of the priest hole. And he felt the wall shift. Felt the wooden panel twist and open, revealing a second narrow space. Below it, a passage yawning into blackness.

On hands and knees, Finn scrambled forward in the darkness, his fingers finding the coarse rungs of a ladder. He scrambled down it, ignoring the splinters that bit into his palms. On every side of him were thick slabs of stone. A passage built into the wall, he realised. It felt almost as if it had been put there for him. For this very moment. Perhaps this mysterious, mythical house might find a way to save his life.

When he landed heavily at the bottom of the ladder, he followed the passage on his hands and knees. It smelt of earth, of wood. Smelt like he was being buried alive.

He would deserve such a fate, he thought distantly. He had killed someone. Run away instead of facing up to his actions. He did not deserve the freedom that Highfield House had inexplicably granted.

But then there was moonlight. The sigh of the sea. Finn scrambled towards the pale, hatched light that marked the end of the tunnel. Perhaps he did not deserve freedom, but he would seize it with both hands anyway.

A rusty grate blocked his path. Wriggling onto his back, he shoved at it with his bare feet until it gave way. And out he scrambled, gulping down the salty air.

He didn't look back as he charged onto the beach. Didn't glance back to see if he had been followed. Wind tore at his shirtsleeves, but his body was blazing. Footsteps drummed in his ears, the sound distorted by fear and fever. He couldn't tell if the soft pounding of feet against earth were his alone.

He slid through the pebbles on the edge of the water. A lamp glowed not far from shore. Ward's barque.

The ship would not save him. The ship would only lead him to the gallows. He ran around the curve of the island, seeking the place where the mainland was closest. Moonlight guided him, but not well enough; he stumbled over rugged dunes and tussocks of grass, slipped into puddles that reached the hems of his breeches.

The tide was high. Tonight Lindisfarne was an island again, and his only way off was to battle the rising German Ocean.

He was in the water before his thoughts caught up to him. The sea closed in over his head and he kicked hard against the current. He thrashed through the water, through the cold and the dark, towards the vague shapes of the mainland.

Finally, the sea grew shallower and he stumbled up the beach. He knew this part of the world well. There were houses here in Beal; a tavern. Surely someone would offer him dry clothes and a little food. Enough to see him out of Northumberland and into a life where Henry Ward would not find him.

Finn stumbled to his feet, turning to look back at the dark mass of Holy Island. Lamps from the village broke the blackness, and beyond them, a pale glow that marked Highfield House. And far beyond that, so distant he was not sure if he was imagining it, was the flickering eye of the firebasket warning ships away from Longstone.

For several moments, the silence is thick, punctuated by the irregular breath of the flame inside the lantern. The hull of the ship groans.

"He was like that," Eva says finally. "Terrifying. I barely remember him. I can't recall what he looked like. Or sounded like. All I remember is that he frightened me."

But this comment, Finn knows well, from the hardness of her eyes and arms held stiffly across her chest, it is no absolution. And why should it be?

"I'm sorry," he says. It feels like a foolish thing to say. Foolish, but achingly necessary.

Eva looks up. "I know." Her eyes are glistening. "You would never have told me, would you," she says. "If I had not come out here looking for you, I never would have known."

He shakes his head. He feels like a coward. But the least he can do is tell her the truth. "No," he says. "I never would have told you."

He tries to catch her eye. Tries to read her. But he cannot do it. She has taken on a sudden blankness.

"Ward will kill you for this, won't he." Her voice is strangely level, hollow.

"Probably. I'm sure he wishes to avenge your mother."

"And is that what you believe you deserve?"

Finn thinks of that airless priest hole, of that tarnished blade pressed to his throat. He thinks of the crack of Oliver's head striking the bed, a sound that has stayed with him for the past twenty years. It might be what he deserves, but that survival instinct in him has not faltered. "Perhaps it is," he says. "But I want to live."

Eva raps on the door of the cabin she and Finn are locked in. "I wish to see the captain," she calls. "I need to speak with him."

The door clicks open at once, reminding her she is not the prisoner. Ward's steward nods at her to exit the cabin, then locks the door behind her. Without speaking, he leads her back through the passage towards the great cabin. Their footsteps click rhythmically and Eva focuses on the sound, to keep her thoughts from running away.

Oliver, the brother never spoken of. Oliver, who she believed had succumbed to smallpox like her father, a swift and unremarkable death. Why had her mother lied? To hide her shame over inviting Ward and his crew into the house? Her shame over inviting Finn into the house? Or was an unremarkable death just easier than the truth?

On one hand, there is clarity. This, of course, is why Finn had pulled away from her in Bamburgh. Why he had erected the walls around himself the moment he had learnt her name. How she longs for her old ignorance; ignorance in which his coldness came only from believing her a government spy. Now that seems far too easy.

When they reach the great cabin, the steward knocks loudly. "Captain. Miss Blake wishes to speak with you."

Footsteps sound across the boards and Ward pulls open the door. He gives her what looks to be a genuine smile. "Please come in."

She does. Their dinner has been cleared away, but the smell of roast meat lingers, mingling with the remnants of wine and the ever-present breath of the sea. Ward closes the logbook on his desk and gestures for her to return to the table. He sits opposite her.

"What is it you wish to speak about, Eva?"

She stiffens at his familiarity, both his informality and the genial way he is looking at her. Like he knows her. Knew her. Like he was walking the halls of Highfield House for far longer than just one night.

She senses that Ward feels his own guilt for his part in Oliver's death. After all, it had been because of him that Finn was in Highfield House in the first place. And while he cannot hope to make it up to Abigail, perhaps treating her daughter well is the least he can do.

Or perhaps she is being naïve. She knows nothing of this world of pirates and privateers that Ward and Finn are so entangled in. Before coming to Holy Island, she had known no world but the rigid life laid out before her in London. But she knows she should not trust a man like Henry Ward easily. And she knows she must act if she is to get what she needs. She cannot just stay locked in that cabin like a rabbit in a trap. How long might it be until Ward's kindness runs out?

She folds her hands in front of her on the table. Squeezes them together to steady herself. "I should like to be taken back to Holy Island. I've heard what I needed to hear from

Mr Murray."

Ward nods slowly. "I see." A smile flickers in the corner of his lips. "You sound just like your mother, you know. She used to speak in the same detached manner as that when she sought to hide her emotions."

Eva tries to quell her irritation at the ease with which he has read her. "I'm nothing like my mother."

Ward's smile broadens, warms. "You're more like her than you know. She could be reckless too. And here you are putting yourself in danger by following the man you love out here."

Something flips in Eva's stomach. "You think I love Finn Murray?"

"Loved, perhaps. At least until you discovered what he was keeping from you. Why else would you risk your own safety by coming all the way out here?"

Eva looks at her tightly clasped hands. Ward's claim is one she cannot allow herself to bring to the light. At least, not now. "Well. It's as you say. He has been keeping things from me."

Ward nods. "Yes. And it's a damn shame. He had such potential, that lad. I believed he had the makings of a fine and decent man. I was sorry to see him throw it all away on one foolish mistake."

Eva squeezes her eyes shut. She cannot allow her thoughts to venture near Finn's decency, or his mistakes. All she can do right now is focus on the conversation at hand. Focus on remaining in Henry Ward's good graces.

"You are leaving Mr Murray to his own devices, then," says Ward.

Eva meets his eyes. "He killed my brother. And thought

done, Eva knew she had to help him do so. Had to take this precarious fondness Henry Ward seems to have for her, and use it to their advantage.

The plan is dangerous, desperate. Could well end in both their deaths. But it is their only chance of leaving this ship together.

"You do not wish to watch the punishment?" asks Ward.

"No." The tears that spill are not an act. But the captain eyes her, and for a moment, Eva's panic intensifies. Perhaps his trust in her is not as secure as she had imagined. But then he turns to his steward. Hands him a key.

"Take her to the great cabin. And pour her a drink. She looks as though she needs it." He turns to Eva. "I shall have one of the men take you ashore once the punishment is complete." He gestures to the men at the pulley. "Drag him under."

The crewman leads her down the passage with excruciating slowness. Eva thinks of Finn below the surface; thinks of the weights at his feet pulling him down; the men on deck with ropes in their hands, dragging him beneath the razor-sharp hull of the ship. Her breath becomes even more ragged. She forces herself to breathe steadily so as not to give herself away.

He has the knife, she tells herself. A way to cut himself free. Desperate, dangerous—but a way nonetheless.

The steward unlocks the door of the great cabin and gestures for Eva to enter. She steps inside, her eyes moving instinctively to the bank of windows at the stern of the ship. The steward walks to the sideboard and uncorks the half-drunk bottle of wine. Fills a shallow cup and sits it on the table. Eva nods her thanks.

"Anything else you need, Miss?"

"No. Thank you." She wills him to leave. If they are to manage this escape, they cannot waste seconds. The moment the men at the pulley feel the ropes lose their tension, they will know Finn has cut himself free. And they will come looking.

After what feels an eternity, the steward steps out of the cabin, locking the door behind him. Eva grabs a chair by the legs and rushes to the window. Swings wildly. Glass explodes into the ocean and the sound seems to echo across the ship. Surely it will be only seconds before Ward comes for her. Terror weakens her legs. She has never swum in her life. And the moment she leaps from this window, she will start sinking to the ocean floor.

She cannot allow this thought to take hold. She pulls her cloak from her shoulders and flings it onto the floor. And she leaps out into the sea.

Dark water closes in over her head, the shock of the cold seizing her chest and snatching her breath. *Keep kicking,* Finn had told her, as they had planned their escape while locked in the cabin. *Just keep kicking. I will come to you.* She surfaces briefly, gulping down air, catching a glimpse of a slivered moon. And she kicks and she kicks, her skirts tangling around her legs. The water pulls her down, sucking the last of the moonlight away.

CHAPTER THIRTY-FOUR

Finn slices through the last of the rope and kicks towards the surface. He opens his eyes, but the water is like ink around him. A part of him is grateful for the darkness; by now, the men will know he has freed himself, and they will not hesitate to shoot. He bursts through the surface. He is close to the great cabin. Through stinging eyes, he can see the windows are shattered. Eva is in the water with him, somewhere. But he can see no sign of her.

Frantically, he dives below the surface again, eyes open, though he sees nothing but black. This, of all outcomes, would be by far the worst—if he is to survive only to have her drown. He longs to call out to her, but he knows he can do no such thing. And then the water shifts around him. He feel the ripples of her kicking and flailing. And he thrashes towards her, reaching, straining into the darkness.

He dives below the surface and his fingertips brush her body. Feels her grab a fistful of his shirt. He pulls at her, wraps an arm tight around her waist. And he kicks hard. His lungs and legs are burning, her heavy skirts dragging them towards the bottom. At last they break through the surface, gasping down lungfuls of the cold night air.

In the faint light of the ship's lamps, he meets her eyes. Sees a wordless mix of terror and relief. She wraps her arms around his shoulders, breathless.

Finn digs his fingers into her collar and kicks towards the longboat trailing behind Ward's barque. It's a dangerous ploy; deadly. He knows the moment Ward sees them, he will start shooting. More than anything, Henry Ward hates being deceived. Especially by those he has put his trust in.

Finn pushes Eva towards the boat. "Grab the side," her tells her breathlessly. "I'll climb in and pull you up."

Reluctantly, she relinquishes her grip on his shirt and grapples at the gunwale. Her eyes dart up at the lamplit shape of the barque. Finn pulls on the gunwale, causing the boat to rock, rock enough for him to haul himself from the water and scramble aboard.

As his knees hit the bottom of the longboat, the first shot comes. He hears Eva's murmur of shock. He grabs her arms and pulls her from the water. Lurches forward and unties the rope latching the longboat to the ship. "Get down," he hisses.

But the shooting has stopped. Suddenly, the night is quiet, eerily still. Finn wraps his hands around the oars, but does not dare lower them into the water. Not yet. He knows there is every chance Ward is trying to lull them into a false sense of security.

"Go," Eva whispers after a moment. "Go."

And he does. He lowers the oars into the sea and begins to pull away from the ship.

He knows he ought to feel relief. But he doesn't.

Ward is watching. Calm and still at the stern of the ship. And Finn knows then, with certainty, that they have only escaped because Ward has allowed it.

He looks up to meet his captain's eyes. There's a look there that he knows all too well. A look that tells Finn this is not a pardon. This is a game.

He has let him go now because he wants him to fret. To suffer, to watch the horizon as he lights the firebasket each night, and wonder when the lamps of the *Eagle* will again shine over Longstone.

He has let him go because he knows Finn has trapped himself out there on his shard of an island. Tied himself to the firebasket to atone for his mistakes.

And perhaps he has also let him go because Abigail Blake's daughter is sitting in the longboat beside him. Perhaps he will not risk another of her children losing their life on account of his crew.

But Finn is certain that once Eva is no longer at his side, Ward will come again. This is who he is: shrewd and calculating. He will see this as a fitting punishment: a life of watching, of waiting, of wondering when he might next appear. Wondering when his desire to avenge Abigail Blake and her son might finally drive him to pull the trigger.

Eva can know none of this. He does not want her to know it is likely her presence that has kept Ward from firing. Does not want to put her in the middle of this poisonous thing between himself and his former captain.

Besides, he can't quite find a way to feel that fear he knows Ward is trying to instil in him. Because somehow, against all reason, Eva is here beside him with an oar in her hand. She shuffles along the bench until her shoulder presses hard against his, as though unable to believe that they have both lived to see the morning.

CHAPTER THIRTY-FIVE

The sun has risen by the time they return to Longstone. The morning is clear and the sea is glass, pink light pushing through the thin layer of clouds on the horizon. Birds are wheeling around the far end of the island.

They had found Angus and Michael Mitchell waiting in the skiff, not far from Ward's ship. In the rising sun, the *Eagle* is still visible. A watching silhouette, but motionless. At least for now.

The two boats bump against the jetty on Longstone, and Finn ties Ward's longboat up beside the skiff. He climbs out ahead of Eva and offers her his hand. She holds tight to him as she steps from the boat. And then, after a moment of hesitation, she lets her fingers slide from his.

Shivering in her wet clothes, Eva goes to the bedroom and finds the dry skirts and petticoats she had flung over the end of the bed before they had gone to Bamburgh. They have been folded clumsily and placed on a chair in the corner of the room. With frozen fingers, she hurries out of her sodden clothing and climbs into her dry things.

She is still straightening her neckerchief when Finn comes barrelling through the door. There is a look of urgency in his eyes that says he does not care that he has caught her in a state of near undress.

He closes the door behind him. And he comes at her suddenly, pulling her close. For a moment, Eva lets herself sink against him. His dry clothes smell faintly of woodsmoke, and the linen of his shirt is rough against her cheek.

After a moment, he pulls back to look her in the eyes. "That was madness. You could have died."

"As could you." With a little distance, she can see the insanity of the plan she had set in motion. Sees how fortunate they had been to survive. And she sees how impossibly grateful she is that Finn is standing here in front of her. Alive and unharmed.

She brings a hand to his bristly cheek. "I don't blame you for what happened, Finn. I know Oliver's death was an accident. Just like Donald Macauley's." And for now, perhaps, the two of them have escaped punishment. But she has no thought of how long their reprieves might last. The shadow of the *Eagle* is still imprinted on the horizon. And government spies are about to descend on Highfield House, covering for her crime.

She lets out a breath. "How do you do it? Live with another's death on your shoulders?"

Finn doesn't speak at once. He rests his forehead against hers, tucking coils of wet hair behind her ear.

"You just carry on," he says finally. "You just carry on and hope that you might be able to do some good. Something that might pay for your mistakes in some small way."

And Eva sees then that the firebasket, and this teetering cottage in the sea is not just about Finn's father and his three uncles lost on the Knavestone. It is also about her own brother; faceless and half-forgotten to her, but always at the forefront of Finn's mind.

Impulsively, she pulls him into a kiss. His fingers slide through her wet, tangled hair, making her sigh against his lips. And she sees things as they are. Sees that this is a kiss goodbye.

Because surely this is too big to ever climb over. How could she take Finn to her family, knowing what she knows? Nathan had seen him with Oliver that night. Is there a chance he might recognise him? Unlikely as it seems, she could never take that risk. Could never keep the truth from him and Harriet, or expect them to forgive Finn as she has done. And how could she ever expect Finn to set foot in Highfield House again, after the horrors he had experienced there?

She steps away and meets his eyes. "I'm sorry," she says. "I need to leave." And he gives a faint nod; one of understanding. She blinks away the tears that threaten to escape. And she says, "Take me home."

Finn guides the skiff towards the beach at Emmanuel Head. The same place Martin Macauley had raised his musket on him and splattered his blood across the shingle at the top of the beach. Today there is only stillness.

Eva looks up at the house. A thin line of smoke is rising from the chimney above the kitchen.

She swallows hard. Stands. Finn shifts, readying himself to climb from the boat and help her ashore.

"No," she says. "I can manage."

And as she climbs over the gunwale, she cannot muster more than a tiny smile goodbye.

Nathan is waiting for her at the front door. No doubt he had seen her coming.

She pauses on the front path for a moment to steel herself. To cobble together an explanation for the way she had fled the house so impulsively last night.

She meets her brother's eyes challengingly as she approaches the door. She will not allow herself to be scolded by him, or made to feel guilty. Because Nathan has been lying to her from the beginning. He knows the truth about Oliver's death; has always known. He had been outside the door when it had happened. Had deliberately kept it from her when she had asked about their past in the house.

Before she can open her mouth, he says, "Go and tidy yourself, Eva. You've a visitor."

She frowns. "Who?"

"In the parlour," he says. He eyes her bird's nest of wet hair. "Make yourself presentable first."

She goes upstairs to her room, dumping her wet clothes on a chair beside her bed. She has nothing else to change into, so she quickly combs her wet hair and re-pins it at her neck. Sponges the grime of the ship from her skin.

When she opens the door of the parlour, she finds Matthew Walton waiting.

Eva freezes in the doorway. She had never expected to see him again.

He stands at the sight of her, a rueful smile on his lips. "Miss Blake." He is a polished piece of London in a striped justacorps and dark blue breeches, lace at his throat and wrists. The dark curls of his wig are tied back with a length of black ribbon. He smells strongly of orange flower.

The sight of him here in Highfield House, with sea wind thumping the shutters, feels oddly disjointed.

Eva stays planted in the doorway. "Why are you here?" She does not attempt to inject any warmth into her voice. This thing between them has always been one of formality. Walton swallows visibly and gestures to the armchair across from him. He wrings his hands together and tugs at the hem of his coat. "Will you sit? Please?"

Hesitantly, she perches on the edge of the chair. Folds her hands neatly. "Nathan's letter reached you already?"

"No. He told me he had written. But I've not yet received it. Although I can imagine what it might say. I'm here on my own accord." Walton shifts forward in his seat. "I acted foolishly. Rashly. Once you had left London, I had much time to think. And I came to see that with great clarity." He pauses for a moment, as though waiting for her response. When it doesn't come, he says, "I'm truly sorry, Miss Blake. And if you are still willing, I would very much like to make you my wife."

Eva waits for the relief. The sense that things might be returning to the path they were supposed to follow. It doesn't come. She presses her lips into a thin line. "You are in love with my sister," she says matter-of-factly.

Walton lowers his eyes for a moment. "Of what consequence is that? You and I both know ours will be a marriage of practicality." His eyes meet hers. "But it will be strong one. A wise one." He reaches forward and tentatively takes her hand. "Eva. I agreed to marry you because I can see what a bright and promising young woman you are. I admit that I lost sight of that for a time. And I'm sorry. You deserved better. And you shall have it."

Eva lets out her breath. Walton is like an actor on a stage. Polished and perfect, with these fine words rolling off his tongue. Over and over, on that interminable journey from London to Holy Island, she had longed for Matthew Walton to see his mistakes like this. To see the value of what he was giving up. Now his words just feel empty.

A marriage of practicality. She supposes that is what she has always been destined for.

He squeezes her fingers. "I could make a good life for you, Eva. A secure life. One that would be of great benefit to your family too. Is that not what you want."

Eva gets to her feet and goes to the window. The wind through the grass is making the dunes breathe. She hears Walton's footsteps behind her.

"I need a good, respectable wife," he says. "And you need the security of a husband. It seems to me that this is an arrangement that will benefit us both. Is that not why we agreed to it in the first place?"

"I would not have agreed to it if I had known the way you feel about Harriet."

"Harriet is of no concern to me. And nor should she be to you." He puts a gentle hand to her shoulder, turning her to face him. "My loyalty will be to you, Eva. I know I cannot expect you to believe that now, after the way I treated you. But I hope you will come to see that in time. And I hope the fact that I have come all the way up here to see you in person might show you how much I regret sending you away."

Eva closes her eyes for a moment. Everything he has said is right, of course. This marriage is what this family needs. It will ease the pressure of selling the house. Ease the pressure on Nathan. Perhaps allow him to regain a little of his warm and easeful self.

In spite of everything, her marriage to Matthew Walton feels inevitable.

She hates that her life might be considered as such. But this is who she is, isn't it? As Samuel Blake's oldest daughter, her role has always been this. To marry a man whose wealth will dig this family out of poverty.

She hates the inevitability. And she hates the ache in her chest that comes when she thinks of that towering cottage on Longstone.

But she and Finn are an impossibility.

She thinks of the arrangement with Joseph Holland that Nathan has agreed to in order to protect her. She owes her brother this, she realises. Owes him a little peace of mind. Owes him the connections that will come with linking her family to the wealthy, well-respected Waltons.

She cannot find the words to accept Matthew's renewed proposal. But she finds herself nodding in agreement.

CHAPTER THIRTY-SIX

Eva shoves her wet clothes into the bottom of her duffel bag. They will likely be ruined when she gets to London, but she cannot bring herself to care. The rest of her wardrobe is waiting at Walton's townhouse, almost as though it has been expecting her return.

She knows she should not feel so empty. Things have been righted, and she will have the life she had always planned to have. Matthew's apology had seemed genuine, and she knows she is doing the right thing by Nathan and the rest of the family. The sooner she and Matthew return to London and begin their life together, the better.

She hates the thought of leaving without so much as a goodbye to Finn. She knows she has no hope of making it out to Longstone to see him, but perhaps she might at least pen a letter. Have Harriet take it to Julia to deliver when she next calls on her brothers.

Of course, things are better this way. Even though it does not feel like it. At all.

She looks up at a knock on the door. Nathan is standing in the doorway.

"Matthew tells me you have agreed to return to London with him."

She nods. Doesn't look at him. "It's the right thing to do."

He comes towards her. "Thank you, Eva. I'm grateful. Very grateful." He puts a hand to her shoulder. She manages a short smile, knowing how hard the gesture is for him. The look of gratitude, of relief in Nathan's eyes convinces her she is doing the right thing.

He pulls away and perches on the edge of the bed. "What happened last night?" he asks.

"Finn Murray was in trouble," she says shortly. "He needed my help."

Nathan frowns. "What kind of trouble?"

She shakes her head.

"You've been putting yourself out a lot for this Mr Murray," says Nathan. "Doing things I never imagined you doing. Is there anything I ought to know?"

Eva grabs the books from her nightstand and shoves them into her duffel bag. "I have agreed to marry Mr Walton. That is all you need to know."

But the moment she speaks, she realises she is wrong. There is far more she needs to share with her brother. She has no idea how a privateer like Henry Ward might have met their mother, and what would have driven her to invite him into their home. But somehow, this man is inexorably linked to their past on Holy Island. And she needs to know how much of this Nathan is aware of.

"Finn was taken by his old privateering captain," she tells him. "He tried to force him back into his crew." She winces at the lie. "But we managed to escape the ship." This is dangerous, of course, speaking of Ward and Finn in the same breath. Eva cannot bear for Nathan to know it was Finn who had caused Oliver's death. "The captain," she says carefully. "Henry Ward. He told me what happened to Oliver." Something almost imperceptible flickers across Nathan's eyes. "He was here at the house with his crew the night Oliver died."

For a moment, Nathan doesn't speak.

"You know all this, don't you," says Eva.

Finally, he faces her. "Yes. I was watching through the keyhole. Oliver fought with a cabin boy from Ward's crew. Oliver attacked him and the boy retaliated."

Eva's stomach twists. "That was why we left the house, wasn't it. Mother was mad with grief over Oliver. She was desperate to leave."

"I believe so," Nathan says after a moment. "We stayed to bury Oliver, of course. But after that… I've always believed that was why we left. I don't think she could handle being here any longer."

Eva stares into her knotted hands. Is that really all there is to it? They had torn out into a freezing night, without so much as a horse. Had her mother truly been so addled by loss she would be that reckless? Put her children in such danger? Or is there a part of the story they are missing?

"Why did you not tell me about Oliver when I asked why we left the house?"

Nathan sighs. "I'm sorry. I thought it for the best. What good would it have done if I'd told you?"

Eva doesn't respond. She supposes he is right. But she cannot help feeling betrayed.

She thinks of that night; herself tucked into the very bed she is sitting on now, oblivious to all that was taking place three doors down the hall. She thinks of Finn, of Nathan, of her mother. Thinks of Oliver, an almost mythical figure on the fringes of her memory.

For long moments, she and Nathan sit in silence. She can tell her brother's thoughts are back in that night too. Eva is almost glad to be leaving this house, and the poisonous air the past has left in its passages. But that life in London she had planned out so carefully, it feels so hollow. It seems like such a banal and empty existence to live a life not lit by the Longstone firebasket.

She stands suddenly and smooths her skirts. "I ought to go. I don't want to keep Matthew waiting."

Nathan nods. He stands; follows her to the door. "Take care, Eva. Be sure to write once the wedding plans are in place. We will do our best to attend."

She nods. Swallows heavily, forcing away tears. She picks up her bag and walks deliberately from the room, refusing the pull to look back at the islands behind the glass.

She makes her way downstairs, searching for Theodora and Harriet to make her goodbyes. Through the window she sees her niece rolling a hoop outside the house. Eva passes the kitchen, looking for her sister.

The door to Harriet's workroom is open a crack. Eva knocks lightly. When there is no response, she pushes open the door and tiptoes inside.

She finds her sister asleep in the old chair in the corner of the room. She is dressed in her nightshift and robe, her hair hanging loose over her shoulders. Paint flecks her hands, her arm draped over the chair, fingers reaching towards the half-drunk glass of whisky on the floor.

Eva turns to the painting that sits on the easel. A dark stripe has been slashed across the middle, blocking out the fine lines of sunlight Harriet had spent so long crafting.

Eva's heart lurches. Pristine and polished Harriet. How far has she fallen that she might allow herself to be seen like this? Is it the oppressive smallness of Holy Island that has poisoned her? Perhaps a little. But Eva knows Harriet had shown glimpses of this even while she had been flitting around London with a champagne glass in her hand. The light had begun to be sucked out of her once she had become a wife, a mother.

Eva kneels beside her sister, placing a hand over Harriet's thin white wrist. She does not want to wake her. But nor does she want to leave without saying goodbye.

She can't pull her eyes from the painting. From the anger and grief it expresses.

And in that dark and tainted artwork, Eva sees her own future. Sees this life that Harriet has taken on, at their brother's behest. Sees what being a dutiful sister, wife, mother has done to her. And this life she has agreed to, this life that has been laid out before her for as long as she can remember, Eva sees now that it will lead her to her own ruined canvas.

Suddenly there is not a sensible thought in her head—only this: that she cannot live the life she has spent an eternity planning. This polished life with the polished man in the parlour who smells of orange flower and loves her sister.

It is a betrayal to Nathan. A betrayal to her mother. To Oliver. To her whole family. She sees that, and it pains her. But for the first time in her life, she also sees something that she wants. Desperately. Passionately. For the first time in her life, she wants to break the rules.

She goes for the door, avoiding Matthew in the sitting room. As she passes the cart house, she hears Theodora call to her. She keeps walking, avoiding the questions, pretending not to hear.

She walks with a new sense of deliberateness, down the narrow path that cuts through the middle of the island.

She goes to the harbour, pulls her pouch from her pocket and puts coins in the hand of the first fisherman who agrees to take her to Longstone.

Printed in Great Britain
by Amazon